GLADIATOR
SON OF SPARTACUS

'The bloodline
of Spartacus continues.
His son will lead us
and fulfil the destiny
and dream of his father . . .'

Books by Simon Scarrow

GLADIATOR: FIGHT FOR FREEDOM

GLADIATOR: STREET FIGHTER

GLADIATOR: SON OF SPARTACUS

www.gladiatorbooks.co.uk

SIMON SCARROW

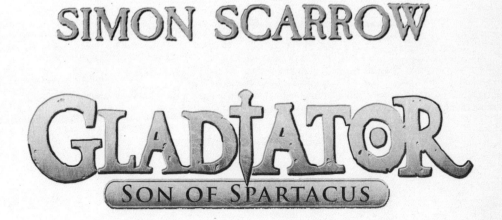

GLADIATOR
SON OF SPARTACUS

PUFFIN

PUFFIN BOOKS

Published by the Penguin Group
Penguin Books Ltd, 80 Strand, London WC2R ORL, England
Penguin Group (USA) Inc., 375 Hudson Street, New York, New York 10014, USA
Penguin Group (Canada), 90 Eglinton Avenue East, Suite 700, Toronto, Ontario, Canada M4P 2Y3
(a division of Pearson Penguin Canada Inc.)
Penguin Ireland, 25 St Stephen's Green, Dublin 2, Ireland (a division of Penguin Books Ltd)
Penguin Group (Australia), 707 Collins Street, Melbourne, Victoria 3008, Australia
(a division of Pearson Australia Group Pty Ltd)
Penguin Books India Pvt Ltd, 11 Community Centre, Panchsheel Park, New Delhi – 110 017, India
Penguin Group (NZ), 67 Apollo Drive, Rosedale, Auckland 0632, New Zealand
(a division of Pearson New Zealand Ltd)
Penguin Books (South Africa) (Pty) Ltd, Block D, Rosebank Office Park, 181 Jan Smuts Avenue, Parktown
North, Gauteng 2193, South Africa

Penguin Books Ltd, Registered Offices: 80 Strand, London WC2R ORL, England

puffinbooks.com

Published in Great Britain in Puffin Books 2013
001

Text copyright © Simon Scarrow, 2013
Map and illustrations by David Atkinson

The moral right of the author and illustrators has been asserted

Set in 13/21.3 pt Bembo Book MT Std
Typeset by Palimpsest Book Production Limited, Falkirk, Stirlingshire
Printed in Great Britain by Clays Ltd, St Ives plc

British Library Cataloguing in Publication Data
A CIP catalogue record for this book is available from the British Library

HARDBACK
ISBN: 978–0–141–33872–9

TRADE PAPERBACK
ISBN: 978–0–141–33873–6

www.greenpenguin.co.uk

ALWAYS LEARNING   **PEARSON**

For Anita Smith,

with the profoundest respect

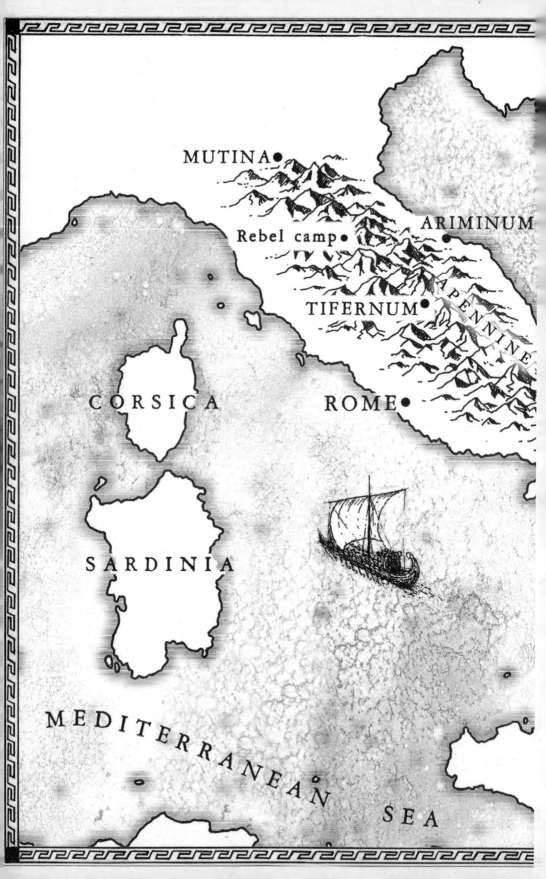

MOUNTAINS

• Porcino's ludus
  (Capua)

SICILIA

ITALIA
59 BC

1

The raiders came shortly after nightfall, emerging stealthily from the belt of cedar trees that stretched along the slopes of the hill above the villa. Over fifty of them, armed with a mixture of swords, spears and clubs. Some had armour: chain-mail or old bronze cuirasses, and helmets and shields in a wide variety of designs. Most of the men were thin and gaunt, used to a life of hard labour and perpetual hunger. Their leaders were different: powerfully built individuals who carried the scars of their profession. In contrast to the other men, their armour was ornately decorated and well cared for. Before they had escaped from their owners these men had once been gladiators – the most deadly fighters in all the lands ruled from Rome.

At the head of the small force rode a broad-shouldered man

with tightly curled dark hair. He sat astride a fine black mare, part of the spoils of another villa attacked a month before. A livid white knot of tissue stretched across his brow and nose, the scar of a wound received only a few months earlier from a centurion in command of a patrol that had been ambushed. The patrol had been part of the force sent out from Rome to track down and eliminate the bands of brigands and runaway slaves who were hiding deep amid the Apennine mountains. Many of the fugitives were the survivors of the great rebellion led by the gladiator Spartacus some twelve years earlier, and they still carried his legacy close to their hearts. That revolt had nearly brought Rome to its knees and ever since the Romans had lived in fear of another bloody uprising. Thanks to the wars that they had been fighting outside Italia, it had not been possible to complete the destruction of the surviving rebels and over the years their numbers had swollen by thousands. Escaped slaves, together with those who had been set free by the rebels' raids on the villas and farming estates owned by the richest men in Rome, now made up the large army of freedom fighters.

Soon, the leader reflected with a thin smile, they would be strong enough to carry out more ambitious attacks on their Roman masters. He had already made his plans. The time would come when once again a gladiator would lead an army of slaves against their oppressors. Until then, the leader was content to carry out small raids, such as the one this night, to unnerve the wealthy men who controlled Rome, and to inspire the oppressed slaves eking out their miserable lives in the houses, fields and mines stretching the length and breadth of Italia.

The leader's keen eyes scrutinized the dark shapes of the buildings and walls lying before them. For two days he and his men had been watching the villa from the shadows of the trees. It was typical of the farming estates owned by wealthy Romans. There was a grand house to one side, built round a courtyard within which neat flower beds and gravel paths ran round pools and fishponds. A wall separated the house from the low, plain buildings where the slaves, overseers, guards and agricultural tools were accommodated along with the granaries and store-houses where the produce of the estate was amassed before it was sent to market. The resulting profit would be added to the fortune of the owner living in Rome, heedless of the sweat, toil and suffering of those who made him rich. Round the whole collection of buildings ran a ten-foot wall, built to keep the slaves in and any threats out.

As they had lain in concealment, the raiders had noted the

routines of the villa and the coming and going of the chain-gangs and their guards as they worked the fields and groves that surrounded the complex of buildings. The leader's rage had burned in his veins as he watched the overseers cracking their whips and using their clubs to beat the slaves who moved too slowly. He would have liked to charge his men down from the trees there and then to cut down the guards and set the slaves free, but he had learned the value of patience. It was a lesson that Spartacus had taught him many years before.

The first thing in any fight was to watch your enemy closely and learn his strengths and weaknesses. Only a fool launched himself into a fight without such preparation, Spartacus had insisted. So the leader and his men had waited, noting the times when the guards had been changed on the walls and gate of the villa. They had counted the guards, how they were armed and which building in the compound served as their barracks. They had also discovered a small section of the wall that was cracked and crumbling behind a spruce tree, barely visible from a distance. The men on watch rarely passed by that section of the wall, and that was where the raiders would strike.

Now they moved silently across a freshly ploughed field and into a square grove of olive trees close to the outer wall of the villa. Ahead, the leader could see the bright flames of the brazier burning above the gatehouse, providing illumination for the guards, and warmth on this cold January night. Smaller flames flickered in the darkness atop the watchtowers at each corner of the wall, and the figures of the lookouts were visible as they huddled in their cloaks and stamped their booted feet to stay warm, their spears resting against their shoulders.

'Slowly now,' the leader murmured over his shoulder. 'No sound. No quick movements.'

His order was relayed in whisper from man to man as the raiders crept through the trees and approached the damaged section of the wall. The leader held up his hand as they reached the edge of the grove, and his men stood still. Then, beckoning to six of the nearest raiders, the leader dismounted and handed the reins of his horse to one of his men. He undid the clasp of his cloak and laid it across the saddle. It would be foolhardy to enter a fight encumbered by the thick woollen folds. Underneath the cloak he was wearing a dark blue tunic with a black leather breastplate inlaid with the silver motif of a wolf's head. A short sword hung from a baldric across his shoulders and his forearms were protected by studded leather bracers.

He turned to the others. 'Ready?'

They nodded. 'Yes, Brixus.'

'Then let's go.'

He stepped cautiously out of the treeline into open ground. The spruce tree loomed tall and dark seventy paces away. A small watchtower was the same distance further along the wall and a lookout stood black against the glow from the brazier behind him. Brixus stepped out and crossed the grass towards the wall. He limped as he walked, the result of an injury to his hamstring many years earlier in his last arena fight. The small party of men slipped out from the trees and followed him, stealing across the ground like shadows. Only the faintest rustling of grass accompanied their progress and soon they were beneath the scented boughs of the spruce tree, beside the wall.

'Taurus, by the wall,' Brixus whispered, and a huge figure leaned his back against the plastered surface and braced his boots in the soil as he cupped his hands. At once one of his companions, Pindar, a lithe, tall man, jumped up, and with a grunt Taurus lifted him towards the top of the wall. His companion quickly worked a brick loose and passed it down to one of the men waiting below. The brick was carefully lowered to the ground and then the next was passed down. Soon Pindar had removed all the bricks that had worked loose and had to pull out his dagger to work at the mortar holding the others in place. The work proceeded slowly and the leader limped out a short distance, then knelt down to keep watch on the man at the lookout tower. He still stood there, hands out, warming them over the flames of the brazier. Eventually he took his spear and slowly paced along the wall in the direction of the fugitives.

'Keep still,' Brixus whispered as loudly as he dared, and then eased himself down into the grass, pressing his body to the ground while keeping watch on the approaching sentry. His comrades froze and Pindar flattened against the wall. The sentry continued towards them and then, not more than twenty feet from the gap, he stopped and turned to stare out over the wall towards the trees. Brixus prayed that his men were keeping still and out of sight as they waited in the shadows there. There was no sign of alarm from the sentry and after a moment he turned and began to make his way back towards the brazier.

'All right,' the leader breathed. 'Carry on.'

Brick by brick the gap was enlarged until it was only a short distance above Taurus's head.

'That'll do. Up you go.' Brixus gestured to the small party of men. Taurus hoisted them in turn up towards the gap, and they crept over the wall and dropped down inside the compound. To their right lay the wall of the villa with a small gateway providing access between the house and the working section of the complex. A separate, more impressive gateway led into the villa from a treelined avenue, so that influential visitors to the estate need not pass by the squalid slave quarters. In other directions lay the slave barracks and those of the overseers and guards. Beyond them loomed storehouses and granaries.

Brixus took one last glance at the sentry to ensure nothing was amiss, then turned towards the trees and cupped a hand to his mouth. Taking a deep breath, he let out a low owl hoot, three times. An instant later he saw the rest of the raiding party creep out from the trees. They went down into the grass and bent low as they moved towards the spruce tree.

This was the moment of greatest risk, thought Brixus. If the sentry was alert, he could not help but see so many men swarming out of the darkness. It was up to Pindar to deal with him. Before the men were halfway across the open ground, there was a soft thud and when the leader looked up at the wall the sentry had disappeared. Brixus breathed a sigh of relief as he rose up and waved the men on before limping over to Taurus.

'My turn, old friend.' He smiled in the darkness and saw

the dull gleam of the big man's teeth as he responded. Then, placing his boot in the large paws of Taurus, the leader clambered up and through the gap.

On the sentry walk he looked to his left and saw Pindar dropping from the wall, leaving the body of the guard sprawled behind him. On the ground below, the other men of the advance party knelt in a shallow arc, keeping watch. Brixus lowered himself over the side of the walkway and then dropped the last two feet to the ground. Above him he could hear the first of the second group climbing through the gap, and hurriedly moved aside. One by one the raiders dropped down into the compound and joined the men spread out in an arc. With a strained grunt Taurus pulled himself up and crawled through the gap to join his comrades.

Brixus drew his sword and looked round at his men as he raised the weapon. In response they grasped their weapons and held them up to show that they were ready.

'To the guards' barracks.' He spoke just loudly enough for them all to hear. 'Go in hard. Show no mercy.'

There was a low growl of assent from Taurus and muttered comments from the others, then the leader led the way along the side of the wall, keeping to its shadow as he limped towards the barracks, a hundred paces away. The muffled sound of voices carried across the compound, light-hearted chatter interspersed with the cries of glee and groans of men playing a game of dice. There was no sound from the slave barracks. They would be too exhausted to do much but sleep after they had eaten their evening ration of barley gruel. Besides, Brixus reflected, most slaves were forbidden from talking in such estates, for fear that it might encourage them to plot against their masters.

They were no more than fifty feet from the entrance to the barracks when the door suddenly opened and a finger of rosy light spilled out across the compound, revealing the men hurrying along the base of the wall. Two guards stood in the entrance to the barracks holding empty jars, which they were taking to the well to refill. They stopped dead and stared at the raiders before one of them reacted.

'Alarm!' he shouted, then turned towards the door and repeated the cry. 'Alarm!'

Brixus turned to his men and thrust his spare hand towards Pindar. 'Take your men and clear the walls of sentries. The rest of you, follow me!'

He thrust his sword towards the entrance of the barracks and bellowed as loudly as he could into the cold night air. 'Attack!'

2

A party led by Pindar ran to the steps leading up on to the wall and made for the nearest of the sentries. In the compound, dark figures raced towards the barrack doors, a savage roar tearing from the throat of each man as the raiders surged forward. Brixus did his best to keep up, but was hampered by his old wound and swiftly overtaken by most of his men. The two unarmed guards who stood at the entrance quickly recovered from their surprise and, dropping their jars, they turned and raced back inside.

Roused by the commotion, the first of the defenders had already reached the barrack doors, armed with a short sword and dagger. Barefoot, he was a well-built man with grey hair and lined features. From the swiftness of his reaction and the steady manner in which he planted his feet squarely on the ground, it was clear he had once been an experienced soldier. He glanced at the wave of men converging on him and then shouted back over his shoulder.

'To arms! Form up on me!'

A handful of men managed to join him before the raiders charged into them. The ex-soldier neatly ducked a swinging club and slammed his sword into the side of the first raider, knocking him off his feet. He collapsed with a groan, clutching his side, and tripping up one of his comrades who sprawled in front of the guard and was despatched with a swift thrust between his shoulder blades.

Despite the courage and example of the ex-soldier, the guards outside the barracks were outnumbered and in moments the raiders had cut down two of the defenders and forced the rest back inside the entrance. Over the shoulders of his men and the flickering gleam of blades, the ex-soldier could see that the rest of the guards had armed themselves to join those at the open door. Only a handful of men on either side could fight in the narrow gap, and as each casualty fell he was quickly replaced with neither side gaining the advantage.

Outside, Brixus hissed a low curse. He had hoped to surprise his enemy quickly enough to burst in upon them and slaughter the guards in their barracks before they could arm themselves and form ranks. It was too late for that now and he had to change his plan before he lost too many men. His fellow gladiators were the only men he knew he could depend on. The rest were escaped slaves who had joined his growing band, keen to wreak their revenge on their former oppressors, but lacking the training and discipline of seasoned fighters. If they saw too many of their comrades fall, then their courage would probably fail them.

Sheathing his sword, he stepped round the men crowding the entrance and grasped the edge of the door.

'Stand back!' he ordered those nearest him. 'You and you, help me close this door.'

With men on either side, Brixus began to push. At first there was no resistance, but as the defenders saw what was happening, the ex-soldier bellowed an order. 'Hold the door open!'

While the desperate fighting continued in the narrow gap, the raiders braced their boots and shoved the rough wooden surface with all their strength as the defenders resisted from the other side. The door slowed down and then stopped.

'Taurus!' Brixus called out through gritted teeth. 'Over here! Now!'

The giant plucked one of the raiders aside and threw his

weight against the door beside his leader. At once it began to move again, steadily closing until the gap was too narrow for anyone to pass through. The pale shaft of light cast from the lamps shrank and then vanished as the door closed on the frame.

'Hold it shut,' Brixus ordered and gestured to the nearest of his men to help Taurus, before he drew back and looked around the compound. A short distance away, beside one of the granaries, he saw a heavy cart. Summoning several men, he hurried across the compound and grasped the yoke. Straining against the dead weight of the vehicle, the raiders pulled it across to the barracks where the door shuddered under the impact of bodies and weapons from within. The cart was manoeuvred close to the wall and worked along the door, pinning it in place. The guards could only open it a small way, enough to let out a sliver of light.

'What now?' asked Taurus.

'Take your men and get some dry feed from the stables, then pile it up round the barracks. The rest of you, cover the windows. Don't let any of them out.'

While the barracks was surrounded and bales of hay piled up against the walls, a handful of the guards guessed the fate that the raiders had in store for them and tried to escape through the small windows set high in the building. Seeing them, the raiders thrust their spears up, forcing the men back inside. Once Brixus was satisfied that preparations were complete, he ordered oil to be poured over the combustible materials and told Pindar to light a torch from the brazier above the gatehouse. When Pindar returned he handed the torch to Brixus, who limped up to the cart blocking the door.

'You inside, hear me! Throw out your weapons and surrender.'

There was a brief pause before a voice answered. 'And let ourselves be slaughtered like cattle? No chance. I'll die like a man.'

'Then die you will,' Brixus shouted back. A cold smile flickered across his lips. 'Let your deaths be a beacon to every Roman and slave alike. For liberty!'

He stepped forward and applied the torch to the straw piled up beneath the cart. The flame caught at once and spread through the dry lengths with a light crackle, then a growing roar, as the flames licked up and burned fiercely. They spread round the edge of the barracks and smoke billowed into the air, the lurid orange clouds lit up by the savage fire.

There were shouts from inside the barracks, and cries of panic as the men appeared at the windows, but were beaten back by the heat. The raiders stood in a loose circle about the burning building, dark figures silhouetted against the brilliant glare of the flames, their long shadows stretching behind them into the darkness. Before long the flames had caught the roof timbers, and sections of tile collapsed inside. There were no more shouts, just piercing shrieks of agony muffled by the occasional sharp reports of timbers bursting. The screams continued for a while and then there was only the roar of the fire.

Brixus climbed up on to the edge of the well and surveyed the small crowd before him, their faces lit up by the slowly dying fire of the barracks. To one side stood the steward who ran the estate for his wealthy master, with his wife and two sons barely in their teens. They looked down at the ground, afraid to meet the eyes of their captors. Brixus turned his attention back to the crowd. Their expressions were mostly fearful, but some looked at him with hope in their eyes. They would be the easiest to recruit to his side, Brixus reflected as he gathered his thoughts and prepared to address the slaves who had just been released from the long, low shed where they were shut in when not at work in the fields and groves of the estate. As the locking bar had been withdrawn and the doors opened, the familiar stench of sweat and human waste billowed out from inside and he cursed the Romans for treating these people little better than animals.

Holding his torch aloft, Brixus had entered the building, fighting back his nausea as the slaves cowered away from him. Most of them were chained together by the ankle to prevent any attempt at escape when they were out in the fields. Only a handful – children and older men and women – had their irons removed. They wore little more than rags, soiled and torn, and their filthy skin was covered in bruises and scars from the beatings of their overseers.

'I am Brixus,' he announced. 'A lieutenant of Spartacus. I have come to set you free.'

He turned to his followers. 'Get the chains off them and lead them out of here. Keep 'em together so I can speak to them when they're ready.'

Now the slaves stood before him, anxious to learn what would become of them.

Brixus drew a deep breath and spoke loudly to be heard over the distant crackle of the flames still consuming what was left of the barracks.

'Your lives of back-breaking toil are over, my friends. There will be no more whips. No more chains. No more slowly starving on the thin gruel provided by your masters. See how well they lived while you endured so much suffering, exhaustion and hunger?' He thrust his arm towards the steward and his family.

The slaves glanced towards the man who had controlled every aspect of their lives and there was silence before a voice muttered angrily. Others joined in, waving their fists.

Brixus raised his hands and called out to them. 'Enough! Enough! You will have your revenge shortly. For now, listen to me.'

When they had fallen silent, he continued. 'As I said. You are no longer slaves, but free. Now you may choose what to do with your lives. You are masters of your fate.'

'What happens when news of this attack gets out?' a voice asked. 'They will come here and punish any slave they find.'

'Then come with us,' Brixus replied.

'And go where? The Romans will hunt us down like dogs.'

'No, they won't. I told you my name. I am Brixus, loyal to what Spartacus died for. When the rebellion ended I survived, along with many others. When I escaped again I made for the hills and mountains of the Apennines and joined those of the slave army who still remained in hiding. Since then we have been adding to our number by raiding the estates of those who call themselves our masters, and setting their slaves free. I lead but one of the bands of rebels who hide in the mountains. The Romans have tried to hunt us down, but we have eluded them. Now we are fighting back, hunting them down in turn and destroying their patrols and burning their outposts to the ground. They are becoming afraid of us. Every Roman soldier we kill, every villa we destroy, every slave we set free adds to their fear.' Brixus paused to give emphasis to his next words. 'One day soon we will be strong enough to rekindle the rebellion that Spartacus once led and there will be a new war against those who would keep us as slaves.'

There were excited cries of approval from the crowd, then an old man at the front took a step forward.

'I too fought for Spartacus. But we were an army. Tens of thousands of us. And the Romans still beat us. You are the leader of a band of runaways and brigands. What chance have we got if we join you? What freedom do you really offer? A few months as fugitives in the hills, in the depth of winter, before we are hunted down, caught and punished. Last time they crucified thousands in order to teach us a lesson. How much greater do you think their anger will be a second time?' The old man turned to his comrades and raised a hand to draw their attention. 'I say we'd be better off here. When the soldiers come, we'll explain that we had no part in tonight's action.'

'You old fool!' Brixus shouted him down. 'Do you think they will listen to you? No. It will make no difference to their desire for revenge. They will make an example of you just the same. Stay here and you will die.'

'We all die, Brixus,' the old man replied. 'One way or another.'

'Then all that matters is how you die,' Brixus replied. 'You can choose to spend the rest of your days living in your own filth, surviving on scraps at the whim of your masters, or you can seize your freedom here and now. Be your own master. Taste the sweet air of freedom. Of course there is a price, as with all things that are worth having. You will have to fight to stay free. Better to fight on your feet than spend your life grovelling on your knees to some fat Roman pig. What is your death now but simply an end to suffering? An end to a life that has no value. Together we can stop this. Have freedom instead of slavery. But only if we have the courage to fight for that freedom. Who here will join me?'

'Me!' a voice cried out and was instantly echoed by many others. The old man looked over his shoulder and shook his head in dismay.

When the shouting had died down Brixus spoke again. 'Brothers and sisters, the age of slavery will soon come to an end. The bands of rebels will join together and the dream of Spartacus will become a reality.'

'Spartacus is dead!' the old man shouted back.

'Yes, he is dead,' Brixus acknowledged. 'But his dream lives on. And more than his dream. The bloodline of Spartacus continues. Soon, very soon, the rebels will be united and fighting together under one banner and one leader, and that leader will be one who is fit to assume the mantle of the great Spartacus, for he is none other than his son! He will lead us and fulfil the destiny and dream of his father, the same dream that is shared by every slave in the Roman Empire.'

'The son of Spartacus?' The old man shook his head. 'It's not possible. I was there. He had no son.'

'The son was born shortly after the end of the rebellion. He bears the secret mark of Spartacus. I have seen it. I have met the boy.'

The crowd had fallen silent, listening to his words with rapt attention, hope burning in almost every face.

'Where is he?' some cried out. 'Where is the boy?'

'I know where he lives,' said Brixus. 'He follows in the footsteps of his father, and already it is clear that he will become as great a gladiator as Spartacus in his time. Greater perhaps. He is still young. But when the time comes he cannot avoid his destiny. He will answer the call, and lead us all to freedom!'

'Freedom!' his followers shouted and the cry was echoed by the newly liberated slaves. Even the old man joined in, his eyes sparkling with emotion. Brixus allowed the cheering to continue for a while before he raised his hands and called for silence.

'There is one last task before we leave this place tonight.' He turned and pointed to the steward and his family. 'We must show the Romans what fate lies in store for those who would oppress their fellow man. Bring me the youngest boy.'

One of his men strode over to the family, grabbed the boy's arm and wrenched him away. He struggled to free himself, reaching out a hand towards his mother as her face wrinkled with grief. The steward held her back as he spoke clearly and defiantly to his son.

'Show no fear to these scum. No tears. Remember, you are a Roman.'

Brixus laughed, and some in the crowd jeered.

Set in front of Brixus, the boy stood as tall as he could manage and tried to look calm and defiant.

'Are you afraid of me?' asked Brixus.

'No.'

'You should be. What is your name?'

'Lucius Pollonius Secundus. Though you can call me young master.'

Brixus smiled. 'Arrogant to a fault. You are a true Roman. The question is, are you a clever Roman, Lucius? Do you think you can remember every detail of what has happened here tonight?'

'I shall never forget it.'

'That is true.' Brixus nodded. Then he turned to Taurus. 'Crucify the others. This one is to be chained to the foot of his father's post. He will be the one to tell Rome that a new rebellion is coming, and this time the heir of Spartacus will lead us to victory, and the annihilation of Rome.'

3

'Do you think Caesar will win the vote?' asked Marcus as he looked in through the window of the Senate House.

As usual with any important vote, the windows and arches were packed with bystanders who had come to witness the debate and cheer on their heroes or jeer those senators who were unpopular. It had rained hard that morning and the air was cold and clammy. Marcus pulled his cloak tightly about him. He wore the hood down, despite the weather, so that he could follow the noisy proceedings in the Senate House more clearly. His dark curly hair badly needed a cut, but for now was held back by a leather strap about his forehead and tied off at the back. Even though he had recently turned twelve he was tall for his age and well built, as could be expected in a boy who had spent nearly two years of his life training to become a gladiator. There was a hardness about his expression that was unusual for his age, and came with the scars like that he bore above his right knee.

An idyllic childhood on the Greek island of Leucas had been cut short when he and his mother had been kidnapped by the hired muscle of the moneylender Decimus. Shortly after they were separated and while his mother had been taken to spend the rest of her life as a slave on a farm in Greece, Marcus had been bought by a lanista – the owner of a gladiator school – near Capua. His training had been brutal and relentless, until he had been picked to fight in front of Julius Caesar. By chance he had saved the life of Caesar's niece, Portia, who had fallen into the pit during his fight with two wolves.

Since then he had been brought to Rome to serve in Caesar's household, and spy on his enemies. For that he had been awarded his freedom. But that was months ago and at first Marcus had assumed that he would be swiftly reunited with his mother. However, it was not to be. Despite Caesar making enquiries to find out where she was being held, there had been no news of her and Marcus was growing restless. His heart ached whenever he thought of his mother, and imagined her chained to other slaves and forced to work in the fields of the villa owned by Decimus. He could not rest while she remained a slave. Nor could he be content until he had taken his revenge on Decimus for all the suffering inflicted on himself, his mother and Titus, the man who had raised Marcus like a father. Marcus decided that if there was no progress by the end of the month, then he would ask Caesar's permission to look for her himself.

Despite being a freed man, Marcus had soon discovered his new status entitled him to less liberty than he first imagined. Those who had been slaves owed a debt to their former masters and were expected to honour any requests for further services, all part of the peculiar customs of the Roman people. It was a far cry from the simple way he had been raised on Leucas.

Time was running out for Marcus. His former master had completed his year serving as one of the two consuls and would shortly be leaving Rome to take command of the armies and province of Cisalpine Gaul. If he was to get any further help from Caesar to find and free his mother, then it would need to happen soon, before the newly appointed general left Rome. But first Caesar had to survive an attempt by his political enemies to have him prosecuted for abusing his powers during his year in office.

Today they would vote on whether Caesar should be put

on trial. The arguments for and against the motion had raged all day and Caesar had risen from his bench several times to address his accusers. As ever, Marcus had been impressed by his former master's public-speaking skills. He had used reason, rhetoric and humour to challenge his opponents and win the support of senators, as well as the majority of the public watching. But was that enough?

The grey-haired man standing beside Marcus tilted his head slightly to one side as he considered the boy's question. Festus was in charge of Caesar's private bodyguard, a small force of army veterans, ex-gladiators and street fighters who were tasked with his safety when he passed through the crowded streets of Rome. Marcus was the youngest member of the bodyguard, but had won the respect of the others for his courage and skill with weapons.

'Hard to decide. The master is popular enough with the people. His land reforms last year have helped many. But they won't have a say over what happens to him. That's down to the senators alone.' He paused and a smile creased his weathered face. 'But I dare say that most of them will not be willing to risk the anger of the mob by putting Caesar on trial. The only danger is that Cato will manage to sway their opinion.'

Marcus turned his gaze to the surly-looking senator sitting on the front bench opposite Caesar. Cato wore his usual plain brown toga to show that he held true to the plain virtues and traditions of the forefathers of the Senate. In the previous year he had bitterly resisted the reforms of Caesar and the two men remained enemies.

One of the new consuls, Calpurnius Piso, was chairing the debate and now stood up to speak. The other senators and the spectators fell silent out of respect for his office as he cleared his throat.

'My fellow senators. I am mindful that there are barely two hours left before the day is out. We have heard the arguments for and against the motion for the last three days and I move that we now vote on whether Caesar should be put on trial.'

'Now we'll find out,' Marcus muttered.

'Don't be so sure,' said Festus. 'You haven't reckoned on our friend Clodius.'

Marcus nodded, recalling the violent young man who had organized the street gangs that had served Caesar's interests the previous year.

'I forbid!' a voice announced loudly.

Everyone's eyes turned towards one of the men sitting on the tribunes' bench. The tribunes, elected by the people, had the power to oppose any decisions made in the Senate, but it was a power rarely exercised. Now, Tribune Clodius rose to his feet and held out his hand. 'I forbid the vote.'

At once Cato was on his feet, pointing his finger accusingly. 'On what grounds?'

Clodius turned to the senator and smiled. 'I don't have to give you reasons, my dear Cato. I simply have the right to forbid a vote. That is all.'

Cato glared across the floor of the Senate House. 'But you have a moral obligation to explain your decision. You must give your reasons.'

'Must I?' Clodius turned to the consul.

Piso sighed and shook his head.

'Bah!' Cato fumed. 'The tribune is abusing his power. If there is no good reason to forbid a vote, and there isn't, then it is not right that he should do so.'

'It may not be right,' Clodius countered in a matter-of-fact tone. 'But, nevertheless, it is my privilege. And there is nothing you can do about it.'

His words provoked howls of anger from Cato's supporters, and, Marcus noted, many of the other senators looked angry, even some of those who normally supported Caesar. He turned to Festus.

'I think Caesar is making a mistake. He shouldn't rely on Clodius.'

'Perhaps, but why risk losing the vote?'

'The master is risking more than losing the vote.' Marcus gestured towards the angry scene on the Senate floor. The shouting continued for a moment before Piso's clerk rapped his staff on the marble floor. Gradually the noise died away and Piso nodded his head towards a tall figure sitting midway between Cato and Caesar.

'The floor is open to Senator Cicero.'

Marcus leaned forward against the window frame. He wanted to make sure he didn't miss a word. Cicero was one of the most respected of the senators and had not yet chosen which side to support. Whatever he said now might well sway opinion behind Caesar, or turn the Senate against him.

Cicero strode purposefully into the open space in front of the consul and turned to face the waiting senators. Marcus could sense their tense anticipation, but Cicero, who was a master of every trick in the book of public speaking, waited until he had complete silence before he began.

'Honoured senators, let us not open old wounds. There are few of us here who can forget the terrible strife and violence that accompanied the age of Marius and Sulla. And none of us want to return to that time, when every senator was in fear of his life and the streets of our great city ran with blood. Therefore, let us approach our present difficulty with a spirit of compromise.'

Marcus saw Cato shake his head and make to rise from his seat. Cicero gestured for him to remain seated and, reluctantly, the other man eased himself back down. Meanwhile Caesar looked on, his face cold and expressionless.

'Few can deny,' Cicero continued, 'that there are justifiable grievances on both sides. Caesar's consulship was a time of great division, due to the nature of the laws he introduced, and even I question some of the tactics used to impose his will. But the present attempt to bring him to trial smacks of political motivation. Of course, I am sure that the Senate would give him a fair hearing and their ultimate decision would be guided by both reason and a sense of justice.'

Festus snorted with derision. 'Who does he think he's fooling?'

'Shhh!' a stout man at his side hissed.

'However,' Cicero resumed, 'since Tribune Clodius has exercised his right to deliver a veto, then we cannot vote on whether there will be a trial. The tribune is within his rights to withhold his reasons for his decision, but I say to him that his act exhibits the kind of frivolity for which he has become notorious. He risks fuelling the divisions that already place the unity of this House under great strain.'

Clodius crossed his arms, leaned back in his chair and smiled.

'It is well known that Clodius is a follower of Caesar and that fully explains his decision. But there is nothing that can be done, or should be done, to force the tribune to change his mind. The moment we step down that path we undermine the very traditions and laws that have made Rome the great power that she is. Nevertheless, Caesar has an obligation not to be seen to abuse the rules. Therefore, I suggest that we agree the following compromise.' He paused. 'Last year Senator Cato put forward a suggestion that Caesar be given the responsibility for hunting down the remains of Spartacus's army. At the time there was no vote thanks to the riot that someone instigated outside the Senate House.' He looked meaningfully at Clodius before he continued. 'As it happens, I have had news today of yet another attack, this time on the estate near Tifernum, belonging to a member of this body, Senator Severus.' He gestured towards a ponderous bald man sitting on the front row.

'That's right.' Severus scowled. 'The scum burned my villa

to the ground, butchered my staff and set free all of my slaves. It's an outrage!'

'Quite.' Cicero nodded. 'These raids have been increasing in number and scale. The bands of rebels are now a major threat to the security of farms and villas on either side of the Apennines. Their leader – some thug by the name of Brixus – is attempting to unite the slaves into one army under his control. He even claims that the son of Spartacus is alive and will become the figurehead of a new rebellion. That's utter nonsense, of course, but the fools who follow Brixus are willing to believe anything.'

Marcus felt an icy tingle at the back of his neck. He had met Brixus before, at the gladiator school where he had first been trained. Marcus had discovered Brixus's secret: that he had been part of Spartacus's inner circle. For his part Brixus had discovered an even bigger secret: that the young boy was the son of the former slave leader, and therefore the enemy to all of Rome. Although Marcus had deliberately positioned himself in Caesar's household as a way of finding his mother, he lived in fear that his true identity would be discovered. So far he'd managed to divert attention from the brand of a wolf's head mounted on the tip of a sword that was burned on his shoulder and linked him to Spartacus, but the news of Brixus's rebellion unsettled him. He glanced warily at Festus and the latter caught his eye and cocked a questioning eyebrow.

'What's the matter, Marcus? You look like you've seen a ghost.'

'It's nothing.' Marcus forced his expression to remain calm even though his heart beat quickly within his breast.

Cicero drew a breath and continued. 'These brigands must be dealt with. If Caesar agrees to take responsibility for destroying them, Cato, will you agree not to pursue your attempt to force a trial of Caesar?'

Before Cato could reply, Caesar was on his feet. 'I object! I already have other duties to attend to. I take up command of my army this spring. I have no time to waste on hunting down a handful of ragged slaves. I have far more important things that concern me.'

'More important than the security of Italia?' asked Cicero.

'No . . . Of course not,' Caesar blustered. 'Nothing is more important than that. Only –'

'Then you will surely accept this task?'

Caesar pressed his lips together, struggling to contain his frustration as Cato stood up and addressed the House. 'If Caesar will accept, then I shall be content to withdraw my motion that he be brought to trial.'

There was a ripple of applause and nodding of heads from the other senators, and Cato bowed his head graciously before stretching out a hand in the direction of Caesar. 'I have given my ground, Caesar. Will you now do the same?'

'Oh, the master is not going to like this,' Festus muttered. 'Better brace yourself for some shouting once we escort him back to his house.'

Marcus was watching Caesar, hoping that he would refuse to accept Cicero's deal.

Caesar nodded slowly. 'Very well. I accept. I will take command of a force to track down and destroy these rebels at the earliest opportunity. I swear to you that I will find this slave, Brixus, and bring him before this House to decide his punishment. I will crush the legacy of Spartacus once and for all.'

His words were cheered by the senators, and they were joined by those watching from the windows and doorways. But Marcus was silent. The very last thing he wanted was for Caesar to capture Brixus. What would his former owner do if he found out that Marcus was the son of Spartacus, the bitterest enemy that Rome had ever faced?

4

Festus was proved right. The moment that Caesar and his entourage entered his house, and the door to the street closed behind them, he flew into a rage. Marcus had never seen him so angry.

'Damn that man, Cicero! Damn him to the darkest pit in all Hades! Now I shall be forced to undertake some wild goose chase when I should be with my legions in Gaul.'

Clodius shrugged and examined the fingernails of his right hand. 'Then perhaps you should have refused, or at least given me the nod to intervene with my veto.'

'No. That is a power that should not be overused. We had to use it to stop the vote. To use it again against Cicero would have been too much for the Senate to stomach. Even my own supporters have a limit to their loyalty.' Caesar gritted his teeth. 'Now Cato has me where he wants me: stuck in Italia when I could be starting my campaign to conquer new lands and win glory for Rome.'

'Not to mention yourself,' Clodius added.

Caesar glared at him for a moment and then sighed wearily. 'Whatever you may think of me, I know that Rome is my first and only master. My life is dedicated to extending her power in the world.'

'Whatever you say, Caesar. Still, that leaves you with the problem of this man, Brixus, and his followers. What do you intend to do about it?'

'Just as I said. I intend to track them down, as well as every other band of rebels and runaways. Those we don't kill I will at least be able to sell.' Caesar pursed his lips. 'So there might be some benefit to be gained from this damned sideshow.'

Marcus felt his blood surge in his veins. Much as he had come to admire Caesar, the man was still a Roman through and through, which meant that he regarded slavery as a natural part of his world. He paid no attention to the suffering and humility of the slaves he encountered. For Marcus, who had been born free, the loss of his liberty had been the most terrible thing that had happened to him. It had meant the loss of his home, the man who had raised him, his mother, everything

37

that had any value. After that he had become simply one item amid the possessions of his owner, Lucius Porcino, the lanista of the gladiator school.

There he had been brutally treated, had Porcino's brand burned into his chest and been beaten and bullied by both the trainers and some of the other slaves. The memories of those days still haunted his dreams so that he sometimes woke with a start, bathed in sweat and trembling. One dream particularly troubled him: a recurring claustrophobic nightmare in which he relived his last fight as a slave. Then he had faced another boy from his school, Ferax, a youth from Gaul who was the leader of the boys who had made Marcus's life a misery.

In reality Marcus had won the fight, and Ferax had been knocked to the ground and forced to admit defeat. But when Marcus's back was turned the Gaul had leapt to his feet and tried to kill him. Only Marcus's fast reflexes had saved him and killed Ferax. But in the nightmares it was Ferax who triumphed, thrusting his sword again and again and again into Marcus's body as his brutal features twisted into a savage, spitting snarl.

Marcus hoped that it was the last such fight he would ever be involved in. But while Caesar had granted him his freedom, his former master still expected Marcus to continue with his training so that he might one day return to the arena and win fame and fortune as a professional gladiator. As the man who had paid for his training, Caesar would win the support of the Roman mob. Meanwhile, Marcus served under Festus in the bodyguard and had been required to swear that he would serve and protect Caesar for as long as he was his servant. It was Marcus's understanding that as soon as Caesar's agents had located his mother and arranged for her to be set free, then his obligations to his former master would be fulfilled.

And what then? He had little clear idea of what they would do with their lives after that. Once, he had thought they could return to the small farm on Leucas and continue the life they had lived before their little world was torn apart. Now that he was nearly two years older and more experienced, Marcus knew that could never happen. The farm had been taken by Decimus to cover the family's debts, so he and his mother would have to build a new life somewhere else. In many ways it would be for the best. It was impossible to have his old life back. The farm would be filled with painful memories, a constant reminder of what had been lost – the idyllic innocence of a childhood protected by two adults who loved him. All of that was gone now, and could never be recovered.

'The four legions assigned to me are in camp close to Ariminum,' said Caesar, drawing Marcus's attention back to the present. 'They are still preparing for the coming campaign; training recruits to bring their numbers up to full strength. I'll use the veterans for the job. They're good men. More than a match for the rabble skulking in the mountains. Ten cohorts should be enough to defeat Brixus.'

'Ten cohorts?' Clodius cocked an eyebrow. 'No more than five thousand men? Are you sure that's sufficient?'

'Of course.' Caesar flicked his hand dismissively, as if swatting an insect. 'It will all be over very quickly. The survivors will be taken to Rome, along with Brixus – or his body – and I shall make sure to reap my reward. The mob will cheer me, and Cato will have to swallow that stubborn arrogance of his and join in the applause. I can hardly wait to see his face.'

'Then let us hope that you will not have to report a defeat when you next face the Senate.'

'Defeat?' Caesar looked astonished. 'That's unthinkable. Impossible.'

'I hope so. When do you intend to leave for Ariminum?'

'At once. I'll take the Flaminian Way. It's the most direct route.'

'That's true,' said Clodius. 'But is it wise? It'll be hard going at this time of year, and you will be crossing the mountains where these rebels are hiding out.'

'I imagine they will be hiding in their caves, huddled over their fires. I shall be safe enough and besides I cannot afford any delay. The sooner the matter is dealt with the sooner I can turn my attention to far more important victories and conquests. I will leave at dawn. Festus!'

The leader of his bodyguard stepped forward and bowed his head. 'Yes, master.'

'I shall take you and six of your best men.' Caesar's gaze flickered towards Marcus. 'And you, young man. I suspect I shall need to call on your knowledge and skills once again. After all, you trained alongside gladiators. You know how they think, and you know how they fight. Yes, I am sure you will be very useful.' He turned back to Festus. 'I'll also need my scribe, Lupus. See that it is all arranged.'

'Yes, master.'

Caesar turned back to Clodius. 'I wish I knew precisely what I am up against. If this man, Brixus, is an escaped gladiator, then he will be a dangerous opponent. Even more dangerous if there is any truth to this rumour about the son of Spartacus joining forces with Brixus. If it's true, then the son must be found as soon as possible. Found, and then eliminated. Every slave in the empire must be made to realize that Rome never rests until its enemies are completely and utterly crushed.'

'Yes, Caesar. I will see to it.' Clodius nodded.

'I also expect that you will look after my interests here in Rome in my absence. I will expect regular reports of the proceedings of the Senate.'

'Don't worry. I will. Now I'd better leave you to your preparations.'

'Farewell, my friend.' Caesar smiled as he clasped the younger man's arm.

Clodius smiled back and then turned to leave the house. Once the door had closed behind him, Caesar's smile faded and he shook his head as he muttered, 'Thank the Gods that he isn't the only supporter I can rely on.'

Marcus could not help nodding in agreement and Caesar's eagle eye caught his gesture.

'So, you share my opinion of Clodius? That is good. I have always known I could rely on your sound judgement, my boy.'

'Yes, master.'

'Well then, we are about to face a new adventure, Marcus. You may have fought in the arena, and on the streets of Rome, but this will be your first campaign, maybe even your first real battle. I expect that you are looking forward to it, eh?'

Marcus forced himself to nod and Caesar punched him lightly on the shoulder.

'Just as I thought. You're a natural warrior through and through.' His expression became serious. 'I meant what I said about needing any advice you can give me . . . Now go and pack your kit and get an early night. We've got a long, uncomfortable ride ahead of us. Crossing the Apennines in winter is not easy.'

'I'll make sure that I pack some warm clothes, master,' said Marcus.

'Good. At least there's one thing to look forward to. My niece will be with her new husband at Ariminum. He's serving with the Tenth legion. I'm sure that Portia will be glad to see you again.'

'I hope so,' Marcus answered with feeling. She was one of the few people he had come to regard as a friend since arriving in Rome and he had missed her when she left Caesar's household to marry the nephew of General Pompeius, one of Caesar's closest allies. Together with Crassus, they were the three most powerful men in all Rome. It was an uneasy alliance, as Marcus knew only too well after having foiled a plot against his master by Crassus. A plot that had involved Decimus and his henchman, Thermon, the man who had murdered Titus and kidnapped Marcus and his mother. There would be a reckoning one day, Marcus vowed. The blood of Thermon and Decimus would run from his blade.

He thrust thoughts of revenge aside and bowed his head to Caesar.

'With your leave, master?'

'Yes, you may go. Goodnight, Marcus.'

Lupus had already heard about the journey by the time Marcus reached the small cell that they shared in the slave quarters of the house. Even though Marcus had been given his freedom he had no means of paying his own way and was obliged to remain in Caesar's house, sharing the same food and conditions of those who were still slaves. It suited him for now. After all, the only thing that mattered to him was waiting for Caesar's contacts in Greece to discover where his mother was. So he was content to stay close to Caesar and hear the news as soon as it reached Rome. Or Ariminum, as would now be the case.

'Ariminum.' Lupus smiled. He was a small thin boy, nearly four years older than Marcus, but could have passed for the same age. His dark hair was cropped short and he spoke with the usual quiet humility of those who had been born into slavery. 'I can't wait to see the place. It's supposed to be a beautiful city, close to the beach. Where the wealthy Romans go to relax.'

'I doubt it will be quite so pleasant in the middle of winter,' Marcus replied.

'Pleasant enough. In any case, a welcome change from Rome.'

Marcus nodded. The capital might be the heart of the empire, a vast city with grand buildings, public baths and every entertainment imaginable, but it was also crowded, with stinking narrow streets, and when summer came the air was stifling. The fresh air of the coast would indeed be welcome. But this would be no holiday.

'I doubt we'll have much time to take in the pleasures of Ariminum,' said Marcus. 'Caesar wants to complete his task as swiftly as possible. I imagine that we'll be there just long enough for him to muster his troops and then we'll be marching into the mountains. You'd better get used to the idea of living out in the snow, rain and wind.'

Lupus shuddered at the thought.

'And it won't just be the elements to contend with,' Marcus added. 'There will be fighting. Caesar thinks that he'll crush the rebels easily. I'm not so sure. They may lack training, but they'll be fighting for their lives, for their freedom. That will make them very dangerous.'

Lupus stared at him anxiously. 'I don't like the sound of

it. Why does Caesar need me to come along? What good would I be in a fight? I wouldn't know how to use a sword. Probably be more of a danger to our side than theirs.'

'It's not your sword Caesar needs, but your pen. He will want a record kept of his exploits. Something he can use to build his reputation later on.'

'Oh, good,' Lupus responded with a relieved expression. 'I suppose I'd better start packing.'

While his companion rummaged through his small chest of stationery Marcus began his own preparations. In addition to his sword, throwing knives and dagger, he took his gladiator cuirass down from its peg on the wall and carefully wrapped it in an old blanket before placing it in his kitbag. He also took a bronze buckler and the reinforced skullcap that Festus had made for him the previous year, leather bracers and a padded tunic to wear under his armour. Once all his fighting kit was packed he moved on to his clothing.

As he worked, his mind was distracted. So far, only his mother and Brixus knew the truth about his father's identity. And now it seemed that Brixus was spreading the word that Spartacus had a son and that the son would take up his father's cause. No doubt some Romans would refuse to believe it, thinking that Brixus had simply invented the story to win support for his cause. But there would be plenty of others who believed it, making Marcus's secret that much harder to keep. Caesar had already seen the brand on Marcus's shoulder but had not been able to place it. There might come a time when Caesar made the link between the brand and the rumour and realized who Marcus was. If that happened, then he would be put to death.

Marcus trembled at the thought. Not just out of fear for himself but also for his mother. Without him, what hope did she have? If Caesar were to find her after discovering Marcus's identity, then surely she would be killed too in the name of revenge?

There was a further matter that disturbed him. He had no wish to take part in any campaign against rebel slaves. If anything, he would rather fight alongside Brixus, against those who made people into their property. It was a doomed cause. Even if Brixus were to unite the bands of runaways and brigands, what hope would they have against the might of Rome? Caesar was desperate to crush them as quickly as possible. Even though he said he would only need five thousand men, the equivalent of one legion, there were three more legions he could use as reinforcements. The slaves' only hope would lie in finding an inspirational leader who combined the qualities of a great warrior, a wise general and a formidable personality. In short, a man like Spartacus. With such a man to lead them, tens of thousands of slaves would escape to swell the ranks of the rebellion, and at last Rome might meet her match. But Marcus was still a boy. If Brixus had plans for him to follow in his father's footsteps, then he would surely disappoint.

Marcus felt a sick sensation in the pit of his stomach. He felt trapped. He was marching to battle at the side of Caesar, to fight slaves whose fate he had once shared. And all the while he would live in fear of Caesar discovering his secret. If Brixus was captured and brought before the victorious Roman general, he'd be sure to recognize Marcus. Would he then betray him, either openly, or under torture?

The more he thought about it, the more anxious Marcus became. Once he had completed his packing, he extinguished the oil lamp and lay down on his bedroll to get some sleep. On the other side of the room Lupus lay on his back, snoring lightly. Marcus folded his arms behind his head and stared up into the darkness. Despite everything that had happened to him since being torn from his home and family, he knew that his greatest challenge lay ahead.

5

The small party of horsemen left Rome by the Flaminian gate at first light. Caesar wore a plain brown cloak as he rode at their head, not wanting to attract attention. He had written a brief note to the Senate, announcing that he had set off to destroy the rebels. By the time it was read out, the riders would be many miles from Rome and it would be too late for his political enemies to summon him to explain his plans. Cato and his allies would have been sure to use every trick in the book to delay Caesar. It surprised Marcus how often politicians put the advantage of their faction above the interests of Rome as a whole.

He cast a glance at Caesar riding at the front of the column. He was even more ambitious than the rest, keen to crush the new slave rebellion quickly so that he could proceed to win glory for himself in Gaul. Despite his misgivings about his former master, Marcus knew that Caesar always rewarded those who served him well. Marcus's victory in the fight against Ferax outside the Senate House had added to Caesar's reputation, enabling him to pass new laws improving the lives of ordinary Romans and removing some of the bitter tensions in Rome that could lead to a new civil war. Marcus had every intention to remind Caesar of his promise to help free Marcus's mother from slavery in return, and that meant staying at his side.

Marcus was riding with Lupus at the rear of the column. Having been raised on a farm, he had learned from an early age how to mount and ride a pony. By contrast Lupus was a poor horseman. He clung to his reins and leaned forward against his saddle horns as if he might fall from his mount at any moment.

'Sit up straight,' Marcus advised. 'The saddle horns will hold you in place. If we have to break into a trot or gallop, then clamp down on your thighs and heels and hold on.'

Lupus shot him a cross look. 'Easy for you to say.'

'Surely you've ridden before?'

'Oh, yes. I've had a few goes on the cook's mule, and some of the ponies on the master's country estate last year. But that's all.'

'I see.' Marcus sucked in a breath to cover up his disappointment. 'Well, I'm sure you'll get the hang of it soon enough.'

'Thanks for the encouragement,' Lupus replied tersely, as he hunched forward again and gripped the reins for dear life.

The road soon left Rome behind and as they crested the brow of a hill Marcus turned in his saddle to look back. Grey clouds were approaching from the west and already the great city was in shadow. The city comprised an ugly sprawl of buildings covering the seven hills, above which hung a filthy pall of woodsmoke. Marcus was glad to be out in the fresh air of the country with its clean scents. He would not miss Rome. Aside from the discomfort of its gloomy alleys, stench and the constant noise, there was the danger of street gangs and the bloodthirsty fickleness of the mob, as well as the endless plots and conspiracies of politicians. With a click of his tongue, he urged his horse forward and caught up with the rear of the column as it continued east, towards the snowcapped slopes of the Apennines.

It had been an unusually cold winter. The open countryside was bleak and the seasonal trees were stripped bare of leaves and stood gaunt and still, like splintering cracks against the leaden sky. The frequent showers of rain and a passing storm had left the fields waterlogged, while puddles gathered in the ruts and dips of the road. At first there were plenty of farms and villages along the route, their inhabitants living comfortably off the crops, fruit and meat that they sold at the markets in Rome. But as the day wore on, there were fewer buildings visible and they rode through unspoiled woods interspersed with much smaller farms and the occasional cluster of rural dwellings that could scarcely be called villages. The ruddy-faced inhabitants, who were outside cutting firewood or taking winter feed to their animals, paused with curious, and sometimes suspicious, expressions to watch the riders passing by and then continued with the unchanging routines of country existence.

After a brief rest at noon they set off again. The road entered the foothills of the mountains that ran down the spine of Italia, just as the clouds darkened the skies above, and with them came the first drops of rain. The riders hunched down inside their capes and pulled the hoods up as the rain pattered on the road. Marcus hoped that it might be a passing shower, but the rain continued to fall, and grew heavier. Despite the animal fat that had been worked into the cloaks to help water-proof them, it was not long before the riders were soaked through. The air was already cold and now the gentle breeze made it even colder.

Marcus could not prevent himself from shivering as he gripped the reins and clenched his teeth in concentration. He spared a glance at Lupus and saw that his companion was shaking uncontrollably as his teeth chattered.

Lupus caught his eye. 'Wh-when is the master going to stop and take sh-sh-shelter?'

'What shelter?' Marcus gestured at the landscape on either side of the road. There was nothing but rocks and stunted trees to be seen, and ahead the road entered a dense forest of pine trees. 'Perhaps up there.' He pointed at the treeline.

But when they reached the forest Caesar continued riding, and while Lupus muttered curses at his master, Marcus resigned himself to the discomfort and misery of the journey. The road continued through the trees and, as the slope increased, the route began to zigzag up the hill into the grey mist that shrouded the view of the surrounding landscape.

As dusk encroached on the dismally lit world, the horsemen finally reached the gates of a small town. Caesar presented his senator's ring to the cloaked sentries and they were ushered through the gate and into the street beyond. There were only a handful of travellers' inns in the town and only one of those large enough to take the entire party and stable their horses. Night had fallen before the needs of the mounts had been seen to and then Marcus, Lupus and the others joined Caesar and Festus inside where they sat at a bench close to the fireplace, sipping heated wine. They had already changed into dry clothes, and their riding cloaks, tunics and boots were drying by the fire.

As the drenched figures huddled close to the flames, the landlord of the inn came rushing out from a narrow doorway behind the counter.

'Ah, gentlemen, you must be chilled to the bone! Get those clothes off and sit you down. My wife and girls will see that they are dried. We've more racks in the kitchen. Just hand 'em to me and once you're dry and changed we'll bring you some nice hot stew.'

Marcus and the others gratefully peeled off their wet over-clothes and heaped them on the counter before rummaging through their saddlebags for dry garments. The cold had left Marcus with numbed hands and feet and he now rubbed his palms together in front of the fire until feeling returned to his fingers. Lupus simply stood with a vacant expression as he held his hands out towards the flames.

'Don't put your hands too close while you can't feel them,' said Marcus, 'or they'll start burning before you realize it.'

'I just want to be warm again,' the other boy muttered. 'By the Gods, I wish I was back in Rome.'

'Well, you're not. And you'd better get used to it. Caesar's on campaign now and where he goes the rest of us will follow.'

'Then let's hope that he deals with these rebels quickly and we get this over with.'

'Over with?' Marcus could not help smiling. 'This is just the beginning. When – if – he defeats the rebels, then Caesar aims to make a name for himself in Gaul. There'll be years of campaigning before he's done.'

Lupus lowered his hands and turned towards Marcus with a bleak expression. 'Years?'

The innkeeper returned and gathered up the bundle of wet clothes, taking them back into the kitchen. A squat, heavily built woman with a dark complexion soon emerged, carrying the wooden handle of a heavy cauldron. At once a rich aroma filled the room and Marcus felt his stomach rumbling as his appetite awoke. Behind the woman came a young girl, no more than eight, Marcus guessed, struggling under a large tray piled with wooden bowls and spoons.

The woman set the cauldron down on the counter and her daughter placed the bowls beside it. The first two bowls were filled with a ladle and the girl carried them across to Caesar and Festus. Having grown used to the deference with which Caesar was approached in Rome, Marcus could not help a soft gasp as Festus received the first bowl, and then his master, before the girl turned back to serve the others. Festus glanced anxiously at Caesar, but the great man just chuckled and waved his hand dismissively. He leaned forward and sniffed the stew.

'And what have we got here, innkeeper?'

The owner of the inn ducked out of the kitchen. 'Sir?'

'What's in the stew?'

'Goat. No shortage of that around the town!' the man said cheerfully. 'I do hope it's to your liking.'

Caesar tested a spoonful and nodded. 'Indeed it is. Just what a man needs after a day on the road, eh, lads?'

The men voiced their agreement, and as soon as they were served moved to a table on the far side of the room to avoid encroaching on their master. Marcus and Lupus were the last to take their bowls. As they headed towards the table where the bodyguards were bent over their food, Caesar called out.

'No. Over here. Join us, Marcus. You too, Lupus.'

They turned and crossed towards the table where the two men were seated.

'What does he want with us?' Lupus asked in a whisper.

'No idea,' Marcus replied softly.

They set their bowls down and each pulled up a stool, sitting nervously under the piercing gaze of Caesar's dark eyes.

He gestured towards their bowls and spoons. 'Eat up, boys. Tonight we are a happy band of travellers. We've left Rome and all those stiff social manners behind for a few days. Life has become a lot less complicated and that is the way I like it. We've escaped from those scheming rascals in the Senate and our task is simple and direct: track down and destroy this man Brixus and his rabble. That is all.' He took another spoonful of stew and chewed quickly on a chunk of meat. 'Damn fine stew this. Must remember to eat goat more often, right, Festus?'

'Yes, master.' The leader of his bodyguard bowed his head.

Marcus tucked in, his spirits rising with every mouthful of the richly flavoured meal. After a moment even Lupus got over the fact that he was sharing a table with his master and began to eat. At length Caesar pushed his empty bowl aside and leaned back against the cracked plaster wall behind his stool. He was silent for a moment and then folded his hands together.

'I've just remembered. I've seen this town before, years ago. I was only a tribune then, in the early days of my soldiering. I had just been appointed to one of the legions in Crassus's army and was riding to join him with a cohort of allied cavalry. We stopped at this town for the night. I didn't stay here. One of the local magistrates put me up for the night.' He paused. 'It was as dismal a place then as it is today.

Anyway, we rode on the next day and I never thought I'd be staying here again.'

Festus finished his bowl and wiped the back of his hand across his mouth. 'Crassus? Then that must have been when he was fighting Spartacus, master.'

'Indeed it was. That's what set my mind to it. Thinking about the enemy we face now. Last time I arrived just in time to witness the final great battle, when Crassus crushed the rebel army.'

'Crassus?' Marcus could not help being surprised. 'I was told that it was Pompeius who ended the rebellion, sir.'

'Pompeius?' Caesar cocked an eyebrow and chuckled. 'No, he reached the scene shortly afterwards, just in time to mop up the survivors of the main battle. I had the fortune to be witness to both battles, if you can call Pompeius's action a battle. Skirmish more like. Not that he described it that way to the Senate. Oh, no. He sent them a report stating that it was he who had put an end to the rebellion and killed Spartacus. As if Crassus had been doing nothing for the previous two years. That's Pompeius for you. He'll claim all the credit that he can.'

Marcus leaned forward and stared at his master intently as a peculiar anxiety to know more gnawed at his heart. 'You said you were at both battles, sir?'

'That's right. After the first one, Crassus sent me to find Pompeius and request that he block the survivors' escape route. He did that right at least.'

Marcus felt his pulse quicken. He had rarely heard Titus, the retired centurion who had raised him, talk of the rebellion. The brutality and hardship of the campaign had scarred Titus for the rest of his life. Now Marcus had a chance to discover more about his true father.

'What was it like, sir? What happened?' Marcus swallowed nervously. 'Did you ever see Spartacus himself?'

'So many questions.' Caesar smiled faintly. 'Well, there's nothing else to do in this place but talk.'

Lupus discreetly reached for his satchel and pulled out a waxed notebook. Caesar shook his head. 'No need for that. I am not anxious to record my part in the slave revolt for posterity. The sooner the whole episode is forgotten the better.' Lupus nodded and returned his writing tools to his satchel, while Caesar closed his eyes for a moment to collect his thoughts, then began. 'It was a war like no other I've ever seen, or heard of. Neither side took many prisoners and the slaves showed no mercy to any slave traders or overseers who fell into their hands. Of course, most of this I got second hand from the men who had been fighting Spartacus and his rebels during the earlier years of the revolt. By the time I joined Crassus he had closed in on them, trying to force Spartacus to turn and give battle. He was like a wounded animal: never more dangerous than when they are trapped and know they must fight or die. So Spartacus formed his army up on a ridge across our line of march.'

Caesar stared at the table in front of him and Marcus willed him to go on. Caesar cleared his throat and continued, his voice a little lower. 'Even though we outnumbered them, I could see that our soldiers were nervous at the prospect of a fight. I remember that I did not understand their reaction. They were trained soldiers and well equipped. Many of them were veterans of previous campaigns. When I looked at the rebels I could see that many of them only carried farming tools and wore little or no armour. There were women there too, and even old men and boys. There were several thousand in the centre of the line who were well equipped and were formed up in a disciplined line. Behind them a body of mounted men surrounded Spartacus and his standard.'

'You saw him, master?' asked Lupus, his eyes gleaming with excitement.

'Yes. He rode a white horse and wore black armour and a helmet with a dark crest. Quite a striking figure.'

Marcus felt a surge of pride at the description of his father, accompanied by the regret of never having had a chance to know him.

'As we deployed in our usual formation of staggered units I heard a murmur from the rebel lines. At first I could not make it out, then I realized it was his name. Spartacus . . . Spartacus . . . Spartacus! Rising up until it became a thunderous chant that echoed across the battlefield. Then they charged. Like a wave. I don't remember hearing any signal. It was as if they shared one thought. One instinct. To kill every Roman that stood before them. I don't mind telling you that I felt afraid then. It surprised me at the time, but there was no denying they were a terrifying sight as they came at us.

'They smashed into our leading units, charging straight on to our shields and swords and dying in their hundreds. But they were like wild animals, fighting with their bare fists if they lost their weapons. Even the wounded fought on from the ground where they lay, using hands and teeth. Our first line held them for a while, but not even the best soldiers in the world could withstand such demons for long. The second line moved forward to join the fight. That was when Crassus gave the order that tipped the battle in our favour.' Caesar's eyes glinted as he recalled the moment. 'The rebels had driven a wedge deep into the heart of our battle-line, so Crassus had his last line move out to each side and quickly march round to charge the rebels in the flanks. As soon as the trumpets sounded, our men let out a roar and closed in. The rebels held them for a while, then some panicked and broke away. Then more dispersed and soon they were finished. Our cavalry closed the trap and only a few thousand got away. The rest were annihilated.'

'And Spartacus?' Marcus interrupted. 'What of him?'

'He and his bodyguard covered the retreat of the survivors until our men were too exhausted to pursue them any further. Crassus realized that if Spartacus escaped he would be bound to stir up a fresh rebellion elsewhere. So he sent me to find Pompeius and, ah, advise him to block Spartacus's route.'

'Advise?' Festus frowned.

'One does not give orders to Pompeius the Great.' Caesar smiled. 'Crassus knew that it was too important a matter to risk offending Pompeius and thereby let the enemy slip away. Anyway, I found Pompeius and gave him the message, and remained with him while his men marched on Spartacus. It was all over very quickly. The rebels were exhausted and many were wounded. Yet they formed up round their leader and fought to the end. We only took a handful of prisoners. None matched the description that had been given to us by his old lanista.'

'Did you see him again?' Marcus asked excitedly. 'Spartacus?'

'I saw him with his closest lieutenants. They were mounted on the last of their horses. Just before the fight began they dismounted and killed their beasts, to show that they would share the fate of their comrades. When the last of them had fallen, I joined Pompeius and his officers as they picked over the battlefield. We found some black armour and a helmet. I suppose that his followers tore it off him when they saw him cut down. Many of the bodies were too mutilated to be identified.'

Marcus shuddered but tried hard not to show his revulsion.

'Perhaps Spartacus survived,' Lupus suggested.

'I can't see how he could have escaped. He must have fallen in the final battle. I am sure of it.'

'He would have stayed and died with the others,' Marcus said at once, then looked round at the others quickly. 'At least, that's what I would have done. If I were him.'

Festus laughed and gave Marcus a good-humoured slap on the back. 'A handful of fights under your belt and already you think you're another Spartacus!'

Caesar stared at Marcus. 'I sincerely hope not. The first one nearly destroyed Rome. We would not be able to survive a second Spartacus. Besides, I have grown fond of you, Marcus. It would distress me if we ever became enemies. Then I would be obliged to destroy you.'

He spoke in a matter-of-fact tone but his words chilled Marcus to the core. Not for the first time, he feared that Caesar knew more about him than he realized. But he had to push those thoughts aside, be strong and see this through. He had to be as strong as his father had been. He took a calming breath and addressed his former master.

'I have served you loyally, sir. There is no reason to think that we should ever become enemies.'

Caesar looked at him, then gave a light laugh. 'Of course not. Besides I have somewhat larger and more formidable adversaries to worry about.' He yawned. 'It's been a long day. We're warm and our stomachs are full. We'd better get a good night's sleep. I want us back on the road at dawn, Festus. See to it that I am roused with the rest of the men in good time.'

'Yes, master.'

Caesar rose from the table and rubbed the base of his spine with a grimace. Then he nodded to his companions and climbed a flight of stairs at the rear of the inn that led to the handful of small rooms that were rented to travellers. Festus turned to the boys.

'I've sorted out a room for you two. The innkeeper has space in his cellar. He's put two bedrolls down for you, but says to watch out for the rats. Sometimes they bite.'

'Rats?' Lupus's face went pale.

'He was probably joking, but all the same take care, eh?' Festus stood up and made for the other men to give them their orders.

'Rats,' Lupus repeated. 'I hate rats.'

'Then make sure you push them to the side of the plate,' Marcus joked. 'Come on, I'll make sure you're safe.'

The innkeeper's wife showed them down to the cellar by the light of an oil lamp, then left it on the bottom of the narrow stairs so they could see enough to prepare to sleep. Lupus glanced warily around the shadows in the cellar before he settled down, but despite his concerns he was soon asleep. Once again, Marcus lay awake for a while, deep in thought.

This time he was thinking about Spartacus. Slowly, his heart filled with pride in his father's achievements and the example he had set for those who followed him, prepared to fight and die at his side. Something began to stir inside him. A vague inspiration and more: a sense that it was his duty to honour his father. To be worthy of his name and all that he had achieved in his short life. After all, the same blood coursed through Marcus's veins – the same skill at arms, and the same burning desire for freedom.

6

The next day the small party of riders left the foothills behind as the road climbed into the mountains. The rain had stopped during the night and a hard frost glinted on the ground as they set off. Before noon they had climbed above the snowline, and the rocks and trees on either side were covered by a gleaming blanket of white. But despite the snow, the route was plain to see as they rode on, up into the hills. The heavily laden boughs of fir trees deadened the sound of their passing and added to the unsettling sensation of stillness. The conversation between the riders died away as they kept a wary eye on their surroundings. They had lived in Rome so long they had grown used to the constant noise of the great city. Now the silence was unnerving them. There was only the soft padding of the horses, the chink of the bits and the occasional snort as the animals expelled warm steamy breath from their wide nostrils.

'I don't like this,' Lupus muttered.

'What's the matter?' Marcus tried to sound more confident than he felt. 'Fresh air, peace and quiet and fine views. What could there be to dislike? Apart from the cold.'

'That's bad enough, but there's something else.' Lupus looked from side to side. 'I don't know, but I can't help feeling that we're being watched.'

'Who by? We haven't passed a single dwelling for hours. The last person we saw was that shepherd a few miles back.' Marcus recalled the solitary figure holding a staff who had watched them from the top of a small cliff. 'And he ran off the moment he saw us.'

'Yes,' Lupus pondered. 'I've been wondering about that. Why did he run?'

'He was just nervous. A party of horsemen appears and he fears that they might be brigands. That's why.'

'Perhaps there's something else to it.'

Marcus looked at him. 'What are you saying?'

'Perhaps he wasn't a shepherd. Maybe he was a lookout.'

'And who would he be looking out for?'

'People like us. Travellers. Easy prey for a band of brigands.

Or worse, the rebels. Supposing that man was a lookout, and he's reported us?'

Marcus glanced over his shoulder, down the road to the point where it turned back on itself and was lost in the trees. There was no sign of movement. He shrugged as he faced the front again. 'If there was anything sinister about him, then I think we'd know about it by now.'

Lupus was silent for a moment. 'I hope you're right.'

Both boys fell silent again, but Marcus was starting to share his friend's anxiety. A mile further on they cleared the treeline and the road climbed towards a narrow pass between two rocky peaks hidden by wreaths of cloud. Marcus breathed a sigh of relief at leaving the confines of the forest. On either side the ground was littered with stones and rocks and afforded little cover for an ambush. Up ahead, the men were talking again and Marcus felt encouraged by their return to the earlier easy conversation and exchange of jokes. Even Lupus seemed more relaxed. The road began to narrow and Marcus allowed his friend to pull a short distance ahead. He needed time to think.

Caesar's comment the previous night was preying on his mind. Despite the debt that Caesar owed him for saving his niece's life, it would mean very little if he decided that Marcus represented any threat to him, or to Rome. Marcus felt he was living on a knife-edge. He must be careful about every comment he made and keep the brand on his shoulder out of sight. He could trust no one, not even Lupus. A wave of bitter loneliness washed over him and he felt the first hot tears at the corner of his eyes. Marcus raised his hand and cuffed them away angrily. He could not afford to be weak, he told himself. He had to be strong if he was to survive. And he had to survive if he was to rescue his mother.

A cold speck brushed his cheek and he looked up and saw that it had begun to snow again, light flecks of white dropping gently from the overcast sky. Ahead, the road came to another hairpin bend, and Caesar and Festus steered their mounts round to lead the column up the new stretch. As Marcus came to the bend, some sixth sense caused him to rein his horse in, and he turned in his saddle to look back down the slope towards the forest.

He saw them at once. Another party of horsemen, twenty or so of them, no more than half a mile behind. They were moving at a slow trot and appeared in no hurry to catch up. Even so, Marcus felt a pang of concern and kicked his heels in as he urged his horse forward.

'Make way!' he warned Lupus, who glanced round with a surprised expression before steering his horse to the side of the road. Marcus trotted by without any comment and carried past the other riders until he drew up alongside Caesar.

'Sir, there's someone following us.' Marcus pointed down the slope, but the lower road was invisible from this point. Caesar glanced down the rock-strewn ground.

'What are you talking about? I see no one.'

'They are there, sir. I saw them plainly.'

'How many?' Festus asked sharply.

'Twenty, about.'

'Where?'

'They were just coming out of the forest.'

'Well, I can't see much thanks to this snow,' Caesar muttered. 'Are you sure about this, Marcus?'

'I am certain, master.'

Caesar stroked his chin. 'You saw them from where exactly?'

'Back where the road turns.'

Caesar sighed. 'Then we'd better have a look.'

The column halted and the three made their way back down the line until they reached the bend and stopped as close to the edge as they dared to peer down the steep slope. Below, the snow was falling hard and it was difficult to make out more than the dim outline of the forest.

There was a brief silence before Festus growled, 'I can't see anything.'

'No,' Caesar added quietly before he turned to Marcus. 'Are you quite certain about what you saw? Tired eyes sometimes play tricks.'

Marcus felt a brief instant of doubt, then shook it off. 'I saw horsemen, sir. I know it.'

'Well, there's nothing down there now,' said Festus. 'Nothing I can see.'

'Nevertheless, I trust the boy's judgement,' Caesar responded firmly. 'I want you to stay at the rear. Keep watch behind us. If you see anything, then let me know at once.'

Festus bowed his head and Caesar was about to turn his horse round when the snow cleared and, as if a veil had been drawn back, the ground beneath came into view again, together with the party of horsemen trotting up the track, closer now than when Marcus had first spotted them.

'Get the men moving!' Caesar snapped. 'Let's get up to the pass. It's a natural choke point. We can wait for them there. If they mean us no good, then that's where we shall make a stand. Go.'

Festus wheeled his mount away and it kicked up a spray of snow as he galloped to the head of the column. Caesar squinted as he scrutinized the horsemen below. 'They're armed. I can see spears, shields, some helmets. Not soldiers from our side at any rate. There's no standard at their head. No sign of an officer. I fear they may be trouble, young Marcus.' He blinked and turned to look at his former slave. 'Well spotted. Once more you serve me well. Come, I want you at my side.'

They trotted back to the head of the column and Caesar waved them forward as he kicked his heels in. There was no need to race ahead of the other men, and in any case the ground beneath the light layer of snow was frozen hard and presented an additional hazard to any horse and rider who slipped and fell. They continued up the slope, and at every corner Marcus looked down to see that the pursuers were remorselessly edging closer. They urged their mounts on, heedless of the risk, and he saw one or two of them tumble into the snow. One went over the edge and tumbled a good thirty feet before landing hard against a rock. The rider lay dazed and the horse floundered in a drift as it struggled to regain its feet. Then they were lost from sight again.

As the road approached the pass it began to level out and Caesar called to his men. 'We're almost there! As soon as we gain the pass, we'll stop and dismount!'

Marcus was about to spur his beast on when he looked back

and saw Lupus struggling to stay in the saddle, his face white and drawn with fear as he clung to the reins. Before Marcus could drop back to help him, Festus drew alongside the scribe and urged the boy on. He looked up and caught Marcus's eyes, nodding as if to reassure him that he would take care of Lupus. Marcus leaned forward and kicked his heels in to catch up with Caesar. Ahead of them crags rose up on either side of the pass, dusted with snow and ice.

They were barely a hundred feet from the narrow opening to the pass when a tall figure stepped out from a rock and strode confidently into the middle of the road. He stood facing the riders, hands on hips.

'What's this?' Caesar hissed as he slowed down and threw up his hand to stop his men ploughing into the back of him. The column slowed to a walk while Marcus's gaze flickered from the man to the rocks on either side and back again. He felt the familiar tingle of apprehension in the hairs at the back of his neck.

'That's close enough!' the man called out when they were no more than twenty feet away.

Caesar reined in and sat tall and imperious in his saddle. 'What is the meaning of this?' he demanded.

Now they were close to the man, Marcus could see that he

was a giant, well over six feet tall. He had thick blond hair that merged with a shaggy beard and blue eyes that twinkled beneath his heavy brows. A wolfskin cloak lay across his broad shoulders and the snout and ears of a preserved head were just visible on the crown of his head. Beneath the cloak he wore a striped tunic and the breeches favoured by the Celts. The head of an axe protruded from the belt that held his breeches up. The man's lips parted in a smile as he sauntered a few steps closer to the riders. Marcus noted that there was no sign of fear in his expression.

'The meaning of this should be plain enough.' The man spoke in a rich booming voice. 'This pass belongs to me and like any owner I want to know the business of those who cross my land.'

'I see.' Caesar nodded. 'And might I ask the name of the man who lays claim to a road which, until now, I understood to be the property of Rome?'

'Please forgive my country manners,' the man replied in a mocking tone. 'I am Mandracus, lord of the lands either side of this pass. That is why I must exact a toll from those who wish to cross my territory. And who are you, sir? I can tell from the cut of your clothes and the haughty accent that you are a well-bred Roman.'

With a soft pounding of hoofs, Festus rode up from the rear of the column and reined in beside his master.

'Who is this peasant? Stand aside, before we cut you down.'

'Enough, Festus!' Caesar cut in. He turned back to Mandracus. 'I am an official crossing the mountains on the business of the Senate. It is a crime to impede my progress.' Caesar smiled coldly. 'However, being mindful of your country manners, I shall not have you flogged, if you stand aside and let us pass.'

Mandracus pursed his lips and shook his head. 'I'm sorry, sir, but I can't do that.'

As the men spoke, Marcus had been watching the rocks on either side of the pass and caught sight of movement there. A face staring at them. Another man in the shadow of a rock, holding a spear and shield.

'Enough of this foolishness!' Caesar snapped. 'Out of my way!'

Mandracus stood his ground and drew out his axe, swinging it loosely at his side. At the signal, more men appeared from behind the rocks and moved out into the path. Marcus saw at least thirty of them. Some looked as solid as Mandracus, but most were thin, their faces pinched by hunger, and desperation gleamed in their eyes. But all of them were armed, with a mix of spears, swords and axes. Their leader gestured towards them.

'As you can see, we outnumber you three to one. And five to one once the rest of my men come up the road behind you. There's no way out.'

Festus's hand slipped to the hilt of his sword and Marcus and the rest of the bodyguard followed suit as they waited for Caesar's lead. The former consul regarded the men in front of him and then folded his arms. 'And what is it that you want from us, Mandracus?'

'There's a certain procedure to be followed.' The brigand smiled. 'First, do you have any slaves with you?'

'Slaves?' Caesar gestured towards Lupus, who was trembling with cold and fear as he sat in his saddle. 'Just my scribe.'

'Then we shall have to deprive you of him. No man is a slave in my territory. Second, I shall have to ask you for any gold or silver you may have, together with your weapons and horses. After that you are free to continue through the pass. Or return the way you came. You will find shelter from the snow closer in that direction.'

'And if we refuse?'

Mandracus's expression hardened. 'Then we shall be forced to kill you all, except the slave, and take what we want anyway.'

There was a brief silence before Caesar spoke quietly through gritted teeth, just loud enough for Marcus and Festus to hear. 'When I give the word, we charge that fool and his rabble. Ready?'

'Yes, Caesar,' Festus and Marcus muttered.

Caesar drew a deep breath and was about to make his reply when he was interrupted by the sound of hoof beats. Marcus turned to see that the horsemen had crested the final rise along the road and were now approaching the pass. They fanned out across the open ground on either side of the road and readied their weapons.

Mandracus shrugged. 'Like I said, you are trapped. You have no choice but to do what you're told, if you want to live. Now throw down your weapons and get off those horses! Do it!'

Marcus concentrated his attention on Caesar as he clamped his thighs to the side of his mount and wrapped his fingers firmly round the handle of his sword. Caesar let out a sigh, as if surrendering to the inevitable, and casually reached for his own weapon. But instead of drawing it out and tossing it to the ground, he snatched it out in a blur and thrust it towards the path as he shouted at the top of his voice.

'Charge!'

7

Marcus flicked his cloak back and ripped his sword from its scabbard. Around him he heard the metallic clatter as the other bodyguards followed suit. Only Lupus was unarmed and he looked on in horror. With a curse, Marcus transferred his reins to his sword hand and groped for the dagger on the other side of his belt. He steered his horse closer to Lupus and held out the dagger by its blade. 'Take it!'

The other boy hesitated briefly before he grabbed the handle and held it in an overhand grip, raising it above his head ready to strike. There was no time for Marcus to tell his friend the correct way to wield a dagger and he spoke through gritted teeth. 'Stay close to me, Lupus. If any of those men get close to you, don't stop to think about it, just stab them or they'll kill you first.'

The other bodyguards surged forward, kicking up a spray

of snow as they followed Caesar. Marcus dug his heels in and chased after them, leaning forward in his saddle and holding his blade to the side of the horse's flank, level and ready to strike.

Caesar's order had taken the brigands by surprise. Their leader was forced to leap aside as Caesar's mount charged directly towards him. The rest of his men were slower to react and the horsemen were in among them before they could get out of the way. The air filled with the thud and clash of blades and spears, and grunts as men struck out with all their strength. Cries of pain and triumph echoed from the cliffs either side of the pass, along with the whinnies of the horses.

Marcus, his heart beating wildly, urged his mount into the swirling confusion of the fight. He glimpsed Mandracus springing back to his feet and raising his axe as he charged at one of the bodyguards. The man saw him at the last moment, too late to react, and the head of the axe slammed down into his thigh, cutting through flesh, muscle and bone. The rider howled with agony and slashed back with his sword, striking a weak blow on his enemy's shoulder. Most of the impact was absorbed by the wolfskin, and the thick folds of the tunic beneath, but it still drove Mandracus to his knees. Gritting his teeth in agony, the rider kicked his good heel in and looked for another attacker.

Marcus urged his mount into a gap between two of the riders and made for a man with a spear who had worked his way round behind Festus and was raising the weapon to strike. Leaning forward in his saddle, Marcus slashed his sword at the butt of the spear, knocking it down so that the tip swished harmlessly over Festus's shoulder. The leader of Caesar's bodyguard caught the blur out of the side of his eye and instantly wheeled his horse round, slashing down at the man who had tried to kill him, and laying open his arm. Another cut to the shoulder put the brigand out of action.

Meanwhile Caesar was surrounded by Mandracus's men and he pulled hard on the reins to make his horse rear up and lash out with its hoofs, forcing his opponents back. It was impossible to keep them all at bay and even as Marcus watched, he saw one of them stab a pitchfork into the horse's rump. A shrill whinny cut through the air and the beast lashed out with its rear legs, catching the man to send him flying. Marcus flicked his reins and drew up alongside Caesar, lashing out with his sword to keep the others back. Caesar acknowledged his presence with a swift nod.

'We have to get out of here. Those horsemen will join the fight any moment.'

Marcus glanced round, past the men locked in combat, and saw the other riders racing up the incline towards them, no more than a hundred paces away. Once they reached the pass it would all be over.

'Festus!' Caesar called out above the din of the fight. 'All of you, on me! On me! We must cut our way through!'

The bodyguards edged their mounts closer to Caesar and formed a loose ring. Looking round, Marcus could see that one was missing, and then he saw a group of brigands bending towards the ground beside a horse with an empty saddle. They were hacking and stabbing at the man on the ground, their weapons dripping with blood each time they came up for another blow. The bodyguard with the wounded leg was swaying in his saddle and moaning through clenched teeth as blood coursed from his wound, splashing on to the snow like exotic flowers. Lupus, who had managed to stay with Marcus, held his dagger up as a snarl distorted his features.

Mandracus had worked his way round to return to his position astride the road leading into the pass. He bellowed to his men to form up either side of him. Those who could did as they were ordered, chests heaving as their breath plumed in the freezing air.

Caesar glanced round at his men, then thrust his sword forward. 'Stop for nothing! Go!'

The small party of riders burst into a gallop, and at the last moment the courage of the brigands failed and most tried to dive out of the way. A handful of the braver men stood by their leader, weapons levelled as the horses charged into them and they were either cut down or trampled. Only Mandracus remained on his feet, swinging his axe from side to side, forcing the nervous riders to swerve round him. Beyond, the road was open and Marcus briefly dared to hope they had escaped. He glanced back and saw Lupus behind him, cloak flickering wildly as he hunched over his saddle, still holding the dagger aloft.

'Keep up!' Marcus shouted.

Beyond his friend he saw Mandracus spin round, draw back his axe and swiftly take aim.

'Lupus! Look out!' Marcus yelled desperately.

Then the axe flew through the air. For an instant Marcus focused on Lupus's confused and fearful expression. Then his horse abruptly collapsed to one side of the road, hurling the scribe from the saddle. Blood sprayed into the air from the shattered rear limb of the horse and it kicked and writhed as it struggled to roll back on to its belly. As it tried to rise up, the wounded leg gave way and the horse fell on to its side with a shrill, agonized whinny.

Marcus reined in, half turning his horse so it stood across

the track. Then he saw Lupus stir. The boy pushed himself up on to his hands and knees, and shook his head. Marcus was about to ride back when Festus called out.

'Marcus! What are you doing? Come on, boy!'

'It's Lupus! He's fallen!'

Festus muttered a curse and turned back, slewing his horse to a halt beside Marcus. They both saw Lupus start staggering towards them. He had lost the dagger and stretched out a hand pleadingly. Marcus beckoned frantically with his spare hand as he sheathed his sword.

'Run!'

Mandracus was already striding along the road behind Lupus, a cruel grin twisting his lips. He stopped beside the horse to snatch up his axe and continued after Lupus as Marcus looked on in horror. Then the spell was broken and he grabbed his reins to ride back and rescue his friend.

'No!' Festus shouted and snatched the reins from Marcus's hands, causing his horse to rise up and snort.

'What are you doing?' Marcus snapped. 'Let go!'

'It's too late. Look!'

Marcus turned. He saw Mandracus lean forward to grab Lupus by the scruff of his neck, then hurl him to the ground. Standing over the boy, he began to swirl his axe, looking up at the two riders watching him a short distance away. Behind him his mounted followers were dashing past, eager to chase down the Romans.

'We can't save him,' said Festus. 'We can only save ourselves, if we go now. Marcus!'

His raised voice jolted Marcus, who took a last despairing look at his friend sprawled in the snow. But he knew that Festus was right: it was too late. With guilt coursing through every inch of his body, Marcus snapped his reins and turned away, galloping after Caesar. The others were already well into the pass, making for the open ground on the far side. Behind them the sound of their pursuers echoed off the walls of the cliff as Mandracus bellowed an order.

'Run them down! Kill them all!'

His booming voice sounded like thunder in the confined space and Marcus glanced back to see the first of the horsemen sweep past their leader. Then there was another sound. A dull crack. Something moved above the pass and drew Marcus's eyes. The mass of snow piled there slowly tilted forward and then broke into large chunks amid an explosion of white that fell into the pass with a roar and a hiss. The horsemen barely had time to look up before the avalanche hit them and swept them and their mounts away, burying them amid a great swirl of snow and rocks. Marcus slowed down and turned in his saddle to look properly as the last of the dislodged snow pattered down. Then all was still.

'Marcus!' Festus called out. 'We must go!'

'Yes.' Marcus swallowed and nodded. 'Yes, I'm coming.'

Festus started to gallop away while Marcus took one last look. He felt a numbing sense of loss. 'Lupus . . .'

Then he breathed deeply, gathered up his reins and turned his horse towards the others. He urged it into a gallop and the mount carried him away from the horror of the scene.

It was pitch-black and impossible to tell which way was up or down when Lupus recovered his wits enough to think. He lay curled in a ball, sensing an open space in front of him in which to draw breath. He was cold and his limbs were numb. Already the air felt foetid and there was a tingling sensation in his lungs as he began to suffocate. For a moment he could not recall how he had come to be in this place. Perhaps, he thought, he had already passed into the shades and this was what happened after death. An eternity locked in a stifling, black, icy void. The prospect filled him with dread and he tried to move. But he could only shuffle his head from side to side as he clawed at the blanket of snow.

'No . . .' he muttered to himself. 'No! NO! I am not dead! I do not want to die! No!'

His shouts were muffled and the effort made it harder to breathe, so he stopped and gasped for air. Then he heard them. Voices. They seemed far away at first but gradually came closer, more distinct.

'Here!' he cried out. 'In here!'

There was a pause before he heard them again, near at hand. Then a scraping sound. He sensed movement around him, and a faint gleam to one side. It became a glow as the sound grew louder, and then there was a rush of noise and light and the flow of fresh air. He gulped down several breaths as a hand grasped him under the shoulders, hauling him out of the snow and ice into the open.

'Mandracus! Over here! I've got one of 'em. A boy.'

Any relief that Lupus felt over his rescue instantly faded as he sat up and took in the scene around him. The pass was filled with a chaotic jumble of snow. There was a man wrapped in furs standing over him. Other men were frantically digging as they searched for their comrades. Some had already been rescued, along with several horses, and they sat nearby, caked in a layer of ice and shivering.

Mandracus picked his way over the debris towards them,

his expression angry and dark. He loomed in front of Lupus and glared at him.

'I lost over twenty of my men, killed by your master and his friends, or buried alive.'

'Please, please don't hurt me,' Lupus begged as he sat trembling.

'Hurt you?' Mandracus frowned. 'I won't hurt you, boy. I've set you free. You are one of us now. For better or worse. Your days as a slave are over.'

Lupus could hardly believe what he had heard. When it did finally penetrate his confusion, he looked up with a surge of hope. 'I'm free?'

Mandracus nodded. 'Of course. Do as you wish. I will not stop you. After all, if you want to escape from me, you would simply run back to slavery. But there is one thing I would know. I want the name of your leader. I have a debt to settle with him. What is his name?' he demanded.

'Gaius Julius Caear.'

'The consul?' Mandracus could not hide his surprise. 'That was him?'

'Not any more. His term of office is over. He's a proconsul now,' Lupus explained. 'On his way to take up a new command.'

'Then what is he doing in the mountains? With such a small escort? Explain.'

'Before he leaves for Gaul, Caesar has been tasked with putting an end to Brixus and his rebels.'

'Oh, really?' Mandracus smiled. 'Tell me, how close are you to your master?'

Lupus struggled to his feet and stood proudly before the man. 'I am Caesar's scribe. I've served him for many years.'

'Good. Then I'm sure you'll have plenty to tell Brixus when I take you to him. He'll want to know all he can about his enemy. Who else was in your party?'

'No one of importance. Just his bodyguards.'

'What about the other boy?'

'Marcus?' Lupus shrugged. 'Not much to say. He's my friend. Marcus was training as a gladiator when Caesar bought him.'

A strange gleam appeared in Mandracus's eyes as he muttered to himself. 'A boy gladiator . . . Where was he training? Which school?'

'Porcino's school in Capua is what he said.' Lupus frowned. 'Why do you want to know?'

'I'll tell you later. But first we must find Brixus. He'll be keen to hear all that you've told me, and more.' Mandracus looked round at the survivors. 'Perhaps this was worth it,' he mused as he turned his attention back to Lupus. 'Perhaps Brixus is right. The time has come to raise the standard of rebellion, and Spartacus, once again . . .'

8

Ariminum was a small town on the east coast of Italia, with a modest port where the river entered the sea. On either side a broad beach of brown sand stretched out for several miles. The water was shallow for a good distance out and Marcus could see why wealthy Romans came here to rest and play in the summer months. But in winter the town reverted to being a quiet backwater where occasional cargo ships dropped anchor and the local fishermen sat on the sand in the shelter of their beached boats, carefully examining their nets. A mile to the north lay the camp of the army that Caesar had been appointed to command.

The twenty thousand men of the four legions occupied an area that dwarfed the nearby town. The camp was in the shape of a vast square, with one legion assigned to each quadrant. A low perimeter wall and ditch surrounded the city of tents, with towers at regular intervals and a fortified gate halfway along each side. Two wide thoroughfares intersected at the heart of the camp where the largest tents stood. Around them stretched row after row of goatskin tents, each shared by eight legionaries. Outside the camp, thousands of men were engaged in drilling and weapons practice.

It was a spectacular sight but Marcus could not summon up any excitement. He sat in his saddle beside the other riders, surveying the scene from the last rise in the ground before the road reached Ariminum. Three days had passed since their lucky escape in the mountains. The man injured in the leg had been left at Hispellum, the first town they had reached. A Greek surgeon there said he would recover, but would be left with a crippling limp for the rest of his life. It was the loss of Lupus that had hit Marcus hard. He had encountered few people he considered friends since being enslaved, and to lose another was a cruel reminder of his loneliness.

There had been Brixus during his days at the gladiator school in Capua. Then Brixus had discovered Marcus's identity before escaping from the school to find his former comrades from the Spartacus revolt. And now they too knew that the son of their hero was alive. When Brixus had revealed the truth, it had shaken Marcus's world to the ground. Titus, the man he thought was his father, and had admired and loved, had been one of the Romans who crushed the slave revolt and killed his real father. It had been hard to accept at first, but since Marcus had learned more about Spartacus his respect for the father he had never known had steadily increased. Respect, but not the affection he had known for Titus. How could it be otherwise?

Then, when he had been brought to Rome, he'd befriended Portia, Caesar's niece, after saving her life. A few years older than Marcus, she had been sent to Rome to be raised by her uncle while her father campaigned in Hispania. Her loneliness and her gratitude to Marcus had drawn them closer than was usual for the niece of a consul and one of his slaves. However, Marcus had always felt a sense of reserve in her company. There were limits to what a slave could say openly in such circumstances. Marcus was a little nervous at the prospect of meeting her again in Ariminum. She would surely have changed now she was married to Quintus, and might not like reminding of her closeness to one of her uncle's servants, even though he had been granted his freedom.

His other friends had been the two boys Marcus had shared a cell with in Caesar's household: Corvus and Lupus. The former had worked in the kitchen, often bitter about the way life had treated him. But he had courage and in the end had given his life to protect Portia. Then there was Lupus. Lupus was a gentle soul who loved his craft and read books too, and even seemed to enjoy them. Now Lupus was gone, and Marcus felt alone again as he grieved for his friend.

'We'll make for the camp first,' Caesar announced, interrupting Marcus's dark thoughts, 'before I arrange for accommodation in Ariminum.'

He waved his hand forward and broke into an easy canter to cover the last few miles. The others spurred their mounts and followed him down the road. A short distance from the town gate they turned on to a side road that led towards a wooden bridge over the river. The autumn and winter rains in the Apennines had swollen the river so that it threatened to breach the banks as it rushed past the pylons supporting the bridge.

As the riders approached the camp, they reached the first group of soldiers exercising at the palus, a wooden stake the size of a man. The legionaries stood crouched before their targets and alternated between thrusting their swords at the posts, and smashing their shields into them. Marcus was familiar with the technique from his days at the gladiator school.

The centurion in charge of the soldiers glanced up but did not salute. His new commander was wearing a simple cloak and no sign of the authority granted to him in Rome. Caesar nodded a greeting as they pounded by.

It was different at the gate to the camp, though. There a timber bridge extended across the ditch and a section of fully armed men stood guard on the far side. Caesar reined in and walked his horse across the bridge, its hoofs making hollow thuds. The duty optio held up a hand and stood in his way.

'Halt! What is your business here?'

Caesar tugged lightly on his reins and reached into the bag hanging from one of his saddle horns. 'Bear with me a moment, I have it here . . . somewhere.'

The optio puffed his cheeks impatiently. 'If you're the grain merchants the quartermaster's been waiting for, then you're late and I warn you he won't be a happy man.'

'No, not grain merchants,' Caesar mumbled as he continued rummaging. Then he smiled as he withdrew his hand and held up a baton, gold at each end with a strip of parchment tightly fastened round it by the great seal of the Senate and people of Rome. 'Here we are! I am Caius Julius Caesar, governor of the province of Gaul and general of this army. I am here to take up my command, under the authority of the Senate.'

Marcus saw the optio's eyes widen as his jaw went slack. Recovering quickly, he stepped smartly to the side, stood to attention and snapped his fist across his chest in salute.

'My apologies, sir.'

'At ease.' Caesar laughed. 'Well, I've never been taken for a grain merchant before!'

'No, sir. Sorry, sir.' The optio's face reddened.

'No need to apologize. We've been on the road for five days. Carry on, Optio.'

Caesar urged his mount forward and led his escort into the camp. Beyond the gate Marcus took in a sharp breath as he saw neat lines of tents stretching out in every direction. Smoke drifted up from scores of campfires and the forges of armourers. The air was filled with the sound of voices, and the shout of orders. Ahead of them stretched a long, wide avenue reaching into the heart of the camp. Some of the soldiers looked up curiously as the riders passed by, but most simply ignored them and continued with their duties, or sat outside their tents tending to their kit or playing dice.

When they reached the large tents at the centre of the camp Caesar was halted by a centurion of the elite unit of soldiers entrusted with guarding the headquarters and the senior officers of the army. As soon as he saw the baton he waved the riders through and they dismounted at the horseline outside the largest of the tents. The eagle standards of the four legions stood on a podium in front of the entrance and were guarded by eight men with bearskins covering their helmets and shoulders.

There was something in the atmosphere that excited Marcus. A heady mixture of sights and sounds, combined with knowledge of the power wielded by Rome through its soldiers. These were the men who had carved out a great empire, defeating other empires in turn. The same men who had worn down and finally crushed Spartacus and his rebels, Marcus reminded himself. His excitement cooled.

At the entrance to the tent Caesar turned. 'Festus and Marcus, you come with me. The rest, wait here.'

Caesar's baton had been spotted by one of the guards at the entrance to the tent and, when they entered, the officers and clerks at the desk on either side immediately stood to attention as the three new arrivals strode through. At the far side of the tent was another flap and a figure hurried in, extending a hand as he smiled. 'Caesar! Good to see you again.'

'Labienus, my old friend.' Caesar grasped his forearm and returned his smile.

'I was expecting to receive you in March. I had no idea you

were coming sooner, otherwise I'd have prepared a fitting reception for a proconsul.'

'I've had enough of ceremonies for a while. Time for me to do some honest soldiering, and leave politics behind. Or at least that's what I had hoped. Now Cicero has manoeuvred me into a nasty little trap.' Caesar looked round at the other men in the huge tent. 'Let's continue this somewhere private.'

Once the flaps were closed behind them Labienus indicated some folding wooden chairs beside the large table that dominated one side of the tent. Caesar gestured at his companions. 'This is Festus, the leader of my personal bodyguard.'

'There won't be much call for you here,' said Labienus. 'There is a unit of the army assigned to protect its general.'

Caesar nodded. 'Even so, Festus and his men will stay close to me. After the events of last year in Rome, I have to be careful who I trust.'

Labienus shrugged. 'It may seem strange to say, but I think you will find you are safer on campaign than on the streets of Rome these days. And who is the boy?'

Caesar turned to Marcus and placed his hand on his shoulder. 'This is Marcus Cornelius Primus, the gladiator. The toast of Rome.'

There was no denying that it felt good to be singled out by Caesar, one of the three most powerful figures in the entire Roman Empire, but Marcus found that he was embarrassed by the praise. He forced a smile before he glanced down for a moment.

'You?' Labienus's eyebrows rose. 'You are that boy? I had thought you would be bigger. Given your reputation. They say you slew a Celt giant in that fight in the Forum. But you are so . . . young.'

'Don't be deceived by what you see,' said Caesar. 'Marcus has the heart of a lion, the speed of a viper and the quick wits of a cat. In time he will make an even greater name for himself. Perhaps the greatest gladiator who ever lived. There is none like him.' Caesar hesitated. 'Well, perhaps there was once. But he is dead now. A great pity. I would like to have seen Spartacus fight in Rome. What a spectacle that would have been.'

'We shall never see his like again,' Labienus agreed. 'For which I can only offer my thanks to the Gods.'

Once again Marcus felt the danger of his situation, and the lure of his father's legacy. If only these Romans knew the truth . . .

Labienus continued. 'I just wish those troublemakers in the mountains realized it and put an end to their rebellion.

Anyway, they will be dealt with in due course. What was that you said a moment ago, about Cicero and a trap?'

'That's why I have arrived earlier than expected. I am required to put down Brixus's revolt, and eliminate what remains of Spartacus's followers. The task must be complete before I am permitted to begin any campaigns in Gaul. It's not going to be easy. I had a taste of what we're up against on the road from Rome. We were ambushed in the mountains and lucky to escape with our skins. I lost one of my men, another was wounded, and my scribe was killed as well.' He paused and turned to Marcus. 'You know how to read and write?'

Marcus had received a sound basic education and nodded. 'Well enough, sir.'

'Then you will take Lupus's place for now. You can do that alongside being a member of the bodyguard, and my expert on gladiators.'

'Yes, sir,' Marcus replied with a flush of pride.

'Good.' Caesar patted him. 'Then see to it that you find what you need for the job from the headquarters staff. If anyone questions you, say that you are acting on my orders.'

'What are your plans for Brixus?' Labienus asked.

'I'll take the best soldiers you have. You'll remain in command here with the rest of the men, preparing the recruits for Gaul. I'll divide my force in two. The commander of the Ninth legion, Balbus, will march his men south to Corfinium, and then work his way north, clearing out each valley as he advances. I'll start from the other end of the Apennines and work towards him. We'll roll them up and crush them between us. I expect it will not take much more than a month.'

'I see,' Labienus mused. 'When do you intend to begin?'

'In two days' time. I want the two columns equipped and provisioned for a month. They'll need to march quickly when we enter the mountains so I can't afford any heavy baggage. Just enough to feed them for a few days at a time. The rest of the supplies will have to be stockpiled in the towns running down the edge of the mountains. You'll need to see to that.'

'Two days?' Labienus puffed his cheeks. 'Yes, it can be done.'

'Can be done?' Caesar frowned. 'Labienus, it will be done.'

'Yes, sir.'

'Then you can give the necessary orders at once. Oh, one more thing. You have a new tribune serving in the Ninth by the name of Quintus Pompeius, the nephew of Pompeius.'

'That's right.'

'I take it he's billeted in the town?'

Labienus nodded. 'He's taken over a slave trader's house

for himself and a rather pretty young wife he's just married. A very nice little filly.'

Marcus felt his anger rise at this disrespectful reference to Portia.

'The little filly is my niece,' Caesar said sharply. 'Very well, my men and I shall stay with her. Once you've given the orders I want a full report sent to me in Ariminum. I need to know the names of my officers and the strength of the units chosen for the job. Also, I'm expecting a man to arrive here in a few days' time. The lanista of the school Brixus ran away from. Clodius is searching for him now. He'll send the man here as soon as he is found.'

'Yes, Caesar. I'll send him to you the moment he arrives.'

'Good, then that concludes our business.' Caesar stood up, followed by Festus and Marcus. 'Now let's find a decent bath-house in the town and get ourselves cleaned up before we descend on Portia and her husband.'

9

'Uncle Caius!' Portia beamed as she saw him enter the atrium. She flew across the tiled floor and hugged him tightly as Caesar laughed. Caesar was wearing a tunic borrowed from one of Ariminum's magistrates, and a slave had cleaned his boots while he and the others had been through the town's largest bathhouse. The steam, massage, scrape and cold plunge had left Marcus feeling clean and refreshed, and he and Festus were wearing the spare tunics from their saddlebags.

'Easy there! You'll crush my ribs.'

Marcus and Festus stood at the threshold looking on, and Marcus felt a pang of envy that he was denied a family. Until he had tracked down his mother and set her free, there would be none of the simple pleasures of such a homely scene.

Caesar took her shoulders and eased her back as he beamed down at her. 'How is my favourite niece?'

'I'm your only niece.' She punched him lightly on the chest.

'Well, there you are then. Still my favourite. And how are you adapting to married life? Where is that husband of yours, young Quintus?'

Marcus saw her smile waver for the briefest instant before she replied. 'Oh, he's down at the officers' club. They've set themselves up in an inn on the harbour front. They're very busy at the moment, as you must know. Getting the army ready for the new campaign. I suppose they are entitled to a bit of fun now and again. But we're happy. Very happy. Although I know that I will not see him for a long time when you take the army north, into Gaul.' Her smile faded as she took his hand. 'Please don't give the order too soon.'

'My dear, empires are not won by men who stay at home with their wives.'

'And men who win empires are not born if their fathers are never at the side of their mothers,' she shot back.

'Hah! You have a sharper mind than half the men in the Senate, and a sharper tongue than the rest of them. But enough of that. I have a surprise for you, just in case you were missing

Rome.' He stepped aside to reveal his two companions. 'Here's Festus, and Marcus.'

'Marcus!' Portia smiled and stepped towards him and took his hands, at arm's length, gave a squeeze and then released them. 'You look well. Fully recovered from the fight with that awful thug Ferax?'

'Yes, mistress,' Marcus replied formally, as was the expected custom between them in front of others. 'I am well. It is good to see you again.'

'Then perhaps we can talk a little later on, when you have all been fed?'

Caesar coughed. 'I'll eat later. There's something I need to attend to first. This officers' club, where is it exactly?'

'Must you go already?' Portia frowned.

'I have much to do. We are on the march against the rebel slaves the day after tomorrow. I need to look at my officers. See what they're like and choose those who will accompany me. I won't be too long, I promise. Meanwhile, you can see that Festus and Marcus are fed, and plague them with questions about events in Rome since you left. I know it's only been a few months, but they've been filled with incident.'

'I will ask. But tell me, how is Lupus? I thought you'd need your scribe at your side.'

Caesar pursed his lips. 'Marcus is my scribe now.'

'Oh. Why not Lupus? I thought he was good at his job.'

'He is . . . was. We lost Lupus on the journey here.'

'Lost?'

'We were ambushed by brigands. Lupus was killed.' He cupped her cheek in his hand. 'The others can tell you the story. I must go.'

Caesar kissed her on the top of her head and turned away to stride through the door into the street. The doorman closed it behind him and Portia was left with the others. She looked from face to face. 'Poor Lupus . . . Come then, to the triclinium. I'll have food and drink brought for us and you can tell me what happened.'

The triclinium of the slave-dealer's house overlooked a long colonnaded garden with a water channel running down the middle, crossed by two small wicker bridges. Dusk had fallen over Ariminum and the air was chilly, so a fire had been lit on a brazier in the middle of three dining couches. Small tables had been set in front of each and a woman slave in a plain brown tunic brought small platters of sliced sausage, olives, honeyed bread and delicate pots of fish sauce to drizzle on their food, together with glass goblets and a jar of watered wine.

For a while they talked light-heartedly about affairs in Rome and the latest scandal to emerge from the world of chariot racing where one of the owners of the blue team had been accused of bribing a stable boy from the green team to poison the feed of the best horses. As a result the races had been cancelled for two months until tempers between the teams' supporters calmed down.

'It's an outrage,' grumbled Festus, an ardent follower of the blue team. 'Typical of the greens. They lose several races and of course it's someone else's fault. Never mind the fact that Barmoris can't drive a chariot to save his life.'

'Oh dear.' Portia made a sympathetic expression. 'It does seem to have upset you.'

Festus stared at her. 'Upset? This is not some minor matter, mistress. We're talking about chariot racing.'

'Of course, I'm sorry.' Portia reached for a dish of stuffed olives and held them out as a peace offering.

'Thank you, but I've eaten enough.' Festus wiped his mouth with the back of his hand. 'If you don't mind, it's been a long day. I'm tired. I think I need a good night's sleep.'

Portia nodded. 'As you wish.'

Rising from his couch, Festus bowed his head curtly and strode out of the room. Portia could not help smiling, and once he had gone she shook her head and muttered, 'What is it with men and chariots?'

Marcus shrugged. Despite having lived in the capital over the last year he had never quite understood the passions evoked by the sight of four teams racing round the Great Circus. He broke off another hunk of bread, dipped it in the fish sauce and began to chew. There was a brief silence as Portia slowly pushed a slice of sausage round her platter with the point of her knife. At length she cleared her throat and spoke without looking up. 'So, what happened to Lupus?'

Marcus finished chewing and swallowed. 'As your uncle said, he was killed in an ambush.'

'I know what he said,' she replied tersely. 'I want to know what happened.'

Marcus paused to recollect the ambush before he responded. 'We were caught in a narrow pass and hopelessly outnumbered. Caesar decided our only hope was in cutting our way through the brigands. So we charged them and escaped. Lupus was bringing up the rear when the avalanche struck.'

'Avalanche?'

Marcus nodded. 'It looked like half the mountain was coming down. It fell into the pass and blocked it, burying everyone in its path.'

'Is there no way Lupus could have escaped?'

'No. I saw it myself. Saw him crushed and buried.'

Portia shivered as she imagined the scene. 'I hope it was quick and painless for him.'

Marcus pursed his lips. He had no way of knowing and was not prepared to put a good face on the tragedy. 'I have been instructed to take his place. I hope I can do half as good a job as him.'

Portia looked up at him and smiled warmly. 'You will do fine, Marcus. I know you will. Nothing is beyond you. I've seen enough of your courage, strength and determination to know that much. Even if your writing skills do not match those of Lupus, they will do very soon. I am sure of it.'

Marcus felt a flush of pride at her words. 'Thank you, mistress. I will do my best to serve Caesar well.'

She smiled, then seemed lost in thought for a moment before continuing. 'I only hope my new husband is as diligent as you.'

There it was again, Marcus thought. That sad tone in her voice. He did not know what to say, if anything. Their worlds were so different and Portia might consider it unacceptable for him to address the subject of her married life. Yet she had also been close enough to call a friend. He cared for Portia and wanted nothing more than for her to be happy. Yet she clearly was not.

'Mistress . . .'

'When there is no one else present, I am only Portia to you,' she said.

Marcus nodded. 'Very well . . . Portia. You don't seem very content.'

'Why should I be? Lupus is dead.'

'But it's not Lupus's fate that upsets you. There's more to it than that.'

'No, there isn't,' she said defiantly, glaring at Marcus and daring him to challenge her. 'I am perfectly happy. Perfectly.'

He sighed and pretended to turn his attention back to the last few morsels on his plate. He selected a small pastry encrusted with salt. 'If you say so.'

There was a silence and then he heard the soft sound of muffled sobbing. Looking up, he saw that Portia had buried her face in her hands and her shoulders heaved as she cried. At once he slipped off his couch and went to sit by her. He hesitated a moment, then reached out a hand and patted her softly on the shoulder.

'I'm sorry, Portia. I didn't mean to upset you.'

She sobbed again, then drew a breath to reply. 'It's not you. It's me . . . It's my fault.'

'What's your fault?'

'I'm not sure.' She raised her head as she sat up, and Marcus's hand slipped away. As soon as Portia's eyes were level with his, he felt her take his hand in hers. The thin dark lines of kohl round her eyes had smudged and her lower lip trembled. 'I try to please Quintus. I try to be the wife he deserves, but he ignores me. I am too young to be his wife, and he is too young to be a husband. I have barely spoken to him this last month. He is out of the house almost all the time, and sometimes does not come home at nights. I've heard that he is losing his fortune in dice games. When I asked him about it, he was angry and threatened to hit me.'

'Why didn't you say something to your uncle earlier?'

'How could I? I know how important this marriage is to Uncle Caius. He needs Pompeius as an ally. Besides . . . perhaps I am just being silly. Maybe this is what marriage is like. If I told my uncle he would be angry with me and tell me to pull myself together, I know it.'

'If Caesar said that, he would be wrong,' Marcus replied firmly. 'You don't deserve to be treated like this.'

'How else should I be treated?' Portia replied miserably.

'Roman girls of my class are raised to forge alliances between men. Traded between men. Why, we are no better off than slaves when it comes down to it.'

Marcus could not help being surprised. He had seen how slaves lived, how they were beaten, abused and treated as just another form of property. The conditions in which they lived were a world apart from the pampered lifestyle of Rome's finest families. Yet there was something in what Portia said. Despite her luxuries, she had no more say in how she wanted to live than the slaves who served her. While other women might choose to marry someone they loved, she had no choice.

Suddenly she put her arms round him and drew herself into his shoulder, beginning to cry again. He reached a hand up to stroke her hair. 'It'll be all right, Portia,' he mumbled, not sure what to say. What words could make it all right for her? 'In time, it will get better. You'll see.'

She let out a soft whine of despair. 'I wish I could tell my uncle. But I can't. All I have now is you.'

She drew back and looked at him with wide, red-rimmed eyes, her face streaked with kohl and her lips trembling. Then she leaned forward and kissed him softly on the lips, and closed her eyes. Marcus nearly recoiled in shock but found that he liked the feeling. A warm gush of affection filled his heart and made his head swim.

Then, with a shudder of anxiety, his lips froze. What was he doing? What utter foolishness was this? If they were seen, he was as good as dead. Portia would be in danger too. Her husband would beat her; he would be within his rights to. Marcus pulled himself free and hurriedly shuffled away from her. Portia looked at him with a surprised expression, before it turned to hurt.

'Marcus, what is it?'

'This is wrong, Portia! Wrong and dangerous. We must not do it.'

'But you are all I have. You are all that is special to me now. The last link I have with the way things were.'

'I know it's hard. But I can't do anything about it. Neither can you.'

'Marcus —'

He held his hand up. 'Please don't! It's too dangerous for both of us.' He stood up. 'I have to go.'

'Stay. Please.'

But Marcus knew that he could not. He strode across to the doorway and paused. Looking back, he saw the hurt in her expression and his heart urged a return to her side, but he hardened himself to speak. 'We must forget this ever happened. For both our sakes. Even our friendship is risk enough. This . . .' He shook his head. 'This is nothing less than suicide, Portia. It must never happen again.'

Marcus turned and left, striding along the colonnade that ran round the garden towards the slave quarters. He clenched his jaw, not daring to look back.

10

As the mud-spattered officers began to arrive for the evening briefing, Marcus set out the waxed tablets and an ivory stylus on the small table to the side of the tent. Overhead a light rain pattered on the goatskin, and in the distance thunder rumbled occasionally. Caesar had sent for all the tribunes and senior centurions he had chosen for the campaign. The tribunes were all young men in finely spun tunics and cloaks, whereas the centurions had a far greater age range. The youngest were in their late twenties and the oldest had lined faces, some bearing the scars of many years of campaigning across the Roman Empire. They were the backbone of the legions, tough soldiers who could be counted on to spearhead the attacks, and be the last men to retreat.

Men like Titus, thought Marcus fondly.

'Don't I know you?'

Marcus looked round to see a muscular youth in his late teens staring at him. He had fair hair, cropped short and already thinning about the temples. His raw good looks would soon be undermined by premature baldness, Marcus decided. He recognized him at once, even though it had been months since their first and last encounter in Rome. It was Quintus Pompeius, Portia's husband. Marcus had disliked the look of him even then, a feeling that had intensified with his awareness of Portia's unhappiness.

'It's possible. I am part of Caesar's household. I serve as his scribe now.'

'Ah, I suppose that's it.' The youth nodded doubtfully. 'But I think there's something else about you I can't quite place. Incidentally, you should refer to me as "master" when you address me, slave.'

'I am not a slave,' Marcus replied coldly, fighting back his anger. 'I have been freed by Caesar.'

'Have you?' Quintus looked disappointed. 'Well, you should not get ideas above your station. I'm a tribune. You should address me as "sir". Is that understood, scribe?'

'Yes . . . sir,' Marcus replied with the slightest dip of his head.

'I'd advise you to show me the proper respect from now on.' Quintus tucked his thumbs into his belt and stuck his elbows out. 'Do you know who I am?'

'Why, have you forgotten?' Marcus asked innocently.

Quintus frowned, and his eyes widened as he realized that he was being mocked. He drew himself up to his full height, a head above Marcus. 'I am Quintus Pompeius. That name should mean something even to a common little dolt like you, scribe. I also happen to be related to Caesar by marriage, so I'd watch your step if I were you.'

He glared briefly at Marcus, then strode off to join the other junior tribunes sitting together in the front row of benches set up for the officers. They talked and laughed loudly among themselves, ignoring the disapproving expressions on the faces of the centurions and some of the senior tribunes. Marcus was certain that Titus would have been equally unimpressed by the young men.

There was a short delay after the last of the officers had taken his seat, then a burly figure with tightly curled grey hair entered the tent and called out in a loud, deep voice, 'Commanding officer present!'

At once all the talking stopped and everyone in the tent quickly rose to their feet as Caesar entered and strode over to a parchment map that hung on a wooden frame. He stood to one side and nodded to the veteran who had announced him. 'Thank you, Camp Prefect.'

The older man remained on his feet by the entrance to the tent, while Caesar turned to survey his officers and glanced at Marcus with a quick smile. 'Please sit down, gentlemen.'

The benches creaked and there was a brief shuffling as the officers made themselves comfortable. Marcus sat at his table and picked up his stylus, preparing to take notes. Briefly, Caesar collected his thoughts before drawing a deep breath and beginning in a clear voice that carried to the back of the tent, above the sound of the rain now drumming on the roof.

'At dawn tomorrow we will leave the camp to march into the Apennines. There we shall hunt down the rebel slaves and destroy their army, and kill or capture their leader, Brixus. You men have been handpicked for this task. Some of you I know and there's a handful I have fought alongside in the past, like Centurion Corvus there.' He gestured to a sinewy officer in the middle row and they exchanged a smile and a nod before Caesar continued.

Marcus, already struggling to keep up, knew that he must confine his notes to only the most important points raised.

'The rest of you have been recommended by Labienus, and

I will expect you to justify his choice. Any man who fails to give me good service will be dismissed from the army and sent home. I will not tolerate cowards, fools or idle hands. Think of this as a chance to test yourselves, and the men you command. There is no better preparation for what is to come when I lead the combined army against the Gauls. I know that some of you think the rebels and brigands of the mountains are only a minor nuisance. You are content to dismiss them as starving wretches, poorly trained and armed, and no doubt the less experienced of you think this will all be over quickly.' He paused and Marcus hurriedly caught up, then sat ready, stylus hovering over the unbroken wax surface of another tablet.

'The truth of the matter is that we are in for a hard fight. My bodyguards and I ran into a handful of the rebels on the road from Rome a few days back. They were clever and boxed us in before we were aware that we'd been trapped. Cleverness is not the only advantage they enjoy: they know the mountains. They know all the paths and will use them to outmanoeuvre us. Therefore my plan is simple: we must send out two columns. One to march south to Corfinium . . .' He turned and indicated the town on the map. 'That column will be commanded by Legate Balbus and most of the Ninth legion will go with him. While Balbus goes south, I will lead the main force north to Mutina, here.' He tapped the map and turned back to his audience, his hands held out wide until he slowly moved them towards each other. 'From either end we will push the rebels back until it is their turn to be caught in a trap.'

He paused to let his next words have their full impact. 'There will be a final battle and this time we must make sure that none of them escapes to keep the legend of Spartacus alive. This time we'll crush the will of every slave that ever thought of rebelling against his master. But let there be no mistake about it, this will be a hard battle. The rebels will be fighting for more than their lives. They will be fighting for the one thing that is truly worth fighting for: freedom. Even though our enemies are slaves, you must treat them with respect. They will fight like nothing you have ever fought so far, and never will again. There are some men in this tent who fought in the last slave revolt and will know what I am talking about.'

Marcus saw a few of the older centurions nod, grim-faced. He hurriedly made some notes on the tablet to catch up with Caesar. At the same time the proconsul's words had chilled him to the bone. This was to be a war of extermination. It would not do to just kill Brixus and his supporters. Caesar was out to destroy the very dream that kept hope alive in the countless thousands of slaves who toiled and suffered across the empire. For the first time Marcus fully grasped what his real father had given his life for. He understood the cause, and why it was worth the price that the followers of Spartacus had paid with their blood. The fact that Marcus would be marching alongside the man who was determined to obliterate even the memory of his father made him suddenly sick to the bottom of his stomach and he had to fight back the bile that rose in his throat.

'Every one of you, and the men you command, will have to march and fight as never before,' Caesar continued. 'I want this campaign concluded before spring comes, gentlemen. I will not tolerate anyone who fails to give me every last ounce of effort. Any such man will be dismissed from the army that I will lead into Gaul.' He stared slowly round the room before his intent expression eased. 'Any questions?'

Quintus raised his hand and Caesar fixed his dark eyes on the youth.

'Yes, Quintus?'

'Sir, you're planning to take half the army to deal with these runaways. Surely the task could be completed with fewer men?'

'And fewer officers too, I suppose?' Caesar smiled faintly, but his eyes remained as cold as before. 'I'd rather take too many men and not need them, than need them and not take them with me. Besides, you are forgetting something. These rebels are led by Brixus, a former gladiator. There are bound to be other gladiators with him and those men will be training their followers. If they have done a decent job of it, then we shall face some of the toughest fighters in the world.'

'Gladiators . . .' Quintus mumbled. 'They're just mindless brutes, sir. All muscle and no brain. No match for a proper soldier.'

'Is that so?' Caesar turned to Marcus. 'Put your stylus down, boy, and come here.'

Marcus did as he was told and stood at the spot indicated by Caesar, directly in front of the junior tribunes. Caesar pointed to him as he addressed the officers. 'This boy, until recently, was training to be a gladiator. A few months ago he won a bout in front of the Senate. I am sure some of you witnessed it.'

There were surprised murmurs from those who had seen the fight but had paid no attention to the scribe at the side of the tent, and now recognized him again.

'This boy is my adviser on gladiators. Even more than that. I have trusted him with my life in the past and would do so again if need be.'

'Him?' Quintus laughed. 'Why, he's just a runt.'

'You think so? I'd place money on him long before I'd ever bet on you.'

Marcus saw the blood drain from the tribune's face as he glared angrily at his commander. 'I'd thrash this boy in a fight, sir.'

'Then let's put it to the test.' Caesar drew his sword and handed it to Marcus. 'Draw your blade, Quintus. Let's see if you are as good with a blade as you think you are. A little fencing bout. Just to first blood.'

Quintus looked astounded. His comrades muttered encouragement and he nodded and stood up, drawing his sword. He took up position ten feet from Marcus and turned to face him with a contemptuous sneer. 'Like I said, no brain, and it seems no muscle either.'

Marcus said nothing but tested the weight and balance of Caesar's sword. The proconsul stepped closer to him and muttered softly. 'I just want you to make an example of him. Go easy. I'm not looking to create a vacancy in the tribunes' ranks or make a widow of my niece. Understood?'

'Yes, sir.'

'Good.' Caesar stepped back, clear of the short stretch of open ground between Quintus and Marcus. 'Begin!'

The tribune looked at Marcus and puffed his cheeks. 'Are you sure about this, sir? I'd hate to damage one of your servants.'

Caesar smiled. 'Why don't you just try?'

Quintus raised his sword and took a quick step forward as he let out a loud shout. 'Ha!'

Marcus barely flinched and stood his ground, staring back intently as he balanced on the balls of his feet, weighing up the tribune. The youth was powerfully built, and could move with speed, but his poise was poor, clumsy even.

Having made his attempt to startle Marcus and failing, Quintus looked towards his cronies and chuckled. 'There! Too stupid to react.'

The moment the tribune's eyes glanced aside, Marcus attacked. He lunged forward, arm and blade outstretched. His opponent caught the movement and swung his blade up to parry the blow. Marcus flicked his wrist, letting the weight of his sword drop and swing under the tribune's weapon. As he continued forward, he ducked low and struck the youth's wrist with the flat of his blade. Quintus let out a strangled cry as the shock of the impact caused him to lose his grip and the sword fell from his fingers. Marcus followed through with the heavy bronze hilt of the sword, driving it into the tribune's stomach with all his strength. Quintus let out an explosive gasp and staggered back, struggling for breath. Marcus calmly stepped forward and, raising the tip of his sword, made a tiny cut on his opponent's cheek.

'First blood.' He smiled thinly, then turned to hand the sword back to Caesar.

The proconsul chuckled as he sheathed the blade and gestured to the astonished-looking tribunes. 'Help Quintus back to his bench.'

Once the wheezing youth was seated, Caesar addressed his officers again. 'If that is what a boy gladiator can do, then you can imagine what an experienced man is capable of. I think we've all learned the lesson. Never, ever take your opponent for granted. The briefing is over. Have your men ready to march at first light.'

He nodded to the camp prefect and the latter shot to his feet and barked. 'Stand to!'

Every officer rose and stood stiffly, except Quintus who was forced to bend forward, still struggling to fill his lungs.

'Dismissed!'

The officers began to file out of the tent, and Quintus angrily shook off one of his friends' hands as they tried to help him. He glared at Marcus as he dabbed the blood from the small cut on his cheek. 'Be careful, boy,' he growled. 'I will not forget this, nor forgive it.'

Marcus showed no reaction but felt a warm glow of satisfaction as Quintus hobbled from the tent. Caesar waited until the last of the centurions was leaving before he patted Marcus on the shoulder. 'Nice work. That one needed to be taught a lesson. More than one lesson perhaps,' he added bitterly. 'He takes too much for granted. I think this campaign is just what he needs to grow up a little and be worthy of the name he bears, especially as he now represents my name too.'

There was a rustle and Marcus and Caesar turned to see the camp prefect holding the tent flap back. 'Begging your pardon, sir, but there's a man just arrived. Says he comes from Marcus Licinius Crassus.'

'Crassus?' Caesar raised an eyebrow. 'Did he say what he wants?'

'Only that he desires to speak with you at once.'

Caesar shrugged. 'Very well, show him in. I'll speak with him briefly. Marcus, gather up your slates and get yourself back to Ariminum. Have Portia's cook feed you well. Then pack your kit and be ready to leave the house before dawn.'

'Yes, sir.' Marcus stuffed his slates into the shoulder bag

and pulled up the hood of his cloak to cover his head from the rain.

During their exchange the camp prefect had ducked his head out of the tent and beckoned to the man waiting outside. A moment later a tall, lean man limped into view. His cloak was flecked with mud and beads of water and what was left of his hair was plastered against his scalp. But as he saw him, Marcus's heart lurched in his chest and he felt a burning rage sweep through his limbs. He recognized the man at once. There was no mistake about it. Decimus. The man who had made an attempt on Caesar's life the year before, and the moneylender whose thugs had murdered Titus and dragged Marcus and his mother off into slavery.

11

Decimus glanced round the tent, barely registering Marcus's presence before he turned his attention to Caesar. He bowed his head and held out a small roll of parchment secured with a seal.

'A letter of introduction from Crassus, sir.'

Caesar took it, broke the seal and unwound the message before scanning the contents. 'Publius Decimus?'

Marcus was watching him closely to see if Caesar recognized the name, but the proconsul's expression did not waver for an instant.

'Yes, sir.' Decimus smiled. 'At your service.'

'Apparently not. You are here acting for Crassus.'

'Indeed, yes.'

'This letter requests that I permit you to accompany my

forces in the fight against the rebels. For sundry commercial purposes . . . That's more than a bit vague.' Caesar frowned. 'Care to elaborate?'

'That would be a pleasure, sir. I am to act as the agent of Crassus in the purchase of any prisoners taken by our soldiers. I am authorized to pay your men directly, and of course you will receive a fifth commission on the value of each purchase, sir. A most generous share, as befits the close ally of my patron.'

'I see.' Caesar rolled the letter up and tapped the end against his chin as he stared at Decimus. At the side of the tent Marcus struggled against the urge to dash across the tent and hurl himself upon the man who was the cause of all his suffering. It took all his self-control to keep himself still as he resolved to remind Caesar who the man was.

The proconsul handed the letter back to Decimus. 'Your patron's terms are most generous. I accept them. I will make arrangements for you to march with the baggage train. I imagine that you have brought some staff with you to assist with the processing of the prisoners and to escort them to a suitable holding depot?'

'Yes, sir. My men are with the wagons outside.'

'Then you can rejoin them. Have one of my clerks direct you to the baggage train and wait for your instructions there,

Decimus. I wish there were time to offer you more hospitality but there is much I have to organize before we leave camp tomorrow.'

'Of course, sir. I understand.' Decimus bowed again and turned to leave the tent. The instant that Marcus judged the man was out of earshot he brushed back the hood of his cloak and rushed across to Caesar.

'Sir! I know that man. He's –'

'I know exactly who he is,' Caesar interrupted with a frown. 'I recalled the name at once. The question is, what on earth is Crassus up to this time? I can accept that he would send a man to buy prisoners. There's a good profit to be made when they are sold on in the slave market in Rome. That's bound to appeal to Crassus. But why send Decimus? He knows that I suspect him of being behind the attempt on my life last year.'

'Does it matter, sir?' Marcus asked excitedly. 'He's in your hands now. Arrest him. Have him questioned. You can also find out what he knows about that plot against you.' He paused. 'And find out where he has hidden my mother . . . before he dies.'

'Before he dies?' Caesar tilted his head slightly to one side. 'I am not going to kill him, Marcus. First I must find out why he's here. There's more to it than buying slaves.'

130

'What if he's been sent to attempt to kill you again, sir?'

Caesar pursed his lips. 'That's a possibility. On the other hand, maybe Crassus is just sending me a subtle message. Reminding me that he still has some hold over me. I must ensure that Decimus is closely watched.'

'I'll do it.'

'No. He would recognize you at once if you bared your face to him. I'll tell Festus to do it. You stay clear of him for now, do you understand?'

'Why?' Marcus growled. 'This is the man who ruined my life. Now he's in our hands. You gave me your word that you would have him hunted down and forced to reveal where he had my mother taken.'

'I know. And I honour my promises, Marcus. But you must not forget your place.' Caesar drew himself up and stared down with an imperious expression. 'I am a proconsul of Rome, and you are my servant. I will not have you speak to me like that again. Not if you want my help. Is that clear?'

For a moment Marcus wanted to shout his defiance into Caesar's face. Tell him that he did not care who Caesar was. All that mattered was saving his mother. Then he took control of his thoughts again, angry with himself for being weak-minded. He was exhausted, but that was no excuse. He had to be strong and control his feelings. Caesar had the power of life and death over him, and the power to determine whether his mother was found and set free, or left to rot in a chain-gang. He could not save his mother without Caesar's help. He took a deep breath and replied bitterly. 'Yes.'

'Yes?'

'Yes, sir.'

Caesar continued to stare at him for a moment before nodding. 'That's better. You must remember your place in this world, Marcus. I will always be in your debt for the services you have rendered me, but there is a limit to what I am prepared to tolerate from you. Overstep the mark again and there will be consequences. Understand?'

'I understand, sir . . . I apologize.'

'And I accept your apology.' Caesar smiled and patted him on the shoulder, as if the tense exchange had been instantly forgotten. 'Don't concern yourself over Decimus. When the time is right he will be called to account for the wrongs that he did to you and your family. In the meantime we should consider ourselves fortunate that Crassus has seen fit to place Decimus in my hands. I wish I knew precisely what Crassus was up to. It's possible that he merely wants to place yet another spy in my camp.'

'Another spy?' Marcus raised his eyebrows. 'You mean there are others, sir?'

'Of course there are. I know most of the identities of those who are working for my political rivals, and my political enemies. I make sure that I feed them enough information to keep their masters happy without giving away my real plans. Just as they have uncovered some of my spies and are careful not to reveal too much to them in turn.' Caesar paused as he saw the shocked expression on Marcus's face. He laughed heartily. 'Surely you aren't really surprised, my boy? Not after all the plots and conspiracies you experienced in Rome last year?'

Marcus flushed with embarrassment. He did not want to seem foolish in the eyes of this man. He had come to admire Caesar, despite the ruthless streak of ambition that ran through him like a marble pillar. He shook his head. 'I'm not really surprised, sir. It's just that I had not realized the full scale of it.'

Caesar shrugged. 'That's politics for you. The greatest game there is. And the stakes are as high as they come. For now, Pompeius and Crassus are prepared to share power with me, but that cannot last forever. There will come a time when the three of us become two, and then one. That will be the best outcome for Rome. A cure for all the petty squabbling that prevents Rome from achieving even greater glory than she already enjoys. All that matters is that I am the last man standing. On that day I will be sure to reward all those who have helped me win power. And you have done far more to deserve my gratitude than most, Marcus.'

'How many years will that take?' Marcus asked anxiously. 'My mother may not survive that long, sir. She has to be rescued before then.'

'And she will be. As soon as I have the opportunity. But I have a greater reward in mind for you, Marcus. What is it that all men crave, no matter their age? Fame and power. For me that is achieved by claiming imperium – the authority and respect that is conferred upon Rome's greatest heroes. For you there is a different route to glory. You have the potential to be a great gladiator, perhaps one of the greatest of all time. For as long as men fight in the arena the name of Marcus Cornelius will be revered. You cannot tell me the prospect does not stir your heart, eh?' Caesar concluded with a smile.

Marcus was tempted by the vision that Caesar held out to him. He knew that he fought well, and took a quiet satisfaction in his skill and the knowledge that Titus would have been proud of him. He wondered what Spartacus would have felt.

Pride, yes. But also shame at the prospect of Marcus fighting and killing in order to satisfy the bloodlust of the Roman mob. Spartacus and thousands of his followers had died to put an end to slavery, an end to gladiator fights and an end to the danger of Rome continuing to extend its brutal power over the rest of the known world. They had sacrificed everything to prevent men like Caesar winning his imperium, a prize that was bought at the expense of countless others buried in the foundations of their fame. The same fate would befall him, Marcus realized. If he ever did become a hero of the arena, then it would only add to the popularity of his patron, Caesar. With a chilling sense of certainty, he knew that was all the proconsul really cared about. Everyone else was a means to that end.

Marcus swallowed and forced himself to nod. 'I can think of no greater honour, sir.'

'That's the spirit!' A faint look of relief flitted across Caesar's face. 'Now go and prepare your kit. It's going to be a tough campaign, even if it will be over quickly. You can use my authority to get whatever you need from the army's stores. Make sure you have a decent supply of writing materials. I have a feeling there will be some interesting things to note down in the days to come. It's a shame that

Lupus is not here to share them with us, but I am sure you will fulfil his duties well.'

'I will do my best, sir.'

'Of course you will. You may go, Marcus.'

He bowed his head, and slipped the strap of his satchel over his head as he left the headquarters tent. Outside, night had fallen and the camp was lit by fires and torches that struggled to stay alight in the steady drizzle. A cold breeze was blowing in from the west, towards the Apennines, and Marcus shivered as he pulled his cloak tighter about him. As he made his way towards the quartermaster's tent, Marcus made a mental note of the supplies he required. Not so much that it would overburden his horse and yet he needed to stay as dry and warm as possible. A spare cloak impregnated with fat and a good tunic should be enough. That and a leather cover for his weapons and writing materials.

Once again his mind turned back to the matter of Decimus. It was a stroke of fortune that Crassus had sent him to join Caesar's army. Now that it was no longer necessary to track the man down, Marcus wondered if there was any way he could force the ruthless moneylender to reveal the location of his mother. Despite what Caesar had said, Marcus intended to keep an eye on Decimus and, if the chance came, there would be a confrontation. Once he had the information he needed Marcus resolved to take his revenge.

The rain stopped shortly before dawn, but the sky remained covered by an endless blanket of dull grey clouds that cast a gloom over the flat landscape around Ariminum. The men chosen by Caesar for his campaign had packed their tents into the allotted wagons. Each man's spare kit was attached to the stout marching yokes, together with his shield. As the order to form up was bellowed across their ranks, the legionaries hefted the yokes and rested them across their right shoulders before taking their place in the column. Marcus heaved his two bags on to the horns of his saddle. One contained his spare clothes and rations and the other his writing implements. His sword hung from his side, and a dagger and throwing knives were in the scabbards attached to his broad leather belt. Swinging up into the saddle, Marcus walked his horse over to join the small group of headquarters staff assigned to accompany Caesar.

When all was ready Caesar gave the order to advance and the long column trudged forward in two sections. The first was commanded by Caesar, the second by Legate Balbus. Cavalry led each of the two forces, followed by the commander and his staff, then their infantry, and the baggage train and its escort came last. Marcus turned in his saddle, hoping to catch sight of Decimus, but it was impossible to make out much detail amid the wagons clustered to the rear of the legionaries.

A small crowd had emerged from Ariminum to line the road along which the army marched. Wives, sweethearts, excited children and some curious idlers stood and watched as the soldiers squelched along the muddy route from the camp towards the road leading north and south. On a warmer day the onlookers might have been cheering but on this cold and miserable morning they mostly stood and watched, only calling out their farewells as they caught sight of a friend or loved one. A small cluster of wealthier spectators stood near the junction where the track joined the road and Marcus picked out Portia, bareheaded, as she watched the cavalry pass by. Her expression lit up as she caught sight of her uncle and waved at him. Marcus saw Caesar acknowledge her with a bow of his head. Quintus was too busy joking with his companions to notice his young wife, and she stared forlornly as he rode past. Her smile only returned as she spotted Marcus and edged to the side of the track.

'Take care of yourself, Marcus.'

He steered his mount to the side of the track, reining in to look down at her. 'I will.'

'Look after my uncle.'

'Him?' Marcus smiled. 'Caesar knows how to look after himself, mistress. Trust me.'

She laughed briefly and then continued in a lower tone. 'And take care of Quintus if you can . . .'

Then she turned and paced back to her place among the other officers' families. Marcus clicked his tongue and flicked his reins, walking his horse quickly to rejoin the rest of the headquarters staff. Ahead, the cavalry of Caesar's force, some five hundred mounted men, had turned north. The rest of the force followed them, picking up the pace now they could march on a paved surface. As the last of the wagons of Caesar's column rumbled after them, Balbus and his men turned south.

Marcus glanced back, momentarily impressed by the spectacle of the two neatly ordered columns marching to war. The air was filled with the din of horses' hoofs, the crunch of nailed boots and the rumble of heavy wagons on the road. Then he recalled the purpose of it – Caesar's plan to crush the rebels and the dream of Spartacus once and for all. Marcus stared at the back of the proconsul sitting erect in his saddle, looking ahead, his mind no doubt fixed on the quest to win fame and glory, whatever the cost.

12

Lupus was close to exhaustion. They had been marching for three days before they reached the main rebel camp. Three days of toiling up steep mountain paths, frequently lost amid the low clouds that shrouded the peaks of the Apennines. Lupus could not hope to recall the route they had taken. He had tried at first, in case he got the chance to slip away and find his way back to the road to rejoin Marcus and the others accompanying his master. Despite the clouds and the occasional blizzards that had shrouded the paths, Mandracus and his men never missed their step and unerringly made their way to their destination. The paths were too difficult for his horsemen so they were ordered to continue their patrol, raiding villas and farming estates to liberate more slaves and loot enough food to feed them. Lupus saw few people along the route. A handful of shepherds, some of whom cheered Mandracus and his band and offered them food and shelter if they needed it. Others simply turned and fled.

They passed through a small village perched above a stream. It was too poor for anyone there to own a slave and they simply watched warily as the rebels passed through. There was no attempt to hinder them, not even to close the small gate in the low crumbling wall that had once protected the village. Looking from side to side, Lupus could see that the people were poor and hungry, and probably lived lives every bit as hard as the slaves passing by. It was clear that the rebels' war was being waged against the rich and powerful. Even though the villagers were freeborn Romans, they had more in common with the rebels than with those who ruled over them.

At last, footsore, hungry and bone-tired, the small column of rebels reached the approaches to the main camp. As the first shadows of dusk settled over the mountains, Mandracus halted his men and called Lupus forward. The boy stood nervously in front of him and Mandracus smiled wolfishly.

'Now you'll see why the Romans can never defeat us.' He waved a muscular arm over the surrounding scenery. They were standing in a shallow valley just above the snow line.

Tree-covered slopes curved up on either side and at the end of the valley where the sides curved round to meet, like half a bowl. There were no signs of settlement or life of any sort, other than a small brook that emerged near the base of some crags to the left. The water gushed over the rocks as it wound its way down to the floor of the valley. In places the water had frozen, leaving glistening ice formations over which the water ran, adding yet more ice. The place felt desolate and Lupus shivered.

At first he had longed for the comforts of Caesar's house back in Rome and silently cursed the day his master had taken him as an escort to Ariminum. But Lupus found there was more to his captors than he had first thought. Initially they had terrified him, and he feared for his life. It took a while before he truly believed they had no intention of harming him. Each night, Mandracus and his men had sat round a fire, eating whatever rations they had found in recent days and talking good-humouredly before they settled down to sleep. They shared their food with Lupus, and treated him with a rough fondness that surprised him.

'You're free now, lad!' Mandracus grinned as they made camp the first night. 'No more masters giving you orders. Here we are just comrades. No masters and no slaves. We live off the land, as well as off those who use slaves to make themselves rich. You'll get used to it soon enough. I imagine you're still feeling a bit anxious, aren't you?'

Lupus nodded.

'Well, don't. No one's going to eat you. Speaking of which,' the rebel leader rummaged in his sidebag and drew out a small loaf of bread and a hunk of cheese. 'Here. Eat this. You need to keep your strength up.'

'Thanks.' Lupus shuffled closer to the fire and let the warmth of the flames seep into his tired muscles. He swallowed the first mouthful and turned to Mandracus. 'What will happen to me after you've taken me to Brixus?'

'That's up to Brixus,' the man replied, then bit off a small piece from a strip of dried beef. 'He'll want to question you about Caesar, and your friend Marcus, before he decides what to do next. I dare say he will offer you the chance to join the rebel army.'

'If I refuse?'

'You won't refuse. Trust me. Once you understand what this is all about. Once Brixus has explained his plans to you, then you'll want to stay and fight with us and put an end to slavery.'

'You seem very sure of it.'

'Let's just say that Brixus can be very persuasive. It's probably wisest not to refuse the offer.'

Lupus nodded and ate some more food before he spoke again. 'I'm not sure that I would want to live on the run all the time. Even though I was a slave, I was treated well enough.'

'Good for you,' Mandracus muttered. 'But most slaves aren't as pampered as you were, Lupus. Most are worked to death. Many in mines and on farming estates. Those are the worst places to be. That's where I was before Spartacus and his men found me all those years ago. Seems like a lifetime now. I've been free ever since. Yes, I've been hunted and I've often wondered how long it will all last. But I am still free, and I have a wife and two young girls, and they have known nothing but freedom.'

'It must be a hard life, here in the mountains.'

'Life is hard,' Mandracus admitted. 'It's a struggle. But we treat each other with respect, we share what we have and we can choose our own fate. That is something a slave can never do. Thanks to people like your former master. And now it seems that he has resolved to crush us.' He stared into the flames and Lupus saw his expression harden when he spoke again. 'Caesar will find that we are a much tougher nut to crack than he imagines. You should be able to give Brixus some insight into Caesar's thinking when he questions you.'

'I'll tell him what I can,' Lupus replied. 'But I don't think it will be much help. Caesar does not take his slaves into his confidence . . . Some perhaps. He seems to have a high opinion of Marcus.'

Mandracus glanced round sharply. 'The boy who was with you at the ambush?'

Lupus nodded.

'Tell me about him.'

'Why? You said earlier that Brixus would also want to know about him. What's so special about Marcus?'

'Just curious. It's probably nothing,' Mandracus replied carefully. 'Brixus has mentioned a boy gladiator he once knew in the past. Your friend Marcus might know something about him.'

Lupus finished eating and held his hands up to the fire, then rubbed them together. 'Not much to tell. The master . . . I mean Caesar, bought him from a gladiator school near Capua over a year ago. Caesar's niece had fallen into the school's arena as Marcus was facing two wolves. He saved her from them and Caesar recognized that he had potential, so he bought him to join us in Rome as part of Caesar's bodyguard.'

'I see. And what does Marcus look like?'

'You saw for yourself at the ambush.'

Mandracus nodded. 'True, but it was only a fleeting glimpse, in the middle of a fight. I can't recall any details.'

Lupus shrugged. 'He's tall for his age, and thin. No, not thin. Sinewy would be a better word for it. He thinks quickly and has sharp reflexes, and he's as brave as they come.' He smiled with pride as he recalled his friend.

The man was also smiling. 'Sounds like someone I used to know . . . Well now, young Lupus. Get some sleep, there's a long march ahead before we reach the camp of Brixus.'

Now they had reached the camp, but Lupus could not see any sign of movement, let alone the rebel army that was growing in strength day by day according to Mandracus. The man laughed at his side, then patted him heavily on the shoulder.

'Follow me.'

Mandracus led the way along a narrow path running beside the stream and they entered the trees at the foot of the crags. A short distance further on the trees gave way to a narrow strip of rocky open ground. Walls of dark rock, dotted with moss, rose up ahead. A waterfall tumbled down into a small pool where the water churned white and wild before it fed the stream running between the trees. Mandracus paused and cupped a hand to his mouth to call up towards the top of the crags.

'Approaching the camp!'

Lupus followed the direction of the man's gaze and saw a figure emerge at the top of the crag, dark against the sky as he looked down at them.

'Who goes there?' a voice shouted.

'Mandracus! Returning from patrol!'

'Mandracus? Then pass, friend!'

The brigand made his way towards the foot of the waterfall, followed by Lupus and the others. It was then that Lupus saw the spur of rock and realized there was a narrow gap in the cliff, a defile, that stretched away at an angle to the waterfall. It remained quite invisible until you were almost at the foot of the waterfall. Two men stood just inside the defile, armed with spears, shields, armour and helmets of the same design used by the Roman legions. They looked relieved as they caught sight of Mandracus and approached to exchange a clasp of hands at their safe return. Then one of them saw Lupus and paused.

'Who is this?'

'Him?' Mandracus chuckled. 'New recruit. And he may have some useful information for the general. Is Brixus in camp?'

One of the sentries nodded. 'He's summoned the leaders of all the bands in the mountains. They've been arriving for several days now. You're the last one. What's going on?'

'Even if I knew, I wouldn't tell you, you big ox! You'll find out soon enough.' Mandracus put a hand on Lupus's shoulder and steered him into the defile. 'In the meantime, get back to your duty.'

The sentries stood aside and the small column of rebel fighters entered the defile. The air was cold and moist from the spray churned up by the waterfall. Lupus shivered as he picked his way forward. Although the path had been cleared enough to permit a horse to pass through, the ground was uneven and the route turned one way and then the next as it wound through the chasm. Overhead, the grey sky was a miserable thin strip caught between the rocks and the limbs of stunted shrubs and small trees growing precariously from the ledges. After about a quarter of a mile the cliffs on either side started to grow apart and light shone into the defile. Then, as they rounded a last bend in the path, Lupus had his first sight of the rebel camp and he paused to take in a sharp breath of astonishment.

Ahead, the path led down a gentle slope into a small valley, seemingly walled in on every side by cliffs and crags. A stream coursed down the far side and crossed the valley floor before it passed underground, heading in the direction of the water-fall. But that was the least remarkable sight that greeted his eyes. Before him lay a vast camp of tents and more permanent shelters. In among the tents were pens for animals and several larger buildings, the nearest of which had its doors open, and Lupus saw a man doling out bowls of grain to a queue of people. In the centre of the valley stood a large round hut, surrounded by an open area ringed with a stockade. Smaller round huts were arranged around the compound.

'There must be thousands living here,' Lupus said. 'Tens of thousands!'

Mandracus smiled at the boy's awed expression. 'That's right. An army of us. Waiting for the day when we will rise up and complete the work that Spartacus began.' He pointed to the largest hut. 'Come, that's where we'll find Brixus.'

He led his men down into the valley. Lupus followed, his eyes switching from side to side as he took in the details of the secret camp of the rebels. Around him the walls of the valley looked impenetrable. There seemed no way in except for the narrow pass they'd come through. *A perfect hiding place*, he reflected. No wonder the slaves had managed to evade the Roman armies sent to hunt them down. The Romans could

149

be unaware that such a powerful enemy was gathering its strength and preparing to attack.

Lupus felt a pang of concern for Caesar and Marcus. They were expecting to fight scattered bands of ragged brigands. They could have no idea what would face them when they marched into the mountains to do battle.

13

January was drawing to an end and winter closed its icy grip around the mountains. Biting rainstorms lashed the foothills and frequently brought hail with them, battering the men of Caesar's column as they made for the town of Mutina that would serve as their base. Cavalry patrolled further into the hills along the line of march, trying to gather intelligence on the location and numbers of the rebels. When they returned they told of wild blizzards howling through the mountain passes and thick ice forming on the roads and tracks that wound across the Apennines. Messengers had been sent ahead to the towns along the road with orders for their inhabitants to provide food and shelter for Caesar's column, while further supplies were stockpiled at Mutina.

Marcus, riding with the headquarters staff, had never

before experienced conditions like these. He had been careful to pick a cloak freshly worked with animal fat and as waterproof as possible. Even so, the cold rain, driven on by a freezing wind, soon penetrated to the clothes he wore beneath and soaked him to the skin. He had also collected a pair of leather mittens, and these too soon succumbed to the foul weather as he grimly followed the other riders behind their leader.

Caesar suffered the same discomforts as his men yet seemed oblivious to the cold. Every so often he would let some of his officers draw alongside and engage them in cheerful conversation. Sometimes about affairs back in Rome, but more often about the glorious future that awaited them all in Gaul once the rebels had been crushed. He even spared a few moments for Marcus to discuss his career in the arena.

'I've decided that you shall fight as a retiarius,' Caesar announced as they rode in a brief spell between rainstorms. Overhead, the sky was clear and bright and the wind had dropped. Fresh clouds were visible above the mountains, waiting to roll down their slopes and engulf the men marching along the road. Marcus had drawn back his hood and was relishing the warmth of the sun on his skin and wet hair.

'You have the right build for a netman,' Caesar continued.

'Slender but strong and you move with speed and grace. I saw as much when you fought Ferax back in Rome. Of course, things might change. Some boys who are thin in their youth pack on the muscle later. If that happens to you, I shall have to reconsider your category. A Thracian or even a Samnite would be more suited to a heavier build. But let's hope you retain your current build. I'd hate to see you lumbering around the arena when you could be giving the crowd a good show with your turn of speed.'

'Yes, sir,' Marcus acknowledged, trying hard to control the fit of shivering that had taken over his body. He was too cold and tired to feel bitter about his former master deciding his destiny. Besides, his mind was fixed on the fact that Decimus was riding with the baggage train. Marcus had caught sight of him on only a handful of occasions since leaving Ariminum and he could not shake the urge to take his revenge. The long days riding had reminded him of all there was to avenge beyond the suffering of his family. Aristides, a slave who had been like a grandfather to Marcus, had also been killed by the moneylender. Even Cerberus, the dog Marcus had rescued from a cruel trader and trained to be his loyal companion, had been clubbed to death by Decimus's men when they attacked the farm. *A simple death would be too good*, Marcus resolved. He must be made to suffer, as his victims had.

'You're not really listening to me, are you?' asked Caesar.

Marcus instantly pushed all thought of Decimus aside and struggled to recall what Caesar had just said. Marcus was vaguely aware of some comment concerning the fortune some famous retiarius had made during the time of Sulla's dictatorship. He cleared his throat.

'Yes, sir. It would be nice to make a large sum of money.'

Caesar stared at him indulgently. 'Marcus, that was a while back, before I began to talk about your training. You're not paying attention.'

Marcus lowered his gaze. 'I'm sorry, sir. I am tired. My mind was drifting.'

'Drifting, eh? You're considering Decimus again, aren't you?'

Marcus thought about denying it but dared not risk being seen through by Caesar again, so he nodded. 'I can't stop thinking about him. And what he did to my family and friends. I'm sorry, sir, but it is eating me inside to know that he is so close but I can do nothing about it.'

'All in good time, Marcus. Remember,' Caesar warned, 'you need my permission to act. For now it serves my purpose to have him close, but not too close, if you understand me. If Crassus has tasked him with doing me any harm, then Festus and my bodyguards, including you, will make his life difficult.'

'Difficult, yes, sir,' Marcus responded. 'But not impossible. Why take the risk? Why not just have him and his men arrested?'

'Because they pose no risk to me at present. If they did, then I would do as you say. But for now I am content to have Festus watch them. If they attempt anything we shall catch them, and then I will have proof of Crassus's treachery. Enough to give me a little power over him, since I doubt the Senate would look too kindly on any man conspiring to murder a proconsul.' Caesar smiled wryly. 'In any case, I am not yet convinced that is his plan. I think Crassus has simply sent the man to spy on me, report back, and make a small fortune for his master in the process. Now that would be typical of Crassus!'

Marcus was not so sure. 'If you say so, sir.'

Caesar's expression became serious again. 'There's one thing that might complicate matters, and that's if Decimus recognizes you. He must already know that you are a member of my household, since that agent of his attempted to poison me.'

'Thermon.'

Caesar nodded. 'So far Decimus has not seen you here and let's hope he assumes that you are still in Rome. If he does find out, then he will know he's in danger.'

'Danger, sir?'

'Of course. You are the only witness to his murder of your father and the kidnapping of you and your mother. If he is ever prosecuted for that crime, then he would face exile or execution. Which means that it would be dangerous for you if he knew you were here. Bear that in mind and stay clear of the man, and his followers. That's an order.'

'Yes, sir.'

Caesar looked at Marcus shrewdly. 'I know you are a freed man now, but you are part of my army in this campaign and that makes you subject to military discipline. An order from your general is just as binding as an order from your master. Is that clear?'

'Yes, sir. Perfectly.'

Caesar nodded with satisfaction. 'Good. Now I need a little time to think about the campaign.' He waved his hand back towards the staff officers riding a short distance behind. Marcus bowed his head and reined in to allow the proconsul to draw ahead. But he could not heed his warning. Much as he respected

Caesar, Marcus had his own ambitions, which he placed above his duty to obey a superior.

The column reached Mutina at the end of the fourth day after marching from Ariminum. The officers and soldiers had already been assigned billets in the town and the horses and mules were led to pens in the livestock market and fed. Marcus remained with Caesar until late evening at the villa of a local magistrate that had been made available to the proconsul and his staff. Waiting for Caesar were numerous reports of the escalating number of raids by the rebels on estates and mines along the entire length of the Apennines. More concerning was the increased boldness and ambition of the rebels' activities. Armed bands were now striking out some distance from the mountains against targets that had been considered safe. Caesar dictated orders to Marcus for the towns running along the mountains to increase their vigilance, ready to deal with any sudden attack. It was late at night before he finished and gave Marcus permission to return to his billet for some sleep. Marcus had been assigned the humble home of one of the magistrate's freedmen, a short distance along the same street as the villa.

As he approached the door of the house, squeezed between

a bakery and a wine seller, Marcus stopped in the street, deep in thought. He was exhausted and the column would be setting out for the mountains at first light. Caesar was right to advise a good night's rest. It might be a long time before he got the chance to sleep in a comfortable dry bed again. But there was no shaking the need to find out what Decimus was up to. Caesar had ordered Marcus to avoid the man, but he had made no mention of avoiding Festus. Marcus smiled to himself. Pulling up the hood of his cloak, he strode past the door of his billet and made for the centre of town.

Mutina had once been an important trading centre between Roman dominions and those of the Gauls and other tribes from the north. Now, with the expansion of Roman power towards the Alps, the town had become something of a backwater, relying more on farms and small industries to generate its wealth. But there was no hiding the fact that the town was in decline. Marcus noticed that some of the houses he passed were in a sad state. The paint on many of the public statues had been neglected and was flaking away to reveal the plain stone beneath. The heart of the town still flourished, however, and the sounds of revelry filled the air as Marcus emerged into the forum.

Every inn was filled with soldiers, and those who could

not get inside stood in the street, sharing jars of wine as they talked in loud, boisterous tones, or squatted round games of dice, gambling with whatever was left of their pay. Marcus guessed that Decimus would not be amusing himself in the company of common soldiers. He was far more likely to be drinking with the officers, men he might have met socially when visiting Rome – men who could one day be useful to him as they rose up the ranks of the Senate.

Marcus stopped outside the first inn he came to and approached a small group of soldiers in their capes who did not yet look too much the worse for wear.

'Excuse me,' he said, pulling back his hood. 'I've been sent from headquarters to find one of Caesar's officers. Any idea where they might be?'

A tall, burly man with thick stubble on his cheeks turned to look down at Marcus. 'Officers? Who cares a stuff for them, eh? Bunch of stuck-up wasters.'

'Oi!' one of his companions called out. 'Leave it out, Publius. Boy's only asking a question.' He pushed his surly comrade aside and stood in front of Marcus with an apologetic expression. 'Ignore him. He's just a grumbler.'

'Too right I am!' his comrade cut in. 'Why aren't we rest-ing up in winter quarters? Ain't right that we've been ordered to get out and fight in the middle of winter. Ain't going to be in good shape when the real campaign starts in spring.'

'Ah, shut it!' his companion said crossly, before turning back to Marcus. 'So what do you want, young 'un?'

'I need to find the staff officers. Have you seen them?'

'Hmm?' The soldier scratched his chin. 'Best try the Jolly Boar. Over there by the Temple of Jupiter. It's supposed to be the classiest inn. That's your best bet.' He looked at Marcus more closely. 'Do I know you? I recognize your face.'

Marcus shook his head. 'I don't think we've met.'

The man frowned and then clicked his fingers. 'Yes! It was in Rome. I was on leave there last year. Saw you fight that Celt boy. You're Marcus Cornelius, right?'

Again, Marcus shook his head. It was already possible that rumours of his fight with Quintus were spreading through the ranks. Marcus was determined to keep his presence secret from Decimus for as long as possible. It would be better to deny his identity for now. . .

'I am just a servant of Caesar,' Marcus replied flatly. The soldier looked disappointed and waved his hand dismissively. 'Off you go then, boy!'

Marcus turned away to head across the forum towards the inn that the soldier had indicated. The owner of the Jolly Boar had set up some tables and benches outside the entrance, and these were crowded with the centurions and optios of Caesar's cohorts. Threading his way through the soldiers, he could not help wondering what shape they would be in come the morning when it was time to march into the mountains.

From inside, Marcus could hear excited chatter and cheering before there was a brief lull, then a crescendo of noise. He squeezed through the door and saw at once that the inn was a lot bigger than it looked from outside, a single open room stretching back a good hundred feet. A counter was set up in the far corner from where a sweaty-looking old man handed jugs and cups to his servants and kept tally on what each table had consumed. The middle of the room had been cleared and a crowd of tribunes, centurions and civilians stood in a ring over a dice game. Marcus knew that if he drew up his hood he would only attract attention, so instead he worked his way round to an alcove and stood in the shadow as he scrutinized the men in the room.

He picked out Quintus easily enough. Portia's young husband was grinning like a fool as he opened his purse. But his smile faded as he groped around inside and his hand came out clutching a small handful of silver coins. He hesitated briefly, before bending down to place his bet. Marcus's eyes then fixed on Festus, sitting on the far side of the room, watching proceedings as he sipped from a bronze goblet. Marcus followed his line of sight to a group of men at a table opposite Festus. He spotted Decimus at once, due to the expensive embroidery on his cloak. A squat muscular man sat next to him, and three more perched on the other side of the table with their backs to Marcus. Two had close-cropped hair; the third was shaven-headed, but the dark hair of an unkempt beard bustled out from each cheek so that he probably looked like a barbarian from the front.

Now that he had them in sight, Marcus stared at Decimus for a while. He recalled vividly the cruel expression in the man's face when the moneylender had told Marcus and his mother of their fate as they lay in a holding cell of the slave market back in Greece. Marcus edged round the room and made his way towards Festus, where he positioned himself with his back to Decimus and the others.

Festus's eyebrows rose briefly in surprise. He leaned across the table. 'What are you doing here?' he growled.

'Caesar's dismissed me for the evening. I thought I'd have a look around the town.'

'Pollux! Do you think I'm a fool, Marcus? You've come to spy on Decimus.'

'How was I supposed to know he'd be here?'

'Where else would he be in a one-mule dump of a town like Mutina? You'd better get out of here before he spots you.'

'I'll go in a moment. But first you tell me what he's been up to. Caesar thinks there's more to his being here than buying up prisoners.'

Festus shrugged. 'If that's true, then there's been no sign of anything suspicious. He sticks close to his men over there and they travel in the wagon. There's been no messages delivered to them, and none sent anywhere.'

'That's all?'

'That's all I've seen.'

'And no sign of Thermon?'

'No. None of 'em look like the man who tried to kill Caesar. See for yourself.'

Marcus half turned cautiously, and looked over the rim of his shoulder. From where he sat, he had a side-on view of the table, and in the dim light cast by the inn's oil lamps he could make out the profiles of Decimus's companions. None had the neatly styled hair and well-groomed features of the moneylender's dangerous henchman. As Marcus watched, there was another cry from the men playing dice and he glanced over towards them. He saw Quintus's face twist into

163

an ashen-faced grimace as he crushed his empty purse in his fist and backed out of the ring of men still watching the game.

'You'd better go,' said Festus. 'Before you are seen.'

Marcus nodded and rose from the table. He paused. 'Keep a close eye on Decimus. He can't be trusted. And he's . . . evil.'

'Evil?' Festus cocked an eyebrow and smiled faintly. 'Well, if he tries to cast a spell on Caesar, I'll be sure to let you know.'

Marcus scowled at him, furious with Festus for being so dismissive. Then he turned and made his way back through the crowded inn. He paused at the door for one last, hateful glimpse of Decimus and stopped dead. Quintus had approached the moneylender's table and was leaning down as he spoke earnestly with Decimus. The exchange was brief, and there was no mistaking the pleading expression on the tribune's face. Decimus was still for a moment, as if thinking, and then nodded. He reached down and took out a heavy purse from under his cloak, placing it in Quintus's spare hand. The tribune looked round nervously before he slipped the purse out of sight under his own cloak. He quickly nodded his thanks to Decimus and hurried back to the dice game.

Marcus remembered Portia's comment about her husband's gambling habit. It seemed even more of a problem than she had feared and Marcus felt a stab of pity for his friend. It was a poor match, her marriage. Forced on Portia for political reasons, it had condemned her to being the wife of a wastrel whose only apparent talent was a capacity to lose at dice games. Marcus felt a moment's sorrow. If Quintus carried on like this, he would only make Portia more unhappy. It was bad enough that he was unlucky, but that weakness was made worse by his lack of judgement.

Only a very desperate or foolish man would ever borrow money from the likes of Decimus. Marcus had learned that lesson only too well. It had cost Titus his life and all that he possessed. Now Decimus had found a new victim, and who knew where that would end.

14

Lupus had been ordered to remain in a simply constructed shack close to the main compound in the heart of the rebel camp. With each passing day he grew more fearful. Despite Mandracus's kindly treatment of him and the promise that he would never be a slave again, Lupus felt he was treated like a prisoner. From the door of his shelter Lupus could see the largest hut in the camp – the one belonging to Brixus, he had discovered. Constructed from crudely cut stone with a manure and mud mixture pressed into the gaps for weatherproofing, and the thatched roof overhanging the walls, it was quite unlike the fine villas of Roman aristocrats, but palatial under the circumstances. A dozen men armed with spears and shields stood guard round the compound, with one assigned to watch over Lupus.

He was eventually summoned by the rebel leader one evening and taken to wait outside Brixus's hut until given permission to enter. The rosy glow of the sun slipped behind the rim of the mountains, and the valley was plunged into shadows as the failing light took on a blue hue. Around Lupus the rebels built up their fires, but none made any attempt to light them as they squatted down, waiting while the sunlight faded.

Lupus began to shiver, and after a moment he addressed the man escorting him. 'Why don't they ever light the fires during the day?'

The man nodded up at the sky. 'Smoke. We light a fire and there's a danger that the smoke is seen and someone gets curious enough to come and investigate. So there are no fires until nightfall. Under strict orders from Brixus. Anyone who disobeys gets flogged publicly.'

'Oh . . .' Despite Mandracus's early reassurance that no harm would come to him, Lupus felt scared of the people around him. Now it seemed that their leader was a man who, despite proclaiming their freedom, ruled his followers with ferocious discipline. The cold mountain air penetrated Lupus's cloak and tunic, and he stamped his feet on the ground as he felt his limbs begin to grow numb. He found himself thinking about Marcus and the others, who would probably be sheltering from the night in some comfortable house in Ariminum by now. As he thought of his friend, Lupus felt a stab of sorrow. Marcus would not be as afraid as he was, or at least would not show it. He had strength and courage, and Lupus knew that he could have coped with his present situation far better with Marcus at his side. But Marcus was not here. Nor were Festus or Caesar. Lupus was alone and no doubt his former companions thought him dead, buried beneath the avalanche. For a moment Lupus felt tears of self-pity in his eyes, but cuffed them away quickly, angry with himself for being weak. *Marcus would never let himself feel afraid like this*, Lupus told himself. He must be more like his friend. Show no fear, and win the respect of the men who had captured him.

At length, as the stars pricked out in the cold heavens above, Mandracus emerged from the hut and looked around for a moment before nodding to one of the guards by the nearest fire.

'It's dark enough. Start the fire.' He glanced briefly at Lupus, then went back inside.

The guard immediately took out a tinderbox from the bag hanging on his shoulder and knelt down by the brushwood piled in a rough cone. Dried moss, straw and twigs filled a small gap at the base of the fire. As he huddled over the tinderbox, Lupus could hear the clatter of flints as tiny sparks fell on to the charred linen inside the box. A faint glow illuminated the man's face as he blew softly, coaxing the tiny flame so that it spread to the other flakes of linen. Then he added some pinches of dry moss and added the contents of the box to the kindling at the base of the fire. It soon caught and spread quickly with a crackle to accompany the hungry orange tongues of the flames. One by one, other fires were lit, dotting the gloom of the valley with rosy glows that illuminated the small figures huddled round for warmth.

'Can I go over there?' Lupus nodded to the fire where a handful of guards stood, spears braced against their shoulders as they held their hands out towards the glow.

The guard cast a longing look towards the fire. 'My orders were to keep you here until I heard otherwise . . . But I don't suppose it can do any harm. Come on. But don't try anything. I'll be watching you, lad.'

'Try anything?' Lupus chuckled bitterly. 'And where would I run? There's only one way out of the valley, and that's heavily guarded.'

The guard stared at him. 'All the same. No funny stuff. All right?'

Lupus nodded, and the man gestured towards the fire with his spear. They crossed the compound and joined the other guards. One of them produced a wineskin and passed it round. The man responsible for Lupus took a swallow, then lowered the wineskin with a satisfied sigh.

'Ah! That warms the heart. Here, boy. Have some.'

He held the flask out to Lupus. For a moment the boy hesitated, then he reached out and took the wineskin with a nod of thanks. Taking out the stopper, he sniffed the contents and could not help wrinkling his nose at the sharp, acidic odour. The men chuckled at his reaction and Lupus forced himself to control his expression. Steeling himself, he put the nozzle in his mouth and raised the skin up as he tilted his head back. For a moment there was nothing and then a jet of the wine sloshed into his mouth, sharp and burning on his tongue. He lowered the wineskin and spluttered, to the accompaniment of laughter from the guards round the fire.

'Rough stuff, eh?' said the guard. 'Even for those of us who aren't used to the wines of the richest households in Rome.' He gestured towards Lupus's plain but well-made cloak. 'It's clear you ain't ever had to work in the fields. You're a house slave. No doubt raised on the fine scraps from the master's table. Never done a real day's work in your life, I suppose?'

Lupus flushed angrily but dared not reply.

'Thought so.' The guard nodded. 'Well, now you're no better than the rest of us. We're all the same here, lad. And you'll fight alongside the rest of us when the time comes.'

Lupus swallowed anxiously. 'If I refuse?'

'Best not to.' The guard drew a finger across his throat. 'You're either with us, or you're one of the enemy. So which is it?'

Lupus felt a shaft of terror pierce his heart. He saw the other men looking at him closely, many with scarred faces, weathered by years of toil or fighting.

'Well?' The man spoke again. 'Are you with us?'

Lupus hesitated, and was about to reply when a figure emerged from the darkness and joined those by the fire.

'What's this? Are you lot teasing our new recruit?' Mandracus chuckled as he stood beside Lupus and smiled at him. 'Ignore 'em, lad. They just like their bit of fun.'

Lupus raised an eyebrow. 'Fun?'

Mandracus placed a hand on his shoulder and steered Lupus away from the fire. 'Anyway, Brixus wants to see you. Now.'

They made their way towards the entrance of the large hut. The lintel over the doorway forced Mandracus to duck as he swept the leather curtain to one side and waved Lupus through. The interior was perhaps eighty feet across, and a fire in the centre provided enough illumination to reach the walls and the framework of timbers that supported the roof above. A woman in an old tunic was using a small knife to cut strips of meat from the carcass of a goat, dicing them up before adding them to a steaming cauldron suspended from an iron frame over the fire. Beyond the fire stood a large table with stools arranged round it. At the far end was a large wooden chair where a man was sitting, scrutinizing the new arrival.

'Lupus, isn't it?'

'Yes, master,' Lupus replied instinctively. Despite the gloom of the interior, he saw the brief look of irritation that flitted across the man's face.

'There are no masters here, Lupus,' the man said evenly. 'No masters and no slaves. Understand?'

He nodded.

'Then come closer. Sit down at the table.'

Lupus crossed the beaten earth and took the nearest stool at the end of the table. Mandracus took the stool opposite. Once they were settled the other man leaned forward and stared at Lupus. 'I am Brixus, general of the rebel army.'

Brixus's hair was dark and tightly curled. A jagged line of

puckered white scar tissue extended from his brow on to his cheek. His eyes were sunken beneath a thick brow and his skin was creased with age. Yet his shoulders were broad and his arms were well muscled. Lupus could imagine that Brixus would have been a formidable fighter in his time. He radiated an aura of toughness and ruthlessness, cruelty even.

'There's no need to be afraid of me.' Brixus smiled, revealing gaps in his teeth. 'We're on the same side. You're going to join the fight to put an end to slavery. Mandracus and his men have set you free from your master, but you can never be truly free until Rome has been humbled and forced to accept terms. That you must know. We are engaged in a fight to the death. Either we triumph over Rome or we are crushed. Do you understand?'

Lupus nodded slowly as he considered the situation, and then grasped the seemingly impossible challenge faced by Brixus and his followers. He felt his pulse quicken as he framed his response, not daring to antagonize the two men.

'Do you really think you can defeat Rome?'

'Why not?' Brixus shrugged his heavy shoulders. 'We came close last time, under Spartacus. But we were divided at the moment of victory. Some wanted to use our advantage to escape from Italia and return home, while others wanted to stay with Spartacus, continue the war and bring Rome to its knees. There were bitter arguments before our army split in two. Divided, we were no longer a match for the legions and were defeated one at a time.' Brixus shook his head sadly at the memory, then eased himself back into his chair before he continued. 'It won't happen this time. There will be no division. No debate. I will not permit it. Together, we will overcome Rome and her legions.'

Lupus chewed his lip before he responded. 'How can you overcome them? You have an army of thousands here. But for every man you have, Rome has ten or more legionaries. You are outnumbered.'

Brixus swept an arm around the hut. 'Do you think this is all that stands in the way of Rome? This is but the largest of the rebel camps. There are many others, all of them waiting for a sign to rise up and follow me. When that time comes we shall be ready for the legions.'

'What will the sign be?' asked Lupus.

Mandracus made to reply but Brixus cleared his throat to warn him off, then called out to the woman stirring the cauldron. 'Bring us a bowl each, and then leave.'

'Yes, master,' she replied and scrabbled for some silver bowls and spoons in a small chest beside the fireplace. She used an iron rod to lift the cauldron off the stand and lower it on to the floor. Ladling a steaming spoon of stew into each bowl, she hurriedly brought them over to set down on the table before ducking out of the tent.

'I thought there were no slaves here,' Lupus said warily. 'What about her?'

Brixus laughed. 'That woman is the wife of a Roman lanista, young Lupus. Or was, until we raided his school, killed him and his staff and set the gladiators and the household slaves free. By all accounts she treated her slaves like animals. Now she's being taught a lesson.' He smiled coldly. 'It's good to see the Romans having a taste of their own medicine, eh? Now, I expect you are cold and hungry, boy. So eat.'

Lupus picked up his spoon and filled it before blowing over the steaming mixture. The rich aroma rising from the bowl made him realize how hungry he was and he tucked in eagerly, relishing the warmth and the full flavour. As he ate, his mind worked feverishly. What did he know that would help Brixus?

They ate in silence, until Brixus finished and pushed his bowl away with a satisfied smack of his lips. He patted his fist against his chest and let out a burp, then smiled as he leaned back in his chair and regarded Lupus.

'Mandracus tells me that you belong – excuse me – belonged to Julius Caesar.'

Lupus hurriedly finished chewing a hunk of meat and swallowed as he lowered his spoon. 'That's right. I was his scribe,' he said proudly.

'A scribe?' Brixus raised his eyebrows appreciatively. 'Then you must be a very clever lad. Clever enough to be taken into Caesar's confidence, a little. Or perhaps clever enough to overhear things that maybe you shouldn't.'

Lupus felt the glow of pride quickly fade to be replaced by anxiety. 'I-I'm not sure what you mean.'

'Of course you are. You're no fool. Besides, I already know that Caesar has been sent by the Senate to find and destroy me and my followers. I have spies in Rome. They attend the public meetings of the Senate and report back regularly. So I know why your former master was making for Ariminum. He means to use the army there to crush us before he turns his attention to the Gauls, no doubt with every intention of enslaving as many of them as he can, and reaping a vast fortune as a result. What I need to know is his plan. You must tell me.'

'But I don't know anything about his plans,' Lupus protested. 'Caesar keeps that sort of thing to himself. All I do is write down what he tells me.'

176

'But you are there when he holds meetings with his supporters, and his allies.'

'Sometimes,' Lupus admitted. 'When he wants notes to be taken.'

'And he has never discussed his plans for dealing with us?'

'Not in front of me.' Lupus saw the ruthless gleam in the man's eyes and could not help trembling. 'I swear I'm telling the truth.'

'There are ways of finding out if you are telling the truth . . .'

'But I am. Why would I lie? You set me free.'

'Indeed. But there are some slaves who are more comfortable with being the property of others than master of their own destiny. It's possible that you might share the sentiments of such miserable creatures, young Lupus.'

'I want to be free. Really.'

Brixus stared at him a moment and then glanced at Mandracus. 'What do you think?'

'He says he wants to be free. I believe him. But he's still getting used to the idea.' Mandracus paused. 'Besides, Caesar keeps his thoughts close. We know that about him at least. So the boy might be telling the truth.'

Brixus stroked his chin thoughtfully. 'Very well. We shall

just have to order our scouts to keep a close watch on Caesar and his army.' He paused and folded his fingers together. 'There is still that other matter.'

Lupus saw Mandracus nod and felt a new wave of anxiety ripple through his guts. What other matter could there be? Then he remembered the earlier comment by Brixus, the one that had caused the rebel leader to send the lanista's wife out of the hut.

'You mentioned a sign. You said there would be a sign that would unite the rebel bands and cause them to rise up against Rome.'

'That's right.' Brixus smiled thinly. 'Clever boy. If we are to stand any chance against Rome we will need a figurehead. Someone to inspire the hearts of every slave in Italia. Someone they would follow to the ends of the earth.'

Lupus swallowed nervously. 'You?'

Brixus shook his head. 'No. Not a lame old gladiator like me. I might command those who live in this valley, and a handful of the other bands of rebels and brigands hiding in the mountains. But my name and my reputation are not enough on their own. We need a more famous name. More than a name, we need a legend. Someone like Achilles, or Heracles, who would inspire people.'

'I see.' Lupus pursed his lips. 'You mean Spartacus?'

Brixus nodded.

'Then it's a shame he was killed.'

'More than a shame, Lupus. It was a tragedy. If you had known the man, then you would understand. He was a great fighter, it's true. But he was more than that. Far more than that. He was a friend to all who met him. He understood their suffering, their desires, and he shared their hatred of slavery.'

'You met him?' Lupus edged forward. 'You knew Spartacus?'

Brixus smiled and nodded towards the other man. 'We both did. We fought at his side. We were part of the small band of companions who acted as his bodyguard from the early days of the rebellion. We stayed with him almost to the end.'

'You were at the final battle?'

'I was there, but I had been wounded and could not fight. I watched from the baggage train. That's where I was captured. Mandracus had been sent to scout for provisions and missed the battle. When he heard that we had been beaten he took his men into the mountains to hide, and found this valley.'

'I remained in charge until Brixus arrived,' Mandracus added. 'Brixus had been my leader in the old days and I was happy for him to take command again. Together we have been building a new army of runaway slaves, arming and training them so we could renew the rebellion when the time was right. The time has come, even though Caesar has forced it on us sooner than we would like. That is why we need to find the figurehead we were talking about. He would be the sign. The one who would cause the slaves of Italia to flock to his standard.'

Brixus and Mandracus exchanged a brief glance before Brixus continued. 'The son of Spartacus.'

Though Lupus had heard the rumours across Rome, he didn't think anyone was foolish enough to raise a rebellion on such a notion. But he was careful not to show his true feelings in front of the two men.

'Then where is he?' Lupus asked. 'Who is he?' He was still confused about his own role in this discussion.

'Before I tell you, Lupus, there are a few details you must know so that you believe me when I tell you his name. I met the boy at a gladiator school near Capua, less than two years ago. He thought himself the son of a retired Roman army officer and the slave woman that the officer had bought, freed and married. Except this woman had been the wife of Spartacus and she was carrying his child in her womb when she was taken by the officer. After his birth she branded the child with the mark of Spartacus, a secret mark that only Spartacus and those closest to him carried. A mark like this.'

Brixus stood up and pulled the cloak and tunic from his arm to reveal the muscle of his shoulder. There at the top of his shoulder blade was a scar, a brand in the shape of a wolf's head pierced by a gladiator's sword. Brixus let him see it for a moment, then shrugged the cloak back over his skin and sat down.

'Mandracus has the same mark, and the heating iron that made it was kept by Spartacus's wife – the same one she used on her child.'

Lupus winced as he imagined the mother branding her own baby. 'Why would she do such a thing?'

Brixus pursed his lips. 'My guess is she loved Spartacus, and all that he stood for, and intended that his son would continue his work one day. The brand served to remind her of this, and would prove his identity to others who had followed Spartacus.'

Lupus frowned. He suddenly realized that he had encountered the brand before, recently. 'I know that mark! I've seen it myself.'

'If reports are to be believed, then I imagine that you have.' Brixus smiled. 'And now that I have explained about the boy who bears the mark, you will know who he is.'

Lupus felt a little dizzy as the realization hit home like a hammer blow. He let out a gasp and whispered, 'Marcus . . .'

'Yes. Marcus. I know that he is with Caesar. We must find him, and bring him here to fulfil his destiny. Once we have Marcus, there will be a rebellion like none the world has ever seen. Roman blood will flow like a river and slaves will be free.'

There was a sudden waft of cold air as the leather curtain was brushed aside by a tall figure entering the hut. In the wavering glow of the flames they could see the man's chest was heaving and his boots, leggings and cloak were spattered with mud. He strode across the hut and bowed his head in greeting to Brixus.

'What is it, Commius?' Brixus asked. 'You weren't supposed to return from your raids until the end of the month.'

'I know, but I have news of Caesar and his army.'

Mandracus leaned forward with an excited expression. 'Out with it!'

Commius nodded and drew a deep, calming breath before he continued. 'We had burned a villa near Mutina and were moving on when we saw a large column of soldiers approaching along the road from Ariminum. We followed them to the town and that night captured a prisoner outside the gates, who we took back to our camp. It didn't take long to get the truth out of him. Caesar has left most of his men in winter quarters. He has taken barely ten thousand men to hunt us down.'

'Ten thousand.' Mandracus sucked in a breath through his teeth. 'That's still too many for us to take on head-to-head.'

'Wait,' Commius intervened. 'He has split his force in half. Caesar and barely five thousand are at Mutina. They are marching into the mountains even now, searching for us.'

'Five thousand?' Brixus rubbed his chin thoughtfully. 'By the Gods, what a chance he has presented to us! His arrogance is typical of his kind. He considers us a rabble, fit meat for a small force of his prized legionaries. Well, we shall punish his mistake, Mandracus. It is time to put our own plan into action. Let Caesar march into our trap. Within a few days we shall have Marcus leading us into battle, and Caesar will be crushed and taken prisoner. Or better still, dead.'

15

'They made a pretty thorough job of it,' Festus said quietly as he prodded the blackened stump of a wooden post. He stepped back, placed his hands on his hips and surveyed the surrounding scene as Marcus dismounted. Marcus tethered the reins to an iron ring set in what was left of the villa's main gate and joined Festus. Before them lay the remains of the buildings and gardens of what had once been the sprawling country home of a wealthy Roman. Now almost nothing stood higher than a man – only heaps of collapsed masonry and tiles and scorched skeletal lengths of timber. Smoke still trailed into the air, wafting up into the haze that obscured the sun. Soldiers were picking their way through the debris, searching for any sign of survivors, or valuables that might be saved from the ruins. Marcus sniffed and wrinkled his nose at the acrid stench of burning.

'I can't see any bodies,' he muttered.

'Not yet. But there will be a few,' Festus replied grimly. 'They would have surprised the place, freed all the slaves and taken what loot they could carry, then set fire to it. The steward of the villa and the guards are probably dead. Their bodies will be under that lot somewhere. Not that there will be much left of them after the fire.'

Both of them were silent a moment before Marcus spoke again. 'We can't be more than ten miles from Mutina. The rebels who did this were taking quite a risk venturing this far from the mountains.'

'Or they're becoming more confident. If so, then Caesar should be worried. Looks like Brixus and his men aren't afraid of the local garrisons any more. Only the largest towns will be safe from their raids if Caesar's plan fails.'

Marcus looked back through the remains of the gate. Caesar was delivering a verbal report of the attack to one of his staff officers before sending him to Rome. It would take several days to reach the capital, where a senator would be informed of the destruction of his property. But there would be other consequences. The burning of the villa would provide Caesar's political enemies with another excuse to attack him in the Senate. Marcus could already imagine the scene with

Cato rising to his feet to denounce Caesar. If Caesar couldn't handle a gang of rebel slaves, what chance had he of taking on the Gauls that threatened Italia's northern frontier? It would be better to recall an incompetent general and send a more worthy replacement, Cato would argue. Meanwhile, Crassus would sit back smugly and enjoy the damage to his rival's reputation.

'What do you think he will do now?' asked Marcus. 'Send for more men?'

'No. He'll stick to the plan. This changes nothing. If he sends for reinforcements, it would be as good as admitting he had made a mistake. You know what he's like. He'll never admit to making a mistake if he can avoid it.'

There was a pounding of hoofs and Marcus turned to see the staff officer galloping back in the direction of the junction where the Via Flamina branched off towards Rome.

Caesar cupped a hand to his mouth and called out. 'Reform column! We're moving on!'

Marcus untethered his horse and climbed back into the saddle. He waited for Festus and the two of them walked their mounts into the road that passed the gate. Behind them, the centurions and optios bellowed at the men to abandon their search and rejoin the column. Once every man was back in position, Caesar waved his arm forward and the cavalry led them along the road that climbed into the foothills of the Apennines. A squadron of cavalry rode a short distance ahead to scout the way and guard against ambush. Behind them came the general and his officers and bodyguards and then the infantry, trudging along four abreast, marching yokes resting on the padding they wore across their shoulders. After the infantry came the small baggage train, carrying a few days' supply of grain and the soldiers' tents, which would offer them some protection against the freezing temperatures up in the mountains. With them trundled the wagon of Decimus, while he rode beside on a horse. At the tail of the column came the cohort of legionaries assigned to serve as the rearguard.

As the column left the smouldering remains of the villa behind, Marcus's sense of foreboding increased. He had begun to doubt the wisdom of Caesar's plan. With little known about the strength of the enemy, it made no sense to start out with a modest force and then proceed to divide it.

The truth about his father's identity was another matter that troubled him. It seemed as if a quiet voice constantly encouraged him to accept the challenge of living in a manner that would make his father, Spartacus, proud. The same voice constantly reminded him of the evils of slavery and the duty of everyone aware of its injustice to stand up and fight those who enslaved other people. And that meant fighting the Roman Empire itself and all those who served it. Especially men like Caesar.

And yet Marcus knew the struggle was not as simple as that. He remembered the tales that Titus had told him when he was a young boy. Titus had fought the Gauls, Parthians and other barbarians, and the vivid descriptions of their atrocities had chilled Marcus's blood. It had also convinced him there were worse people in this world than those of Rome. There had to be a middle way between the traditions of Rome and those who wanted an end to slavery. Or was that just the wishful thinking of a young boy? Yet here he was, riding beside the men marching to hunt down and kill those who opposed slavery. Part of Marcus thought he was on the wrong side. That he should take his chance and run away to join Brixus and his men. But then he remembered his mother. Her best chance of survival rested on Caesar helping Marcus to track her down and set her free. With a leaden feeling in his heart, Marcus knew he was trapped. He had to remain at Caesar's side and serve the Roman general until his mother was safe. After that, finally, he could decide his own future.

The column continued into the mountains, and the road

gave way to a narrow track hemmed in on either side by forests of pine trees enveloped in mists and cloud. The grey skies steadily darkened and there were frequent showers of rain. Marcus hunched in his saddle and daydreamed of sitting in front of a fire at Portia's house in Ariminum when the current campaign was over. There, with Festus and Caesar, he would tell Portia of their experiences, and perhaps she would secretly give Marcus a knowing look.

As quickly as the thought occurred to him, Marcus thrust it from his mind. He must not let himself even think about her in that way. She could never be more than a friend, and then only in private, hidden from those who would be horrified at the prospect of friendship between them.

As the rain gave way to sleet and snow, the column passed the remains of a handful of other small villas that had been raided by the rebels. Only ruins remained, and Marcus sensed the anger welling up in the men around him. When the time came for them to fight, they would show little mercy.

At the end of the first day the column reached a small town perched on a cliff above a stream. While the men set up their tents on the open ground outside the town walls, Caesar and his entourage found accommodation in the house of an affluent mule-breeder. Publius Flavius glumly told his guests about the constant raids on outlying farms and villages in the area. A shepherd had driven his flock into the town the previous day, claiming to have seen a party of rebels – no more than a hundred of them, on foot – making for a villa in a valley not ten miles away. Caesar ordered Marcus to take down the details as he listened patiently, then reassured Flavius that the threat would soon be extinguished.

The following morning the temperature dropped and snow began to fall, blanketing the tiled roofs of the town and drifting across the track that led further into the mountains. Caesar inspected the path with a frustrated expression before turning to issue orders to his closest followers.

'We'll take the cavalry and ride on. The rest of the column will follow as best they can. I'm keen to catch up with those slaves seen by the shepherd. If we can capture them, they'll provide us with useful intelligence about Brixus. With a bit of luck, they might even know where he is.'

Festus puffed his cheeks out and cleared his throat. 'Is that wise, sir?'

'Wise?' Caesar asked tonelessly, but Marcus saw the dangerous glint in his eyes, the prelude to one of his angry outbursts. 'Why would it not be wise, Festus?'

'Sir, it would mean dividing the force yet again.'

'I have more than enough mounted men to take on a hundred rebels. Besides, the infantry and the wagons are holding us up. If we stay together the enemy will escape. I won't let that happen. My mind is made up. Give the orders to the cohort commanders. Meanwhile, the cavalry are to set off as soon as they are ready.'

Festus bowed his head. 'Yes, sir.'

As the head of his bodyguard strode off to relay the orders, Caesar caught Marcus's eye.

'The chase is on, eh, Marcus?'

Marcus nodded, despite his doubts. He agreed with Festus. Caesar was taking a risk. But clearly there was no changing his mind.

'If Fortuna favours us,' Caesar continued, rubbing his hands together to warm them, 'then we might discover where Brixus is hiding by the end of the day. Think on that. We find and destroy Brixus and his rabble, and so break the spirit of those who would follow him. The slaves will learn their lesson. No one defies Rome. Then I will be free to turn my attention to Gaul.'

'Yes, sir. And I can seek out my mother.'

Caesar flashed him a look of irritation. 'Of course. Did you think I had forgotten?'

Marcus did not dare reply, having made his point, and Caesar turned away and called for a groom to bring his horse.

The snow continued to fall through the morning as the horsemen followed the track, often in single file to negotiate the drifts that had formed. On either side the boughs of the pine trees were heavily laden and the dull thrumming of the horses' hoofs was muffled as they rode on. Then, at noon, shortly after the snow had stopped falling, the track descended into a small valley and there was a cry from one of the men scouting ahead. Marcus and the others looked up expectantly as a rider galloped back along the road. He reined in sharply and snow sprayed into the air as he thrust an arm out.

'There's a fire ahead, sir!'

'A fire?' Caesar grasped his reins tightly. 'Then we may have them! Let's go!'

He spurred his horse forward and the rest of the column rippled into motion, horses thundering along the track, their steamy breaths whipped out from flaring nostrils. All thought of the cold disappeared from Marcus's mind as he urged his mount to keep up with Caesar and Festus. The rest of the bodyguard and staff officers galloped behind, followed by the cavalry.

Ahead, the other scouts were waiting on a small rise that afforded a view along the valley. As they crested the ridge, Marcus saw that the trees fell away on either side, with open land ahead, nestling between the mountains. Aged walled enclosures showed that the land had been used as pasture for many years. A stream meandered along the valley floor into a small lake and ahead, beside a mill, stood a collection of farm buildings enclosed by a wooden stockade. Bright flames licked up from the windows in the largest building and black smoke billowed into the still winter air. Marcus could see figures moving, stark against the snow, as they carried off their spoils, piling them on to several small carts and a wagon hitched to mules a short distance from the villa.

Marcus galloped down the far side of the rise to the flat road approaching the farm, not much more than half a mile away. The wind roared in his ears and his heart was beating wildly with excitement. Immediately ahead, the horses of Festus and Caesar were kicking up a spray of snow that made it difficult for him to see beyond them. He urged his mount on, steering it to one side, then saw the distant figures scrambling into activity as they spotted the horsemen charging towards them.

'Don't let them escape!' Caesar shouted. 'I want prisoners!'

Ahead, the men who had attacked the villa were sprinting across the open ground towards the safety of the treeline, abandoning their loot. Even as they raced across the snow-covered fields, Marcus could see most of them would escape well before the Roman cavalry reached the scene. Once they disappeared into the depths of the forest where the snow had not penetrated, there would be no tracks to follow and they could escape. Marcus felt relieved by that.

The last of the rebels had already vanished from sight as Caesar savagely reined in outside the villa. Behind him, the rest of his men caught up and the air was filled with the snorting of horses and chink of bits.

'Decurion!' Caesar thrust his hand towards the first officer to arrive on the scene. 'Take your squadron and go after them. On foot if necessary.'

'Yes, sir!' The decurion snapped a salute and bellowed to his men to follow him as he galloped across to the line of trees stretching along the edge of the valley. Briefly, Caesar turned to look at the villa before dismounting and handing his reins to one of the bodyguards. Festus and Marcus followed suit and joined him inside the wall.

The fire had taken hold of the main building and already tongues of flame were stabbing up into the air between the roof tiles. A large section of the roof gave way and crashed into the blaze with an explosion of sparks that swirled high into the air. One of the adjoining buildings was already alight as the fire spread.

Caesar raised an arm to shield his face from the heat. 'Look for survivors! I'll check this side of the villa. Festus, take Marcus and search the other side!'

Festus pulled Marcus towards the side of the building, where the double doors of a long shed stood open. While Festus strode ahead, Marcus struggled to keep up. As they reached the end of the shed, a wiry man with grey hair lurched into view. A club swung from one arm, and a small chest was tucked under the other. With astonishing speed, he raised his club and slashed at Festus's head. The glancing blow threw Festus into the snow at his feet with a deep groan. At once the man raised the club again, ready to strike at his head.

'No!' Marcus yelled, hurling himself forward. He snatched at the man's bony wrist and both of them tumbled back across the threshold of the shed, sprawling to the earthen floor inside. The impact winded the man but Marcus had rolled to his feet and was ready to strike before the man could rise. Marcus kicked him in the side and smashed a fist on to the back of his head. Raising a hand to protect himself, the man released his club and Marcus snatched it up, then delivered a quick, savage blow across his shoulders. With an explosive grunt the man slumped to the ground, moaning. Marcus stood over him, both hands tightly grasping the club. When he was sure the fight had gone out of the man, he crouched beside Festus and shook his shoulder.

'Are you all right?'

'I'm seeing double and my head feels like a house landed on it,' Festus growled. 'Next stupid question?'

Marcus grinned, then turned his attention back to the other man. Sinewy and tough, the rebel looked in his fifties at least. Marcus regarded him warily. 'Stay down, if you know what's good for you.'

The rebel lay where he had fallen, winded and gasping for breath. Slowly, Festus struggled to his feet and leaned forward, hands resting on his knees as he recovered. Marcus turned at a soft crunch of feet in the snow to see Caesar's grim smile of satisfaction as he walked towards the rebel.

'You got one of 'em. Well done!' Caesar stood over the man and stared down at him. 'Looks like he's on his last legs. If this is the best that Brixus can offer, then we have nothing to worry about. The battle, when it comes, is as good as won.'

Marcus took in the rebel's ragged cloak and boots that were falling to pieces. His skin was mottled and covered in grime, his breathing laboured as he lay on his back. If Festus hadn't been caught by surprise, he would have cut the man down in an instant. Why would Brixus even think of sending a man in such poor condition on a raid? It didn't make sense.

'What if this isn't the best, sir?' he asked. 'The others who were here ran off quickly enough.'

Caesar waved a hand dismissively. 'No matter. We have this one to question. Festus, take him behind the shed and question him. I want to know where Brixus is hiding and how many men he has under arms.'

Festus straightened up and paced over to the rebel. He wrenched the frail man to his feet. Then, drawing his dagger, he dragged him round the corner of the shed and out of sight. By the time the rest of Caesar's officers arrived the first cries of terror and pain cut through the air, only slightly muffled by the roar of flames that consumed the main building some fifty paces away. Tribune Quintus nodded towards the villa wall beyond the burning building.

'One of the decurions found some bodies over there, sir. Looks like the owner of the villa and his family, and their overseers. Their throats have been cut.'

Marcus saw the shaken expression on the tribune's face as Caesar turned to him.

'That's too bad.'

Quintus nodded and hesitated a moment before he spoke again. 'Should I give orders for a funeral or burial, sir?'

'There's no time for that. Once Festus gets the information I need we'll be moving out.'

'What if the rebel won't speak, sir?' asked Marcus. 'What if he doesn't know anything useful?'

'He'll know something. And trust me, he will speak. Festus has never let me down in that regard.'

Before Marcus could respond there was a long, piercing shriek from behind the shed, and then another, followed by a terrified gabbling and pleading before a fresh scream sent a shiver down Marcus's spine.

While the torturing continued, Caesar sent some men to search the buildings for food and wine. When they returned, together with some stools, he and his officers sat down and tucked into the makeshift meal. While Caesar attempted to lighten the mood by talking about the approaching campaign in Gaul, Marcus stood a short distance away and looked on with a growing sense of disgust. He could not block out the cries of the rebel. In the end, he paced away, standing close to the burning building where the roar of flames almost covered up the sounds of torment.

At length the rebel fell silent and a moment later Festus emerged, wiping the blood from his dagger with a strip of cloth cut from the rebel's cloak. As he saw him, Marcus turned away from the fire to rejoin Caesar and his officers.

'Well?' Caesar demanded. 'What did you get out of the wretch?'

'He didn't know, or wouldn't say, where Brixus has his camp, sir. He was part of a separate band that Brixus had ordered to raid this villa.'

'Damn! Is that all?'

'No, sir.' Festus sheathed his dagger. 'There's more. After this raid, Polonius and the others will join Brixus in a gathering of his bands. They are massing to attack the town of Sedunum, at the end of the next valley. Brixus and two thousand of his men will attack at dawn tomorrow.'

Caesar's lips parted in a cold smile. 'How far is it to the town?'

One of his tribunes coughed. 'No more than ten miles, sir.'

Caesar turned to the officer. 'And how do you know this?'

'I have an uncle there, sir. I've visited Sedunum several times.'

'Excellent. How does the land lie around the town?'

The tribune collected his thoughts. 'It is at the end of the valley, with mountains on three sides, and a river crosses in front of the town. If Brixus plans to attack at dawn, he will probably be concealed in the trees on this side of the river, facing the town.'

'Then we have them!' Caesar punched a fist into the palm of his other hand. 'As long as we act at once. We can't take them with the cavalry alone. I need the infantry. They will have to march through the night if we are to corner Brixus against the river.' He turned to Quintus. 'Ride back to the column. Leave one cohort to guard the baggage train. The rest are to drop their packs and march on Sedunum. I'll be waiting a few miles short of the town. Once the infantry have come, we'll attack Brixus and his rabble in their camp. It will all be over before the day even begins.'

'You mean to attack under cover of darkness, sir?' asked Quintus.

'That is the best way to surprise your enemy,' Caesar replied sharply. 'Do you question my orders?'

'Of course not, sir. But is one cohort sufficient to protect the baggage train?'

'Protect it from what? You heard Festus. The rebels are gathering ahead of us.'

'Yes, sir.' Quintus paused. 'It's just that all our supplies, the tents and the packs of the rest of the column will be with the baggage train. If anything happens to it the men will be without food or shelter.'

'The baggage train will surely catch up with us by the end of the day,' Caesar responded. 'I have made up my mind. Now give the orders.'

Marcus felt a nagging doubt at the back of his mind. There was something wrong about this. It was all too neat. He took a step forward, between the officers, so that he was clearly visible to Caesar.

'Sir, the tribune is right. It would be dangerous to put the baggage train at risk. Besides, why would Brixus let himself be caught in a trap?'

'He doesn't know it's a trap,' Caesar snapped. 'Besides, he's just a slave. A brigand. All he's interested in is looting and revenge. He's become too confident. Success has made him arrogant and now he is going to pay the price.'

'But, sir —'

'Enough, Marcus! You are only a boy. Still your tongue. Do you dare to defy my will in this?'

'The boy is right, sir,' Quintus interrupted. 'We cannot risk leaving our men without shelter and food if anything happens to the baggage train.'

Caesar's expression hardened. 'Since you are so concerned about it, Tribune, then you will take command of the baggage. There will be no place for you in tomorrow's battle. No share of the victory. I will not have men who fear for their safety at my side in a fight.' His gaze shifted to Marcus. 'Nor boys who share such fear. Both of you will return to the column at once. And when you have passed on my orders, stay there.'

Quintus opened his mouth to protest, then clamped his jaw shut and bowed his head before turning towards the horses held ready by one of the troopers. Marcus stood his ground, burning with shame at the accusation of cowardice that Caesar had thrown at him.

'What are you waiting for, boy?' Caesar waved his hand. 'Get out of my sight.'

Marcus nodded, his lips pressed together in a thin line. He glanced towards Festus who gave the slightest of shrugs, then turned to stride stiffly through the snow to catch up with Quintus, his heart filled with a sense of foreboding.

16

Tribune Quintus watched the rear of the infantry column marching off into the gloom with an anxious expression. Around him the men of the rearguard were busy picking up the marching yokes of their comrades and heaping them on to the supply carts and wagons. Even the wagon of Decimus had been pressed into service and his men were grumbling as they helped the legionaries. Marcus had raised the hood of his cloak the moment they joined the baggage train and did his best to keep out of sight of Decimus as he followed the tribune.

Quintus was no more than five or six years older than himself, Marcus estimated. His cheeks sported only a faint blur of stubble and he looked no different from the youths hanging around the street corners of Rome. Only he was now in charge of five hundred soldiers and another two hundred mule drivers of the baggage train. As Marcus watched, Quintus raised his thumb to his mouth and chewed on the nail.

A fresh flurry of snow had blown down from the mountain peaks. Very quickly, the swirling flakes swallowed up the departing column, filling the air with a mournful moan and faint swish as the wind disturbed the tops of the laden fir trees on either side of the track.

'You were right to warn him,' Marcus said quietly.

Quintus turned and frowned at him. 'I don't need some ex-slave to tell me that.'

Marcus controlled his anger. 'I apologize if you think I am speaking out of turn. I just thought you should know.'

Quintus glared at him in silence for a moment. 'Just who in Hades do you think you are? You're just a boy. I know you've trained as a gladiator and even won a fight or two, but that doesn't make you an expert in anything. Why on earth Caesar keeps you close to his side is beyond me.'

'I'm not at his side now,' Marcus pointed out.

'But he still listened to you, and holds you in some kind of regard. Just like his niece. Anyone would think you were Portia's little brother from the way she goes on about you,' he said bitterly.

Marcus frowned. So, she spoke about him. Even to the man who had become her husband. He felt a spark of warmth in his heart. That, and the hope for something impossible, then he pushed the thought aside.

'Sir, the sooner we set off after the main column the better.'

'I know that!' Quintus snapped and tugged sharply on the reins as he turned his mount, trotting back down the line to shout at the men. 'Get those packs loaded on the wagons! Centurions! Get your men moving. I want the wagons sent off as soon as possible!'

Marcus watched him for a moment, then looked up at the sky. Thick flakes of snow swirled down from the dark grey clouds and there was no sign of any break in the weather. The track along which the column had marched was already covered by fresh drifts, and Marcus realized they had little chance of catching up with Caesar and the main column the following day.

Once the men had formed up, two centuries marched in front of the wagons, with two more at the rear. The rest of the legionaries were strung out beside the vehicles, ready to clear drifts from the track or put their shoulders to the wheels to push the carts and wagons forward. Quintus rode at the head of the formation, with the senior centurion of the cohort at his side. Marcus remained a short distance behind, to keep out of the tribune's way. He had no desire to antagonize Portia's husband any further.

It took two hours, as far as Marcus could estimate, for the baggage train to reach the rise from where the villa had been sighted earlier that day. Now the blizzard obscured the way ahead and it was impossible to make out any of the buildings. The water at the edge of the lake had frozen and the snow settling on the ice left only the middle of the lake visible.

As they approached the villa, a faint glow through the falling snow revealed that some buildings were still on fire. A short distance further on Marcus could see the dark mass of the mill by the stream and then the wooden stockade surrounding the villa, the outline of the sharpened stakes clearly defined against the glow of the fire within.

'We should stop here for a moment to rest the men and mules,' the centurion marching beside Quintus advised. 'It's hard going, and they're exhausted.'

'If we stop now, they'll not want to continue,' Quintus mused. 'Better we carry on.'

'If we do that, sir, then we'll risk losing men and beasts along the way. Any stragglers we leave behind won't survive the night without shelter.'

'That's their lookout. I have orders to bring the baggage up to the main column as soon as I can.'

The centurion sighed in frustration and was about to speak again when Marcus heard a faint sound to his left, from the direction of the trees. It had sounded like a voice calling out. He flicked his hood back to hear more clearly, tilting his head to the side as he strained his ears.

'Did you hear that?' he interrupted the two officers.

'What?' Quintus rounded on him, the wind fluttering the crest on his helmet. 'Hear what?'

'Quiet!' Marcus snapped. 'Listen! There it is again.'

There was another shout from amid the trees, muffled and impossible to make out, but definitely a voice.

'Could be a wild animal,' suggested the centurion. 'With the wind and all, it's easy to mistake the sound.'

Marcus shook his head. 'There's someone out there, I'm telling you.'

Quintus chuckled. 'Your imagination is getting the better of you, boy. You should have stayed in Caesar's household in Rome where you belong.'

Before Marcus could respond, the sound of a horn cut through the moan of the wind. Three sharp blasts, a pause, then they came again. Along the track the men and vehicles slowed to a halt as faces turned towards the sound with anxious expressions.

'What's that?' Quintus asked.

The horn sounded a third time and a cheer rose up from within the forest. Marcus stared at the shadows along the treeline, no more than two hundred paces away. As the sound of the cheers swelled, he saw movement and the first of the figures burst from cover to charge across the snowy field towards the track.

'Ambush!' the centurion exclaimed, then turned to his men and cupped his hand. 'Form line to the left!'

Quintus stared at the oncoming men open-mouthed, then thrust his jaw out as he drew his sword. He caught Marcus's eyes and nodded grimly. 'Looks like we were right about the risk.'

'Maybe,' Marcus replied through gritted teeth. 'But there's nothing we can do about it now.'

He reached down for the handle of his sword and drew the blade from its scabbard with a sharp rasp.

'Stay close!' Quintus ordered. 'If you're half the gladiator they say you are, I want you at my side.'

The tribune wheeled his mount and spurred it into a gallop back along the track, past the men of the first two centuries who had dropped their yokes and were hurriedly checking the straps of their armour before raising their shields to form a line facing the ambushers. Leaning forward in his saddle, Marcus glanced to his right and saw the white expanse in front of the forest was filled with figures. Thousands of them were surging through the ankle-deep blanket of snow.

Quintus reined in when he reached the wagons, shouting at the thin screen of legionaries to step aside and let him through. Some of the mule drivers had already deserted their positions and were running towards the shelter of the stockade, while others ran blindly towards the stream. The water was raging between the banks and Marcus knew that anyone attempting to cross it would be swept away. There was no escape from the trap that had been set for them. They must close up and hold their ground for as long as possible. As Quintus took up his position by the cohort's standard, close to the wagon where Decimus and his men stood ready with their swords, Marcus edged his horse alongside the tribune. He stared at the wave of men rushing towards them, their mouths open as they let out a deafening roar of triumph. Most were well armed, kitted out with shields, helmets and weapons looted from the farms, villages and small towns that they had attacked. A far cry from the ragged appearance of Polonius, the rebel tortured by Festus.

In that instant Marcus saw it all. The clever trap Brixus had set for Caesar played on the Roman's contempt for the rebel slaves and his desire for a quick end to the campaign. Polonius had been a plant, deliberately left behind to be captured and give the information that had lured Caesar away from his baggage train. It had cost him his life and Marcus could only marvel at the courage of a man who played such a part, sacrificing himself to give his comrades a victory over the Romans. He wondered if any man in Caesar's army would have such courage. Then there was no more time to think: the enemy was upon them.

At the front of the charge the men armed with slings and bows stopped to loose their missiles before charging on. Marcus turned at the sound of a dull crack and saw one of the legionaries fall, his face a bloody mask. He thudded into the snow and kicked out for a moment before losing consciousness. More shot and arrows rattled off the heavy oval shields as the legionaries raised them up. There was a shrill braying as the mules fell victim to the barrage and some of the mule teams began to panic and drag their vehicles out of line. Marcus saw one team veer to the side, thrusting through the legionaries. One man was knocked down, his legs crushed as the cart wheel ran over them. The mule team broke into a trot, careering across the snowy field into the rebel ranks.

'Ready javelins!' barked the senior centurion.

The gap between the two sides had narrowed to no more than thirty paces. Waiting for the centurion's order, the legionaries hefted their javelins and drew their arms back. Marcus saw the centurion narrow his eyes as he timed the moment, his sword held high. With a dull gleam, the blade swept down and he bellowed at the top of his voice. 'Loose!'

The dark shafts of the javelins arced through the snowflakes before striking the figures swarming towards the Roman line. Marcus saw scores of men collapse as the sharp iron heads tore through them. But the attackers did not waver and charged straight into the cohort's shield wall. Sitting in his saddle, Marcus's ears filled with the crash of shields and scrape and ringing of clashing blades, and the grunts of men locked in battle. This was unlike any fight he had ever seen. Worse even than the riots he'd witnessed from the street gangs at the Forum in Rome. And more frightening than the gladiator bouts he had been forced to endure. Those had involved a test of skill, each fighter with only one opponent to concentrate on as they duelled to the death. What was happening now seemed a bloody chaos of hacking, slashing and stabbing along the ragged battle-line.

At his side Tribune Quintus held his sword up and out as he shouted encouragement to the men under his command. 'Hold fast! Drive the slave scum back!'

Then, just in front of the two horses, a rebel burst through the Roman line. An axe in one hand and a buckler in the other, his mouth gaped in a roar behind a wild black beard. He saw the Roman officer and charged forward, swinging the axe above his head and thrusting the heavy blade towards Quintus's shoulder. Marcus acted instinctively, pulling hard on his reins so his horse crashed into the rebel and knocked him aside. The axe swept down, narrowly missing the tribune's boot before crunching into the compacted snow on the ground. Quintus twisted in his saddle and swept his sword down, stabbing deep between the rebel's shoulder blades. The man let out an agonized cry and collapsed face first in the snow as blood spattered the snow around him.

Quintus met Marcus's eyes and he nodded his thanks before turning back to the fight.

Already the rebels' superiority in numbers was telling. Both ends of the Roman line were being forced back as the legionaries tried to avoid being outflanked. But Marcus realized they could not prevent the inevitable for much longer. A harsh cry to his side alerted him to a fresh danger and he snapped his head round to see a lithe figure in a gladiator's cuirass rushing towards him with a spear in both hands, the point aimed directly at Marcus's chest. There was little time to react and he threw his weight back in the saddle at the same time as he thrust his sword out, catching the wooden shaft just beyond the iron point. He was not strong enough to parry the thrust and only deflected the point into the neck of his horse. It punched through the hide and flesh before the bloodied iron burst out the other side. The horse let out a terrified whinny and reared up, wrenching the shaft from the rebel's hands. Marcus held the reins in his left hand as tightly as he could, but he was already leaning backwards and felt his legs slipping out of the saddle.

With a cry he tumbled off, letting the reins go before he crashed to the ground, the impact driving the breath from his lungs. There was no time to recover as the horse reared and kicked, spraying snow into Marcus's face. He rolled away towards the river, then scrambled to his feet, gasping. On either side the legionaries were being driven back through the line of wagons and panicking mules.

'Protect the standard!' Quintus shouted. He turned his horse towards the gilded wreath and red drop that rose above the crumbling centre of the Roman line. Then his horse

213

stumbled and Quintus desperately swung a leg over the saddle, jumping to the ground as the horse fell on its side, a broken leg thrashing out.

Marcus ran to his side. 'Are you all right, sir?'

Quintus nodded. 'We have to save the standard. Stay with me.'

They joined the small group of legionaries formed up round the standard and saw that the senior centurion was among them, fighting the rebels back and shouting to his men in between the blows he struck.

'Form on the standard! On me!'

Those who could obeyed the order and closed ranks with their comrades. In the centre Quintus took stock of the fight.

'We're losing.'

Marcus caught glimpses of the fighting beyond the ring of men around him and saw that the centre of the line had broken. Some legionaries had thrown aside their weapons and were running away, pursued by the rebels, who showed no mercy. On either flank the centuries had closed up into desperate knots as they fought back to back until they were cut down. The men protecting the standard were slowly forced to give ground as they were driven away from the track towards the edge of the small lake.

The centurion forced his way to Quintus's side. 'Sir, we cannot let the standard fall into the enemy's hands.'

Quintus stared back, white-faced, and Marcus saw that his lips were trembling.

The veteran officer took a breath and spoke as calmly as he could. 'We've lost the fight, sir. But we can save our honour. We must not let the standard be taken. If we reach the lake, we can throw it into the depths.'

Quintus blinked and nodded. 'Yes. That's what we must do.'

The veteran turned and called to the men surrounding him. 'We will give ground towards the lake. I'll call the pace. One! . . . Two! . . .'

The small group backed away from the rebels. All the time Marcus could hear the pounding of weapons on their shields and see the men thrusting back with the short sword of the legions. Every so often an enemy weapon found its way between the shields and a legionary let out a cry as he was wounded. Some fought on, even as their blood flowed on to the disturbed snow at their feet. Others staggered back and collapsed, too wounded to stay in formation, and Marcus saw the look in their eyes as they drew their shields close to their bodies and gripped their swords. He admired their determination to go down fighting while their comrades were forced to leave them behind as they fought to reach the lake.

Marcus glanced round and saw there were no more than thirty or so men left to protect the standard. Suddenly there was a shout from nearby.

'Let us through! Let us through!'

He recognized the voice well enough. A moment later Decimus and a handful of his men, breathing hard and holding bloodied swords, stumbled between the shields and stood panting beside Quintus, Marcus and the standard bearer. Behind them the soldiers quickly closed ranks as the rebels continued to harry them. It was impossible to break through the wall of shields and the vicious points of the legionaries' swords, and most of the rebels moved on, looking for easier prey.

'We're almost at the edge of the lake,' the centurion announced as he craned his neck to peer over the helmets of his comrades. 'We'll hold our ground there for as long as possible while I get rid of the standard.'

Decimus rounded on the officer. 'And then what? Where do we go?'

'Go?' The centurion smiled grimly. 'Straight to Hades, that's where.'

'That's your plan?' Decimus laughed. 'Not me. I'm getting out of here. I'll swim for it.'

'In that water? You'd freeze before you reached the far side. You can drown like a rat or die like a man with a sword in your hand.'

Decimus shook his head as he looked round the small formation. 'You're mad.'

Then he saw Marcus for the first time and stared at him with a puzzled expression before his eyes widened. 'I know you! You . . . You're that brat son of Titus.'

For an instant Marcus forgot the battle raging around him. He forgot the imminence of his own death at the hands of the rebels. All he saw was the face of the man who had tormented him and his mother as they stood in a slave pen waiting to be auctioned off. With a feral snarl, he raised his sword and thrust it wildly at Decimus.

'Watch it, lad!' the centurion snapped as he thrust his shield between Marcus and Decimus. The blade cracked harmlessly against the edge of the armour. 'He's one of ours, you fool!' he snapped. 'Watch what you do with that blade!'

Marcus let out a cry of frustration as he saw Decimus move back, two of his men blocking Marcus's way.

The centurion thrust Marcus towards Quintus. 'Keep

this hothead under control. He's more danger to our side than theirs.'

But the moment had passed and now an aching despair filled Marcus's heart. If he and Decimus were to fall here, then all was lost. He would die knowing that his mother was doomed to slavery, worked to death on Decimus's farming estate in Greece. He'd also die without having avenged Titus and the others murdered by Decimus's henchmen.

There was a loud crack and then an oath as one of the legionary's boots went through the ice.

'Hold your ground!' ordered the centurion. 'We make our stand here!'

As his men faced out, the centurion lowered his shield to the snow and reached for the standard. Gritting his teeth, he hacked at the staff with his sword, cutting away at the smooth wood until it was weak enough to snap over his knee. He cast the bottom of the standard aside and moved towards the knot of men clustered at the edge of the lake. With a grunt, the centurion hurled the standard out towards the water. The gold wreath and the red material flew through the air and thudded into the snow-covered ice, sliding a short distance before coming to rest a few paces from the edge of the water.

'Damn it!' the centurion growled. He clenched his fists in

frustration, then suddenly rounded on Marcus. 'You can do it! You're small enough for the ice to bear your weight. Go out there. Push the standard into the water.'

Marcus glanced across the expanse of unbroken snow. It was impossible to know how thick the ice was.

'There's no time to think!' The centurion grabbed him by the shoulders. 'You must go now, before they cut us all down. Go!'

Marcus nodded. If he died then he would do it for a reason. If he could not save his mother, or honour his real father, he would do this in memory of the old soldier he had always loved. He would do it for Titus. He sheathed his sword and slipped through the men standing at the edge of the lake, stepping cautiously on to the ice. The standard was no more than twenty paces away and Marcus paced carefully towards it. On either side he was aware of the fight reaching its bloody conclusion. The Roman cohorts had been shattered by the rebels' ferocious attack and only a few clusters of men remained, scattered along the shore of the lake as they sold their lives dearly.

Individuals had thrown aside their weapons and tried to surrender but the rebels butchered the Romans where they stood or knelt. A handful of legionaries were trying to escape on to the ice, but it had given way beneath them and they floundered in the icy water until their strength gave out.

There was a dull creak under his boots and Marcus stopped dead. The sound eased and after a pause Marcus took another few steps. There was another creak, louder this time, and then a crack. He stopped again, heart pounding, and slowly lowered himself to his hands and knees before continuing towards the standard, wincing as the ice seared his bare skin. He was no more than ten feet away from the standard when the ice began to crack again and Marcus caught his breath. He lowered himself on to his stomach and edged forward slowly. His fingers groped for the red cloth where the cohort's number had been stitched in gold thread. As the ice creaked beneath him Marcus clenched his teeth, clasping the material in his fingers and drawing it back towards him. Taking it in both hands, he turned slowly on to his back and took a deep breath. He counted to three, then hurled it over his head with all his strength.

The sudden movement caused the ice to crack, and water seeped through his cloak and tunic as he heard the splash behind him. Dreading that the ice would break at any moment, Marcus wormed his way towards the edge of the lake until he was confident the ice was thick enough to climb to his feet. He looked back to make sure there was no sign of the standard, then hurried towards the survivors of the cohort banded together by the lake. The rebels massed round them, grim-faced and silent.

'Well done, lad.' The centurion clapped him on the shoulder. 'That took guts. Now the cohort can die with its honour intact.'

'Die?' Quintus said.

'What else?' The centurion gestured towards the rebels. 'They'll charge any moment. It'll all be over very quickly.'

But there was no charge, and the two sides stood their ground, breathing hard from their exertions as they waited.

'Why don't they attack?' Quintus asked, his voice wavering. 'For pity's sake, why?'

Then there was movement in the rebel ranks and a tall figure emerged and strode towards the Romans, stopping two sword lengths from their shields. He carried a long heavy sword in one hand and his dark hair was tied back with a thong. Marcus recognized him at once. It was the same man who had led the ambush of Caesar's party several days earlier. Mandracus glared at the Romans for a moment before he spat to one side and addressed them.

'The fight is over. You have been defeated. Throw down your weapons and you will live. If not, you will be cut down where you stand.'

There was a brief stillness before Quintus lowered his sword and stepped towards the edge of the ring. The centurion stood in his way.

'What do you think you are doing . . . sir?'

'The fight is over. We did our best and lost. It's time to surrender.'

'No!' the centurion growled. 'Do you really think they'll let us live? Better to die like a man than be cut down like a dog. There'll be no surrender.'

'Yes, there will.' Quintus drew himself up. 'I am in command here, not you. And you will obey my orders, Centurion. Now stand aside.'

Marcus saw the glowering anger in the centurion's eyes as he stood still for a moment, then did as he was told. Quintus made his way to the edge of the ring and threw his sword out on to the snow, at the rebel leader's feet. 'We surrender.'

The man next to him followed suit, and lowered his shield to the ground. Another did the same, then the rest, until the surviving legionaries stood defenceless. All except the centurion and Marcus.

'Very wise of you,' said Mandracus. 'Now back to the track in single file. Move!'

With Quintus leading, the unarmed men began to move away from the lake, through the ranks of the rebels who jeered and jostled them as they passed by.

Marcus gazed around him, his mind a turmoil of struggling impulses. His gladiator training had taught him never to give in, yet if he chose to fight and die there would be no chance to save his mother. While he lived, there was a sliver of hope, no matter how small.

'Good lad,' the centurion said. 'You've got more guts than that yellow tribune and the rest of them put together. We'll go down, side by side, like heroes.'

Marcus glanced at him, then at the sea of rebel faces that glared back with hatred. He lowered his sword and spoke softly. 'I'm sorry. I can't do it. I have to live.'

The centurion stared coldly at him a moment, then nodded. 'It's all right. I understand. Better go quickly, before it's too late.'

Marcus stepped away from him, sword arm hanging loosely. As he approached the rebel leader, he let the handle slip from his fingers and heard the soft thud as it landed in the snow. His heart felt heavy at abandoning the centurion to his fate, but while there was a chance his mother lived, that governed every decision he made. Mandracus glanced at the boy as he passed by, then gave him a shove towards the end of the line of Romans being led into captivity.

Behind him, Marcus heard the centurion shout. 'For Rome! For Rome!'

Bodies surged past Marcus on either side. There was a clash of blades and the thud of a weapon striking a shield. Then a cry of triumph and a throaty roar from the rebels that was swallowed up by the snow swirling down the length of the small valley.

17

The surviving legionaries and Decimus and his men had been joined by a handful of mule drivers as they stood on the track guarded by several of the rebels. There they had been securely bound as Mandracus ordered the rest of his men to strip the bodies of undamaged armour and weapons. Any wounded Romans had their throats cut, while the injured rebels were carefully loaded on to the carts and wagons. The dead were carried into the villa, where a pyre was built using any combustible material left from the morning raid.

By the time the rebels were ready to move out it was dusk and the snow had stopped falling. A pale blue hue hung across the valley, where the dark forms of bodies and pools of blood lay either side of the track. The lurid red flames rising from the stockade added to the sombre scene, and Marcus shivered miserably as he and the others awaited their fate in silence. Mandracus took a last look around and swept his arm along the track.

'Move out!'

Marcus waited until the man ahead of him lurched forward, and hurriedly marched a few feet to give himself some slack, then concentrated on maintaining the gap. He thought it strange that Mandracus was leading them in the direction of Caesar. With a brief flicker of hope, he wondered if Caesar might send a message back to the baggage train, so the rider would see them and raise the alarm with the main column. Then, no more than a mile along the track, Mandracus turned off, taking a smaller path that meandered through a forest and headed into the heart of the mountain range.

They stopped for the night in an abandoned village, where the prisoners were herded into a small sheep pen and left without food or water. Around them the rebels found shelter in what remained of the houses and huts of the silent village. No fires were lit, but as night fell the sky cleared and the stars shone like tiny shards of ice.

Marcus explored the pen and found a corner out of the wind containing the musty remains of a pile of straw. He pulled as much of it over his body as he could with his bound hands and sat hunched over his knees, shivering. One by one the other men settled down to endure the freezing night as best they could.

It was impossible to sleep and, in any case, Marcus knew that sleep was dangerous. Titus had told him that once, recalling a campaign he had fought in the mountains of Macedonia. Pompeius's army had been forced to spend several nights in the open and there were men who fell asleep never to wake again. Come dawn their comrades discovered them frozen stiff. Marcus was not going to let the same thing happen to him. As soon as he felt his eyelids droop he sat up stiffly and pinched his cheeks hard.

At some point during the night, he heard someone shuffling towards him in the darkness, then a voice rasped.

'Boy, is that you? In the corner there.'

At first Marcus did not recognize the voice and kept still, holding his breath.

'I know you can hear me, boy . . . It's Marcus, isn't it? Titus told me about you once, when he came to do business with me.'

Marcus felt a familiar anger flare up in his heart. He drew a slow breath to calm his body so that his voice would not tremble when he spoke. He did not want Decimus to think that he was afraid of him. 'What do you want?'

'A word.'

'Why would I want to talk to you, Decimus? After everything you have done to me and my family. All I ever want to hear is you begging for your life before I kill you.'

'Kill me?' Marcus heard a low chuckle, then the man's voice caught as a bout of shivering seized his body. 'You? What makes you think you could ever harm me? I have powerful friends. Men who depend on me. You are just one step up from being a common slave. Be realistic, Marcus. There's nothing you could ever do to harm me.'

'I won't have to. Not now. I just hope the rebels get round to killing you before me.'

Decimus was silent for a moment. 'Fair enough . . . But there's a chance that Caesar might find us first.'

So that's what he wanted to ask Marcus about. He laughed quietly. 'I doubt it. Caesar has his own problems now that he has lost his baggage train.'

'You know him better than I do, Marcus. Do you think he will come looking for us?'

'He might. But it would make sense for him to find fresh supplies and shelter first.'

'But he can't afford to let the rebels get away with taking hostages.'

'Why not? We're dead, Decimus. Face it.'

'No. Why would they take us prisoner if they meant to kill us? Perhaps there is a way out. I have money. I can offer them a ransom for my life. But not yours, alas.'

'And your men? What about them?'

'I can always hire more men.'

Marcus stared at the dim outline of the man, a short distance away. There was no limit to the callousness of Decimus. If only his hands were free, he could throw himself on the moneylender. Without weapons, he might not win a fight with a fully grown man, but he could do him some injury.

'Don't take it too hard, boy. That's just the way life is. These rebels are like any other men. They have their price, and I can afford to pay it.' He lowered his voice to a whisper that only Marcus would hear. 'It's too bad for everyone else. Especially you. A few more years' training and you would have been one of the heroes of the arena. Another little boost for Caesar's reputation. He was right to buy you from Porcino's school. He's as shrewd a man as ever put on a senator's toga. He may turn out to be one of the greatest Romans who ever lived.'

'So why have you been plotting to kill him? You're a Roman. If Rome needs men like him, then why kill him?'

'Because I think Caesar believes that Rome needs him more than he needs Rome. That makes such men very dangerous. In any case, my political beliefs happen to coincide with an opportunity to do business with Crassus.'

'Business?'

'I am a businessman, young Marcus. I do what I do for money. That is why I work for Crassus. He rewards me with tax-collecting contracts. That's how a man gets rich in this world. In return I provide Crassus with the services of my employees who have the skills needed to remove obstacles in the path of his ambition. Over the years I have recruited a few men who have proved very useful indeed.'

'Men like Thermon?' Marcus interrupted bitterly. 'Murderers.'

'Murder is such a harsh word. I prefer to think of it as providing a special service at a premium price.'

'I take it that you and your men did not join Caesar's army to buy slaves then?'

'Why not? Might as well make a little extra on the side.'

'But you were sent to kill him, weren't you?'

'If the opportunity presented itself. I had thought to blackmail that young tribune over there to help one of my men get close to Caesar, but now I have more pressing concerns. I need to strike a deal with these rebel scum and buy my freedom.'

A gust of wind moaned over the sheep pen. Marcus glanced up at the sky and noticed a band of cloud to the north. There would be more snow before the dawn came. But that was of little concern to him. If he was to die, then there was one thing he had to know. One last comforting thought to cling to.

'Decimus, there's something you must tell me.'

'You want to know if your mother still lives?'

'Yes.'

The man was silent for a moment before he spoke again. 'I wonder what would be most merciful to tell you. If I said she was alive, then it would comfort you, until you considered what being alive means to her. You know I sent her to an estate of mine in the Peloponnese. A place where the slaves work until exhaustion or sickness finishes them off. On the other hand, if I told you she was dead, you would know you had nothing to live for. So, my boy, which would you prefer?'

'I just want the truth,' Marcus replied firmly. 'Whatever it may be.'

'The truth . . .' Decimus raised his hands and blew into them. 'The truth is that she still lives. She is too beautiful a creature to kill, and too proud for me not to want to break her.'

Marcus sighed with relief at the news that his mother was alive. Then the rest of the words struck home, a tingle of surprise raising the hairs on the back of his neck. 'You . . . You have feelings for her?'

'Of course. I am only flesh and blood, as your father was. Why would I not be drawn to her as he was? Yet she was his wife. A few years ago, when Titus came to me for a loan, he brought her with him to Stratos. That's when I first saw her. The next time was at the wretched little farm of yours, when I called in person for the first instalment of the loan repayment. Even then, I knew Titus could never repay it and would sink into debt. That's when I made my offer to her. Leave him and come with me and I would write off the loan. Otherwise Titus would lose everything. The farm, Livia, and you. Sold into slavery to pay off the debt.' Decimus chuckled drily. 'And you know what she did? She spat in my face and told me she would rather die than be mine. What do you think of that, eh? Your mother has courage. Even more than that fool, Titus. Yes, I think there is more of her in you than there ever was of him . . . Now she will stay on my estate, working the fields, until the day she begs me for forgiveness.'

The surprise that Marcus had felt gave way to disgust as he listened to the man talking about his mother. The thought of this vile, repulsive snake wrapping his coils round her made Marcus feel sick to the very depths of his stomach. He must not let it happen. He must find a way to escape, or to survive. And if Decimus did succeed in buying his way out of captivity, then as soon as Marcus was free, he would hunt him down. He silently swore an oath to all the Gods that he would not rest until Decimus was destroyed.

The man stirred and struggled to his feet, looming over Marcus in the darkness.

'I've enjoyed our little chat. But something tells me I would be rash indeed to spend the night close enough that you might feel tempted to harm me. Sleep well, young man, if you can. Don't try to take advantage of me during the night. Thermon will be watching you.'

'Thermon? Here?'

'Oh, yes. I always keep him close. Though he has had to change his appearance, thanks to you.'

Marcus's mind raced. Thermon had been in Decimus's party of henchmen all along? He recalled their faces, but at first none reminded him of the man he had only seen clearly on a handful of occasions. Then it hit him. Of course, the bald man with the beard. Biding his time, waiting for the order and the opportunity to strike at Caesar.

Decimus shuffled away, leaving Marcus hunched into his corner, his mind filled with dark thoughts of hatred and revenge.

18

Early the next day, as the sun shone bleakly through a thin mist, one of the rebels came to wake the prisoners. Two men had died during the night. They had shed their armour and cloaks the previous day in an effort to escape and their tunics had not kept them warm enough. In the pale light of dawn they sat hunched up where they had died, their faces frozen into peaceful expressions of slumber.

The rebel kicked them to make sure they were not feigning death, then grunted dismissively before stirring the rest to their feet with further kicks and blows from a thick club in his fist. Marcus and the others rose stiffly, joints cold and painful as they stumbled from the sheep pen to stand waiting in the narrow lane outside. Around them, the rebels emerged from their shelters, stretching and grumbling. Some had already started to eat, chewing on strips of dried meat and the bread they had captured in the wagons. Marcus looked at them, his lips working hungrily. He had not eaten for a day and his belly growled in protest. But no food or drink was offered to the prisoners, and shortly afterwards the Romans were blindfolded as the column began the day's march.

Several hours later, after winding their way along steep and uneven tracks, the column reached the rebel camp. As the captives were led into Brixus's camp, the inhabitants emerged from their huts and shelters to watch the spectacle. The defeated Romans were bound together by a length of rope that passed through their arms. Their leader, the once proud Tribune Quintus, had his hands bound behind his back and stumbled to keep up with the rebel leading them through the camp. Marcus was second in line, bruised and cut from the tumbles he had taken during the day's march.

'Halt the prisoners!' a voice commanded from some-where ahead, and the men behind Marcus shuffled to a stop. There was a pause before he heard boots crunching on the snow beside him, then his blindfold was removed. The morning mist had long since cleared and the sunlight was dazzling. Marcus squinted, his eyes watering. After a moment they adjusted to the light and he looked round in astonishment at the vast camp, hemmed in by the mountains that ringed the valley.

'No wonder we could never find this place,' Quintus said. 'An army could search the Apennines for a hundred years and never guess it was here.'

Marcus looked back the way they had come and saw the path disappear into the cliff a few hundred yards away, as if into solid rock. He recalled the clammy cold of the last stage of the march, and the echo of footsteps and clink and clatter of equipment off solid rock. Quintus was right. The rebel camp was perfectly hidden. The only danger was that a traitor might betray its location. The fact that no one had, only proved that the slaves who flocked to Brixus's banner shared his fervent belief in the cause for which he fought.

When the last of the blindfolds had been removed the prisoners were led through the heart of the camp towards the largest huts nestling in the centre. The route was lined with people cheering the rebel fighters. Their cheers turned to insults and cries of anger as they caught sight of the prisoners, and some scooped up filth from the ground to hurl at Quintus and the others. Because of his size and the simple cloak he wore, Marcus was spared the worst of the deluge. That was targeted at the tribune, his soldiers and Decimus, conspicuous in his expensively embroidered cloak. They soon emerged from the crowded path into an open space in front of a large hut. A cordon of men armed with spears held the crowd back and Marcus breathed a sigh of relief as the hail of missiles came to an end. He forced himself to compose his expression as he stood up straight and examined his surroundings. The hut was the largest building he had seen in the valley and he guessed it must be where the leader of the rebels lived. If this was the main camp, then there was a chance that Brixus himself was here. Marcus felt a surge of hope. Brixus would be sure to spare him, even though Marcus had marched with Caesar. He would have to explain that he was unwillingly involved in the proconsul's campaign, and hoped that would be enough for Brixus to forgive him.

Turning towards the nearest of the guards, Marcus cleared his throat. 'You there. Tell me, is that Brixus's hut? I must speak to him.'

The rebel stepped quickly towards him and backhanded Marcus across the cheek. 'Shut your mouth, Roman! You only speak when spoken to if you want to keep your tongue. Clear?'

Reeling from the blow, Marcus opened his mouth to reply, then closed it at once and nodded, rather than risk more punishment.

Mandracus approached and stopped in front of Quintus, hands on his hips. 'Well then, not so high and mighty any longer, tribune. You and these other Romans. Look at you. Not much older than this boy, barely a man, and already you have that air of haughty arrogance so typical of you Roman aristocrats. Soon you'll see what it's like to be treated as a slave.' He smiled coldly, then turned and made for the entrance to the hut. As he passed the rebel in charge of the prisoners, he gave his orders.

'I'm going to eat. Hold them beside the hut. Then pass the word around the camp. The entertainment begins the moment that it's safe to light the fires.'

'Yes, Mandracus.' The rebel bowed his head in acknowledgement.

As Mandracus ducked behind the leather curtain in the doorway, Quintus edged closer to Marcus and whispered, 'Entertainment? What do you think they're planning to do to us?'

Marcus shook his head. 'I have no idea. But whatever it is, I don't think many of us will survive it.'

By the time the circle of fires was lit in the open area by the round hut, a huge crowd had formed round the compound.

Their faces illuminated by the red flames, they gazed expect-antly at the prisoners. The excited hubbub of conversation reminded Marcus of the atmosphere in the crowd that formed at the Senate House in Rome before the start of an important debate. No, that wasn't quite it, he reflected. It was more like the mood of the crowd in the Forum before he fought the Celtic boy, Ferax. He shuddered at the memory of the terror that had consumed him before the fight began. Partly the terror of facing someone who wanted to kill him, but also terror at the bloodlust in the faces of the crowd pressing in on all sides.

The prisoners had been forced to sit on the frozen ground until darkness fell, their hands kept bound. They had finally been given water and a bowl of thin, greasy stew that was gulped down greedily. After that they had sat in silence, awaiting their fate and forbidden to make a sound or move on threat of a beating.

A hush settled over the crowd and Marcus looked round to see Mandracus emerging from the hut. Wrapped in a long fur cloak, he stood with a silver goblet in one hand, waiting until he had complete silence. Then he drew a breath and spoke in a loud clear voice that carried to the fringes of the crowd.

'I would prefer to wait until Brixus returns to share our entertainment, but we shall have to start without him. As you all know, both Brixus and I were once gladiators. Men torn from our homes by the legions of Rome, ripped from the bosom of our families and enslaved. Then sold, like cattle, to a lanista to train in the art of killing other men – for no better reason than it whetted Rome's appetite for entertainment. Tonight we shall return the favour in kind: these Romans will provide *our* entertainment.' He punched his spare hand into the air and the crowd let out an excited roar.

Mandracus indulged them for a moment while Marcus felt his blood freeze in his veins. So that was their fate.

'Quiet!' Mandracus boomed, gesturing to the crowd to calm down. 'Tonight I give you a feast of entertainment,' he continued. 'A series of fights to the death. The winners of each bout will then face each other until one is left standing. That man, that champion,' he spoke the word in a tone laced with irony, 'will be spared. He will become a slave of the camp, for all of you to use and abuse as you will, until he dies.'

Marcus saw the nearest faces in the crowd nod approval. Some looked at the prisoners and shook their fists, shouting insults, the bitterness of their long years in slavery finding expression in this chance for revenge.

'Let the entertainment begin!' Mandracus called out, and strode over to the Romans. All their armour and cloaks had

241

been stripped from them, and they sat in their tunics and boots. Mandracus gazed over them a moment before raising his finger to point. 'You . . . and you. Stand!'

The two legionaries were slow to react and the rebels hauled them to their feet, dragging them into position, twenty feet apart, in the middle of the open ground. As their bonds were cut, the men stood rubbing their wrists. A sword was dropped at the feet of each man before the rebels backed away.

'The rules are simple,' Mandracus told them. 'You fight to the death. If you go down, then don't bother appealing for mercy. That's it. Now pick up your swords and wait for the word to begin.'

Marcus looked at the two men. One was a wiry veteran with dried blood on his left arm where he had been wounded in the ambush. His opponent was a fresh-faced youth, trembling as he stared down at the sword.

'Pick up your weapons!' Mandracus bellowed.

At once the youth did as he was told and held the weapon out, its point wavering wildly. The veteran did not move. Then he drew himself up and folded his arms.

'I don't take orders from slaves.'

Some in the crowd hooted with derision, but Mandracus simply shrugged and gestured to one of the rebels acting as guards. The man strode behind the veteran and swung a heavy club into the back of his head. The skull gave way with a sharp crack, blood and brains bursting out between the fragments of bone and scalp. The veteran's jaw sagged open as he stood for a moment before toppling face first to the ground.

Marcus averted his eyes from the gruesome scene. Glancing round the group of prisoners, he wondered who his opponent would be. If only it could be Decimus, or even Thermon.

The rebel tucked the club under his arm and grasped the veteran's boot to drag the body aside. Mandracus pointed to another prisoner. 'You. Take his place.'

The legionary scrambled to his feet and as soon as his hands were freed he snatched up the sword and lowered his body into a crouch, prepared to fight for his life.

'Begin!'

The fight was unlike any Marcus had ever seen during his gladiator training. There was no attempt to size up the other man, decide on tactics and test the opponent's mettle with a few feints. The two legionaries rushed at each other with grim expressions to hack and parry wildly, and the sharp ringing of their blades filled the air as sparks flew from the clashing metal. With a cry of pain the young recruit staggered back, clutching his spare hand to his thigh where blood seeped out between his fingers. The older man held back, his chest heaving from the exertion. They stared at each other until a voice called out to resume fighting.

The call was taken up and Mandracus gave orders to a group beside one of the fires. 'Use the heating irons.'

One of the men nodded and leaned down to pick up a metal bar. One end was wrapped in strips of metal; the other led into the heart of the fire. When he raised the bar into the air, it glowed bright yellow, then faded to a lurid red. The man strode behind the wounded young legionary and prodded him with the heated tip. He screamed with pain and lurched forward towards his opponent. Another frenzied exchange of blows followed before the younger man's leg gave way, forcing him down on his knee as he desperately tried to fend off his former comrade's attacks. Then his numbed fingers lost their grip and his sword fell to the ground a short distance away. The other man raised his weapon and hesitated.

'What are you waiting for?' Mandracus demanded. 'Finish him! Or you'll be cut down alongside him.'

The legionary gritted his teeth and shook his head in apology, then thrust the blade into the wounded man's chest. The young man grunted and flung his head back and arms wide. Then, as the sword was wrenched free, he writhed for a moment on the ground before lying still. The crowd let out a bloodthirsty roar and punched their fists into the chilly air. Two of the rebels approached the winner and one took the sword from his hand while the other steered him to one side of the hut.

Marcus felt sick with worry as Mandracus approached the remaining prisoners and looked over the group. None dared meet his eye to risk being chosen for the next fight.

'You . . . Yes, you, and the man next to him. You're up. Move yourselves!'

There were two more fights and Marcus counted fourteen men left in the group. That meant seven fights, and Decimus was still with them. There was a chance yet to avenge himself. As they dragged the fourth body away, Mandracus scanned his finger across the group and smiled. Then his finger stopped.

'You . . . Up!'

Decimus struggled to his feet, shaking his head in mute protest. At once Marcus stood.

'I'll fight him! Choose me!'

Mandracus turned. 'What's this? A volunteer? The plucky lad wishes to take on a grown man. Looks like we finally found a Roman with the heart to put up a fight. Very well then, boy, he's all yours.'

'No!' Decimus called out. 'You can't make me fight!'

'Oh? Why can't I?'

Decimus held out his hands. 'Set me free and I'll make you a rich man. I have a fortune in Rome. Let me live and I will ensure that all of you are handsomely rewarded. I swear it.'

'How interesting,' Mandracus mused. 'And what amount are we talking about for your ransom?'

'Half a million sestertii,' Decimus pleaded, but the rebel did not respond. 'All right then, a million! A million sestertii!'

'Hmmm, now that is quite a fortune.' Mandracus thought briefly. 'We'll wait to see what Brixus says. Take this one inside the hut.'

'Thank you,' Decimus grovelled. 'You won't regret it.'

As he was led away he gave Marcus a smug smile. 'What did I tell you? Goodbye, boy. Give my regards to Titus when you catch up with him in the afterworld. And apologize to Thermon for me. Tell him it was only ever business between us.'

Marcus gritted his teeth and spat out his reply. 'Coward!'

Decimus shook his head. 'No, just a survivor.'

Then he was led away and disappeared through the leather flap into the hut. Mandracus approached Marcus and looked down at him curiously. 'It's a shame to put an end to such courage. But you will die with these others. The question is who to pick for your opponent. I'll be fair so you can put up a decent fight.'

His gaze scrutinized the remaining legionaries and Decimus's servants. All were tough-looking men, except one.

'You, tribune. You're the next youngest, and I dare say you have lived a pampered enough life to provide a poor showing with a sword. Think you've got it in you to defeat this boy?'

Quintus stood slowly, his lips curling with contempt. 'I am not gladiator scum, like you. I will show you how a Roman noble fights.' At the last moment his lips trembled, betraying his true feelings, and Mandracus chuckled.

'Nice try. Like all you Roman aristocrats, you have no heart for a real fight. You leave that to others. Well, not tonight. Not here.' He cut Quintus's bonds and then did the same for Marcus. 'Take your positions.'

Two of the rebels dragged them into the open and turned them to face each other. Swords were thrown down in front of them. Quintus picked his up quickly without waiting for the instruction. Marcus noted that his opponent seemed even more nervous than he felt. He had no desire to fight Quintus or any other prisoner, now that Decimus was removed from the grim contest. But while he still breathed he would fight.

Aiming to survive, his determination was fuelled by the hope that Brixus would set him free. If he protested now he would only share the fate of the man who had refused to fight earlier.

He bent down to pick up the sword, grasping it tightly and instinctively testing its weight and balance as he had been trained. He experimented with a slash and a few cuts in the air before being satisfied he understood how the weapon would handle in a fight.

'Begin!' Mandracus bellowed.

Unlike the previous fights, the two combatants remained still. Marcus forced all thoughts from his mind to concentrate on what lay ahead. Quintus was of average height and slightly built, which meant he had the potential to move fast, but his reach was little better than Marcus's. Like many other young men, he had a fondness for wine and the good life. Even after days on the road, his reactions might be slow compared to those who had trained at a gladiator school. Marcus tried to recall something from their brief fight in Ariminum that would give him the advantage here.

The crowd had become quiet, sensing that this bout would be a different, more subtle kind of contest.

Marcus raised his sword and turned so that he presented his side to Quintus, limiting the size of the target the tribune could strike at. Then he steadily advanced. Quintus lowered himself into a crouch and adopted the same stance, but held his ground and waited for Marcus. The tips of their swords touched and Marcus applied a gentle pressure as he slid his point a short distance down his opponent's blade. Quintus dropped the point, cut under and tapped Marcus's sword aside. Then he feinted with a little jump forward, straightening his arm. Marcus pretended to parry the blow and correctly anticipated that the tribune would cut under his sword again. He knocked it aside, forcing the other sword back with the length of the blade close to his guard, stepping in to Quintus as he did so. The move forced the young man to back off quickly, to prevent Marcus getting too near, and he swept his sword from side to side to block any attacks to his body. Marcus contented himself with flicking his sword so that it nicked the flesh of his opponent's forearm, opening a long shallow gash that looked worse than it was as the blood began to flow. Then he stepped back out of reach and stared at Quintus, trying to gauge his next move.

The tribune backed off and looked anxiously at the cut as the more knowing members of the crowd murmured their approval of the initial exchange. Marcus had won control of the centre of the makeshift arena, a move that he knew would undermine his opponent's confidence. Sure enough, there was no mistaking the glimmer of fear in Quintus's expression as he lowered himself into a crouch again, determined to seize back the initiative.

It was obvious that he would attack even before he began to move, his legs bracing for the explosive charge across the hard ground. Marcus let him come, then ducked to one side as the blade passed harmlessly by his head. The momentum carried Quintus forward, and Marcus lowered his sword to slash it across his thigh as he passed. Both turned to face each other and now there was no hiding the fear in the tribune's eyes. Marcus forced himself to keep his face like a mask: cold, ruthless and unreadable.

Quintus licked his lips and spoke in a low voice. 'Marcus, you can't kill me. Think of Portia . . . She considers you her friend. She trusts you. Would you betray her trust, her affection, by striking down her husband? I love her, Marcus. If I am lost she will be alone in the world.' As he spoke he edged forward, his sword tip lowered, his tone genuine.

Marcus struggled to push the memory of Portia from his mind, but could think only of the words she had spoken to him, and the soft touch of her lips.

With a blur, Quintus charged, his sword sweeping in

a clumsy but deadly arc. Marcus backed off as he blocked the blow and sparks flew. Quintus continued his assault with a vicious flurry of strokes as he growled, 'I will not die! I will win! Win!'

Marcus cleared his mind of everything but the reaction to each attack, and met it with a block or parry, conserving his strength as his opponent wasted energy. Then, as Quintus swung again, Marcus counter-attacked before the tribune could reverse the stroke. Stabbing the blade with all his strength, Marcus went for the hamstring above and behind Quintus's knee. His aim was true but the cold and exhaustion had left him weak, and instead of a crippling blow the sword cut deep into the flesh and muscle without severing it.

Quintus let out a cry of pain and staggered away, bleeding freely. The advantage won, Marcus pushed ahead, feinting and thrusting to force his opponent backwards. Then Quintus's boot slipped on the icy ground. He stumbled and fell on to his back, throwing his arms wide. Marcus leapt forward and stamped his foot on the wrist of the tribune's sword arm, so that his fingers spasmed and the sword fell from his grasp. Marcus kicked it away, then stood over the tribune and touched the point of his blade to Quintus's throat.

'No! I beg you, spare me!' Quintus pleaded. 'For Portia!'

Marcus hesitated. He had concentrated on winning the fight. Not on its aftermath. He stood still, sword arm trembling slightly with the cold.

'What are you waiting for?' Mandracus demanded. 'Kill him.'

Marcus did not move and Quintus closed his eyes tightly, his head tipped to one side.

'Kill him,' Mandracus ordered. 'Or I will kill *you*.'

The rasp of a blade sounded and Marcus saw the rebel striding towards him. He willed himself to strike, to thrust his blade into the tribune's throat, but he could not do it. Mandracus stood to one side and hissed. 'This is your last chance . . .'

When Marcus did not react, he raised his sword.

'Wait!' a voice cried from the crowd. Marcus turned to see a commotion near the track leading to the secret entrance to the valley. He heard a horse's hoofs as the dark figure of a rider emerged into the rosy glow cast by the flames from the fires. Behind him came other figures on foot, some limping and others supported by their comrades. Anxious muttering filtered through the crowd. Mandracus slowly lowered his sword and turned towards the rider.

'Brixus.'

19

'What is the meaning of this?' Brixus demanded as he rode into the open space outside his hut.

The muttering of the crowd rose into a nervous murmur as the men following their leader came into view. Many were wounded and streaked with dried blood, with crudely tied strips of cloth acting as dressings. Marcus stepped back from Quintus and lowered his sword as he turned to watch the new arrivals. The tribune opened his eyes and stared up at the sky, his chest heaving as he gasped at the cold air.

'These are the prisoners we took after the ambush,' Mandracus explained.

'And what are you doing with them?'

'Putting on some entertainment, to raise our people's spirits. But what of you?' Mandracus indicated the straggling column of men following Brixus into the camp. 'What happened?'

Brixus reined in and took a weary breath. 'My ambush did not fare so well. We caught Caesar's column in the flank as it approached Sedunum. They were strung out along the track as I had expected, but they turned and formed into a battle-line before we could close with them. By the Gods, I've never seen men so well handled, not even in the days of Spartacus's revolt. It was as bloody a battle as I have ever fought. Thousands were cut down on either side. But we had the upper hand. Then both sides pulled apart to lick their wounds and draw breath. When I gave the order to charge again . . . my men would not obey. They'd had enough. I had no choice but to retreat into the forest and return here.'

Mandracus heard his leader's report in silence, then glanced past him towards the entrance to the valley. 'Were you followed?'

'Do you take me for a fool?' Brixus snapped. 'Of course not. Caesar sent his cavalry after us but we lost them in the trees. We headed south for half a day before turning back to the camp. We're safe, Mandracus.'

'Safe for now. How many men did you lose?'

Brixus frowned. 'We'll speak in my hut. For now, I want my men fed and rested and their wounds seen to. Give the orders.'

Mandracus nodded, then recalled the prisoners. 'What do you want me to do with the Romans?'

Brixus shrugged as he dismounted. 'They can serve the camp, like the others.' He turned towards Marcus. 'Disarm that one and . . .' His words died away and he froze as he stared at the boy.

Marcus was not sure how to react and returned his gaze in silence.

'By all the Gods, it can't be . . . surely?' Brixus limped closer, his eyes wide in amazement. 'Marcus. It is you. By all the Gods . . .'

'You know this boy?' Mandracus stepped in and took the sword from Marcus's hand.

'Know him?' A smile of delight and triumph spread across Brixus's face. 'This is Marcus. The Marcus. The one I have often told you about.'

'Him?' Mandracus's eyes widened in surprise. 'This runt? This is the son of Sp–'

Brixus rounded on him angrily. 'Quiet, you fool! We'll not speak of this in front of the others. Have the other prisoners taken to one of the huts and placed under guard. No one is to speak to them, is that clear?'

Mandracus nodded and turned to carry out his orders.

'Marcus.' Brixus stood in front of him and clasped his shoulders, speaking in an undertone so that his words would not be overheard. 'I cannot tell you how much good it does my heart to see you again. Come, we must talk. You have arrived at the hour of our greatest need.'

Marcus was aware that the other prisoners were looking at him in astonishment. Then Brixus placed a hand on Marcus's shoulder and steered him towards the entrance of the leader's hut. Behind them, the men of the newly arrived column slumped down on the ground by the fires and began to warm themselves. Marcus could see the weariness in their faces and already there came the sound of wailing as the first casualties were made known, shrill cries of grief that pierced the night sky.

Brixus swept the leather curtain aside and gestured to Marcus to enter. Despite its size and the icy temperature outside, the hut felt warm. A large fire was crackling in the centre, tended by a woman feeding split logs into the blaze. Marcus looked for Decimus and saw him sitting against the wall a short distance from the entrance. He glanced round nervously as Marcus and Brixus entered.

'Who is that?' Brixus demanded, following the direction of Marcus's gaze. 'What are you doing in here?'

'He's one of the prisoners,' Marcus explained. 'The Roman who destroyed my family and sold my mother and me into slavery.'

Brixus thought a moment before he recalled the details of his last conversations with Marcus over a year ago. 'Decimus?'

Marcus nodded.

'The moneylender from Greece? Then what is he doing here?'

'He is working for Crassus. He was responsible for an attempt on Caesar's life last year.'

Brixus raised his eyebrows and shook his head in wonder. 'What's the matter with these stuck-up Roman nobles? Not satisfied with punishing us slaves, they turn on each other! They're scum. Utter scum. No better than the meanest street dogs . . . What do you want me to do with him, Marcus? Shall I have him crucified? Like they crucified those who surrendered at the end of your father's revolt? Or burned alive, perhaps? The people out there would like that.'

Marcus thought for a moment. There was blood on Decimus's hands. Not just that of Titus, but countless others he had cruelly exploited and ruined on his path to riches. The offer was tempting.

Decimus had heard every word and now shuffled forward on his knees. 'I made a deal with Mandracus. He promised to set me free if I paid a ransom. A million sestertii. It could be yours. All yours.'

Brixus regarded him with loathing and disgust before shaking his head. 'Any deal you made with my subordinate is not binding with me, Roman. I know about you from Marcus. It is for him to decide your fate.'

Marcus looked up in surprise. 'Me?'

'Yours is the grievance. You decide.'

'The boy?' Decimus shook his head in disbelief. 'You can't let a boy decide whether I die or not.'

'I can decide what I like. Well, Marcus?'

Marcus frowned. There was still something he could get out of this if he played his part well. He curled his lips into a sneer. 'I would like to see him die, by my own hand. His death is long overdue.'

'No!' Decimus protested. 'Marcus, wait. I'll give you the million sestertii. Enough to set you up for life. You could buy your farm back. Or buy a bigger one. Have slaves of your own.'

Marcus stabbed his finger into Decimus's chest and shouted.

'If you want to live, tell me exactly where my mother is! Which estate did you send her to? Where in the Peloponnese? Speak now! Or I swear I will cut your heart out!'

Decimus flinched in terror at the boy's violent expression and opened his mouth to reply. Then his eyes narrowed and he shook his head.

'I will tell you nothing. If you want to see her again, then you must set me free. That is the only deal I will make with you. My life for hers.'

Brixus stepped over the moneylender and grasped him by the collar of his tunic. 'Say the word, Marcus, and I'll have Mandracus beat the truth out of him.'

'He can try.' Decimus smiled thinly. 'But how will you know I am telling the truth? You need me alive, Marcus. I will tell you where she is, once I am away from this place, and safe. Only then.'

'And he's supposed to trust you?'

'I give him my word.'

'Hah? Your word?' Brixus spat. 'I'd sooner trust a snake. Marcus, kill him. You can find your mother on your own.'

Marcus glared at the moneylender, his heart welling up with despair and frustration. Decimus had the advantage and there was little he could do about it – unless there was some way to hold Decimus to his side of the bargain. He turned to Brixus. 'There is another man among the prisoners who I would have you keep safe. A tall, thin man. Bald and with a beard. His name is Thermon.'

He turned back to Decimus. 'If you fail to keep your word, I will give Thermon to Caesar. He would have some interesting stories to tell about your business interests, as you call them.'

Decimus sucked in a breath through his teeth. 'You learn quickly, my boy. In time you might well be as successful as I am, and a dangerous rival. We have a deal then, and a means to enforce it.'

The leather curtain swished aside as Mandracus ducked into the hut. He saw the others and gestured to Decimus guiltily. 'I was going to tell you about him as soon as I could.'

'Never mind,' Brixus replied. 'I know all about him. Have your men take him away. He is to be kept apart from the others. Guard him closely. He must not escape. And if he tries to, then I want him taken alive.'

'Yes, Brixus. As you wish. Come on, you!' Mandracus hauled Decimus to his feet and pushed him out of the hut.

Brixus turned to Marcus and let out a low whistle.

'A strange day indeed.' Then his expression fell and he

rested a hand on Marcus's shoulder. 'I have bad news for you. There was a boy captured by Mandracus when he ambushed Caesar's party earlier this month.'

Marcus felt a surge of hope in his breast. 'Lupus!'

'Yes, Lupus.'

'Where is he? You said bad news?' Marcus felt a stab of anxiety. 'I've not seen him here. Send for him.'

'I can't.' Brixus pursed his lips. 'He was with me when I marched against Caesar. The last I saw of him was in the battle – just before we charged the Roman line.'

Marcus swallowed. 'Captured?'

'I don't know, Marcus.'

'Or killed?'

Brixus sighed. 'A slave taken under arms faces a death sentence. It would be better if he were dead. Better than crucifixion.'

'Crucifixion?' Marcus's guts turned to ice. 'No . . . Not Lupus. Caesar wouldn't let that happen. Lupus is his scribe. Or was.'

'None of that will matter if he has been captured with a sword in his hand.'

Marcus stood silent, remembering his friend. Then he looked at Brixus with a guarded expression. 'I never took

Lupus for the fighting kind. I'm surprised he was prepared to go into battle.'

'There are many in our camp who have never fought before they joined us. But they soon discover that freedom is a cause worth fighting for, or dying for if need be. That is what your father taught us. Many remember the lesson and honour his legacy.' He placed a hand on Marcus's shoulder. 'When word spreads that a new Spartacus has risen to lead the rebellion, then slaves the length of Italia will flock to join his standard. This time nothing will stand between us and freedom. We will have our victory over Rome.'

Marcus forced himself to smile in response. He felt anxious about the dream that Brixus held out. Though he had come to accept that he was the son of Spartacus, would his blood inheritance be enough to guarantee that Marcus would rise to the same greatness?

20

Brixus released Marcus's shoulder and smiled wearily. 'I am a poor host. What am I thinking? You're cold and hungry, and no doubt exhausted. Come, let's sit by the fire while I send for food and drink, and we can talk.'

He clapped his hands and called out harshly. 'Servilia!'

The woman crouching by the fire cringed like a whipped dog, then scrambled to her feet and scurried across the hut, bowing her head as she stood before him. By the glow of the fire Marcus could see bruises amid the grime on her skin, and the locks of her long dark hair were matted with filth.

'I want meat, bread and watered wine. And dried figs if there are any left.'

'Yes, master.'

'At once. Now go.'

She turned and scuttled to an arch that led into a small lean-to at the rear of the hut. As she disappeared, Brixus led Marcus to the fire where he gratefully sank down on the skins arranged at one side of the hearth. The warmth of the flames felt good and Marcus allowed himself to indulge briefly in the comfort, releasing the terror he had faced in front of the crowd. Even though he was out of danger, it took a while for the tension in his muscles and the trembling of his limbs to subside.

Brixus slipped his sword belt over his head and let the scabbard drop to the ground beside another pile of animal skins. He unbuckled the straps fastening his cuirass and placed that beside his sword, before slumping down with a sigh of contentment.

'Your limp has improved,' Marcus observed. 'Much better than it was back in Porcino's ludus.'

'Well, it was never quite as bad as I made out.' Brixus grinned. 'Once I received the wound I vowed I would never again fight in the arena for the pleasure of the Romans. Even though the injury would have slowed me down, I could not trust Porcino not to make me fight again. I played it up enough to fool his surgeon and he pronounced me unfit for the arena. That's how I was sent to the kitchens.'

'I see.' Marcus nodded. 'But how did you come to be here, in charge of this camp?'

'After I spoke to you that last time, when you were on the road to Rome, I made my way north into the mountains. It wasn't long before I encountered one of the rebel bands. They brought me here. Mandracus was their leader and he had fought for Spartacus in the last revolt, even though he was only a boy at the time, not much older than you are now. He recognized me, and when I told him that the son of Spartacus lived and would one day lead a new rebellion against Rome, he was persuaded to let me take command. After that we increased the scale of the attacks on the enemy and recruited more people. They were anxious at first and slow to join us, but when news of our victories spread, and with that the promise of the heir of Spartacus, they flocked to our side.' His eyes blazed with excitement. 'Marcus, we have over ten thousand men under arms in camps like this up and down the Apennines. With you as our figurehead, that number will grow even more swiftly. Soon we shall march down from the mountains to face the Roman legions on the battlefield, and this time the victory will be ours.'

The slave woman emerged through the small entrance at the side of the hut, balancing a tray stacked with meat and bread in one hand, and carrying a jar and two silver cups in the other. She scuttled across to the fire and set the meal down between Brixus and Marcus, then backed away nervously, out of reach, and stood with her head bowed, in silence. Brixus ignored her as he piled some meat on a wooden platter and offered it to Marcus.

'Here. I expect you're hungry.'

Marcus took the platter and began to eat at once, quickly, tearing at the cold mutton with his teeth and chewing hard. Brixus watched with a smile, then passed him a small roundel of bread and a cup of watered wine. Marcus nodded his thanks and continued eating until his belly felt comfortably full. He eventually pushed the platter aside with a sigh.

Brixus was eating in a more measured manner and looked up. 'Want some more, or something else? Fruit? Fig and date pie?'

'No. I'm fine. Thanks.'

Brixus clicked his fingers at the woman. 'Some more logs on the fire. Then get out and leave us alone.'

'Yes, master.' She hefted some logs from the pile beside the fire and added them to the blaze, before backing away to the side of the hut where she disappeared through the side exit.

As the leather curtain dropped back into place, Marcus stared at it, frowning, before he spoke.

'I thought you were fighting to end slavery.'

'Eh?' Brixus frowned briefly, until he got the point. 'Oh, her. Don't concern yourself with her, Marcus. It's time some Romans learned what we slaves had to endure.'

'I don't understand. Either you are against slavery or you are for it.'

'Of course I am against it. And when Rome no longer claims to own us, then Servilia can go free too. Until then, she is my slave.'

'But —'

'That's enough, Marcus. I will not discuss the matter. She deserves to be treated as she once treated others until there's an end to it. Is that clear?'

Marcus nodded, surprised and a little intimidated by the cruel edge to Brixus's words. A silence fell between them and Marcus stared into the flames, deep in thought. He was worried about Brixus's plan. Apart from the prospect of being the figurehead of the new rebellion, he was unsure that the rebels could overwhelm Rome's legions. Even if tens of thousands of slaves escaped from their masters to join the rebellion, they would lack the training and experience of the legionaries. Only a small proportion of the rebels were gladiators or had some fighting experience. Marcus had seen at first hand the huge advantage that a trained fighter had over a raw recruit, no matter how eager that recruit might be.

'You can't win this, Brixus,' he said quietly. 'You cannot defeat Rome.'

The rebel leader stared back at him. 'And why is that?'

'You know only too well. Look what happened when you went up against Caesar. You were defeated.'

'We were not defeated,' Brixus replied sharply. 'We fought like lions. My followers have the courage to see this through.'

'Courage is not enough. We have both seen that at Porcino's ludus. It takes more than courage. You cannot win without discipline and training. That's why your men refused to charge at the Romans a second time.'

'They will have discipline and training in time. More than enough to match the enemy.'

'But there isn't any time,' Marcus argued. 'Caesar and his men are hunting you down. How long do you think it will take them to find this valley?'

'No Roman has found it yet.'

'That's because it was being used by just a handful of rebels before you arrived. Now there are more, many of whom have been captured by Caesar. One of them is sure to tell him about this valley. The Romans will use torture, or offer a reward, to get what they need. Then they'll blockade the entrance to this valley and starve you and your followers out.'

'Those who follow me would die rather than betray the cause.'

'I wonder.'

'Besides, you are here now. Your name, your legacy, will inspire the devotion of all to the cause of fighting for their liberty. With you at the head of our army, nothing can stand in our way!'

'Brixus, I am not the man my father was.' Marcus stopped and smiled thinly as he touched his chest. 'I am not even a man. How can I lead an army?'

'You won't lead it as such. That is my duty. As I said earlier, you will be the figurehead of our cause. That's all.'

Marcus reflected a moment and shook his head. 'I will not be used like that. I will not be the reason why men, women and children rush to join a futile cause. I will not have their blood on my hands.'

'But I need you,' Brixus insisted angrily, then paused to calm himself. 'I mean *we* need you. Would you betray all those slaves who still believe in your father and what he fought for?'

'I am not betraying them. I simply want to save them from a pointless death.'

'It is not a pointless death, Marcus. While men are prepared to fight, and die, for a cause they believe in, that cause lives on and one day it may triumph. If men do nothing they are simply doomed to a pointless and painful life.'

'But they are still living,' Marcus countered. He felt the truth of Brixus's words but could not accept the suffering and bloodshed it entailed. And he could not bear to be responsible for luring so many people to their deaths. He shook his head. 'No. I cannot do it. In time, perhaps the Romans themselves will put an end to slavery.'

'Pah! You live in the clouds, boy. Rome will never – never – renounce slavery. It is the foundation of all their power. It is slaves who farm their fields, toil in their mines, or shed their blood in the arena. Without us Rome is nothing, which is why this can only stop if we have the courage and endurance to see it through to the bitter end.' His eyes burning with zeal, Brixus leaned towards Marcus and thrust his finger at him. 'Even if we fail, if all of us are crushed and crucified, then our example will kindle the rebellious fire that burns in the hearts of all those who are not free. That is what makes men into heroes, Marcus. Your father was a hero. You have a duty to follow in his footsteps. Or will you betray him? Are you too much of a coward to honour his memory?'

Angrily, Marcus gritted his teeth as he replied. 'I am no coward. I would face any danger, no matter how great, for something I believe in. I do not believe you can defeat Rome. Besides, I never knew my father. He was dead before I ever breathed in this world. I will not be the slave of a dead man's legacy. It is my life, Brixus. Mine. I was raised on a small farm on a Greek island. The man who raised me, the man I loved as a father, was killed in front of my eyes. My mother and I were sold into slavery. That is the story of my life, and I will not rest until my mother is free. That is what I am prepared to fight for, and die for if I must. Only that.'

Brixus looked at him with an understanding expression. 'Of course, Marcus. I can see that. But that is the boy in you speaking. You have had your childhood taken from you and you want it back. Few people in this camp have even had the chance to enjoy what you have known and lost. That is a monstrous injustice. Perhaps you are too young to grasp that. But you will. That is what it means to be a man. To understand there are more important things in the world than yourself, and your dreams.'

'It is not a dream!' Marcus snapped back, his eyes smarting with the effort of fighting back tears. He wished he could explain the pain that tore at his heart every time he thought of his mother. The terrible guilt that ate away at him because he failed to save her. 'I will free my mother. She is all that is important to me.'

'Marcus ... We all have mothers. I lost mine when she was sold by my master. I could do nothing to stop it. Do you think I am any different from you? Was my loss any less than yours?'

Marcus's throat felt too tight to speak. If he tried, he knew his voice would catch and he would choke on a wave of grief and tears. Fortunately, Brixus spoke again, with great sympathy.

'Marcus, join us and you will be fighting for your mother, and every mother and child who has suffered as you have, and more. Is that so much to ask? That is the only question that matters now.'

He reached over and gently squeezed Marcus's arm. 'You are tired. It is best if you rest now that you have eaten and are warm. Stay here by the fire and sleep. We'll talk again in the morning. I'm sure you will see the truth of my words then.'

Marcus looked at him. 'And if I don't?'

'You will.' Brixus's expression hardened. 'There are only two sides in this conflict, Marcus. Those who fight for liberty and those who don't.' He let his hand fall away, then rose to his feet and looked down. 'For the sake of our friendship, I hope you choose the right side.'

21

Lying curled up on the animal skins beside the fireplace, Marcus could not sleep despite his exhaustion. He could not shake from his thoughts the last words that Brixus had spoken. There was no mistaking the threat. He must either agree to be the figurehead for the new rebellion, or he would become the enemy of Brixus. That would put Marcus's life in danger, and consequently that of his mother. Yet if he agreed to do as Brixus demanded, he would be little more than a puppet to dangle in front of his supporters and lure them towards almost certain death.

Marcus was sure the new rebellion was doomed to fail. Even if Brixus did manage to inspire a mass uprising, the vast majority of fighters would be field hands or household slaves who stood little chance of survival against the Roman legions.

It would be a bloodbath. Tens of thousands would die, and after the rebellion was crushed the Romans would rule their slaves with even greater cruelty and suspicion than they did now.

The time was not right for rebellion. Rome was too strong and the slaves were too weak. It would be wiser to wait for a better opportunity, Marcus reasoned. Those who opposed slavery needed to bide their time. *But what if that time never comes*, a voice wondered at the back of his mind. *How long should slaves endure before they seize the chance to throw off their chains? Ten years? Twenty? A lifetime?* The voice mocked him. In that case, it would be better not to even think of rebellion.

Marcus felt torn in two by the desire to fight the evil of slavery and the knowledge that Brixus's struggle could only lead to defeat and death. In the end, he knew what he must do, even though it left a leaden sense of despair weighing down his heart.

The dull glow of the embers provided just enough illumination for him to see his way to the entrance of the hut. Easing the furs back, Marcus warily rose into a crouch and padded across to the leather curtain. He paused and listened, but there was no sound of movement outside. He took a breath and eased the flap aside to peer round the edge. The open space beyond seemed empty apart from a single sentry bending over a small fire, building it up with some fresh logs. The rest had gone out and the dull glows around the valley indicated that most of the other campfires had been allowed to die down to avoid any telltale smoke come the dawn. Overhead, the sky was mostly obscured by cloud and there were only a few clear patches sprinkled with stars. It was likely that more snow was on the way, Marcus realized. A fresh fall of snow would help to hide his tracks.

He watched the sentry squat down and hold his hands out to warm them over the flames flickering about the newly added logs. The man appeared settled for the moment so Marcus slipped out of the hut and, staying low, followed the wall until he was out of sight. Then he paused to remember the layout of the valley he had seen after his blindfold was removed. He retraced the direction from which Brixus and his men had joined the crowd, then saw a distinct dip in the wall of the valley against the lighter background of the night sky. That seemed as likely a spot as any to find the secret entrance.

Checking that all was still, Marcus crept away from the hut and cautiously made his way through the camp. The sounds of snoring and occasional coughs and muttered words issued from the crude huts and shelters that had been constructed. These were accompanied by the shuffling and snorting of penned animals whose warm odour mixed with the slowly fading smell of woodsmoke. Marcus edged stealthily from cover to cover, pausing to make sure he had not attracted attention, while straining his eyes and ears to ensure that nothing stirred ahead of him before risking the next move. Once he had to throw himself flat when a man stumbled from a goatskin tent to relieve himself, waiting until he returned to his shelter with a half-awake grumble.

At length Marcus reached a track at the edge of the camp that meandered down a slope towards the cliffs. He realized that it was the dried-out bed of a small stream and guessed that many years before it had flowed through the chasm in the cliffs that now served as the entrance to the valley. The stream must have found a new course, or had one made for it by the first settlers in the valley.

Creeping round a large boulder, Marcus froze as he heard a quiet exchange from the foot of the cliffs no more than fifty paces ahead.

'Brixus and his lads took a hammering today,' said the first voice. 'I heard he lost over five hundred men.'

'As many as that?' another voice replied gruffly. 'A hard blow for us. But harder for the Romans.'

'How?'

'You heard him. He said they fell right into the trap. They were lucky to escape being completely cut to pieces. Once word of Caesar's defeat reaches Rome they'll know we're a serious threat, and they'll have to consider our demands.'

'You think so? If we really did win, then I doubt we could survive many more of Brixus's so-called victories.'

'Be careful. That sort of talk is dangerous.'

'So's being here. This ain't turning out to be the great uprising we were promised when we joined up. I ain't so sure I'm any better off here than when I was a slave. Leastways, I got fed and sheltered properly. Now, me guts is rumbling all the time and I'm so cold I can't stop shivering.'

'Quiet!' his companion hissed. 'You want everyone to overhear us? What if that Mandracus is doing the rounds, eh? If he heard you mouthing off like that he'd tear out your damned tongue. Now stop your whining and keep watch like we're supposed to be doing.'

The other man grumbled incoherently and Marcus heard the crunch of nailed boots on pebbles as the two sentries slowly paced away from each other, keeping watch over the entrance to the gorge. Straining his eyes, Marcus could just see the outlines of the two men, wrapped up in cloaks and each carrying a round shield on one arm, while a spear rested on their shoulders. Scarcely daring to breathe, he crept closer. The sentries were standing either side of a gap in the cliff face, no more than ten feet across. Beyond, the opening to the narrow gorge was soon swallowed up by inky darkness. There was no way of reaching the gorge without the two rebels seeing him. Marcus forced himself to think through the problem. If he could not get past the men he would have to distract them somehow.

Reaching down, Marcus's fingers groped among the pebbles on the dried-out water course until they closed round one the size of an egg. He hefted it to get some sense of its weight and shape, then hurled it to one side as far as he could. There was a brief silence before the pebble clattered off a rock at the base of the cliff. At once the two sentries turned towards the sound and the nearest of them lowered his spear.

'Who's there? Show yourself!'

When no reply came he glanced over his shoulder to his comrade. 'On me, let's go.'

'You go. Probably just a dog or something. I'll stay here.'

Marcus felt his heart sink and silently cursed the man's timidity.

'No. You come with me!' the other said angrily. 'Now!'

As the two of them cautiously made towards the sound, Marcus half rose from his position and crept towards the mouth of the gorge. He slipped into the shadows as he heard one of them mutter, 'See, there's nothing here. Let's get back to our posts.'

'There was a sound. We both heard it.'

'Like I said, some animal.'

'Hmmm.'

Marcus hurried along the gorge as swiftly as he dared, desperate to put some distance between himself and the two sentries. Around him the sides of the gorge rose up, and only a thin gap showed the night sky. It was pitch black and he had to feel his way with the toes of his boots, hands stretched out in front, searching for any obstacles in his path. But there was nothing and underfoot the ground seemed to be an even layer of gravel. Although there was no wind, the temperature was colder than it had been in the valley and Marcus clamped his jaw tightly to prevent his teeth chattering. He could do nothing about the rest of his body and his limbs shivered violently as he pressed on through the darkness. He was terrified of encountering any rebels positioned within the gorge, but there was only silence ahead.

Trembling with cold and nervous exhaustion, Marcus edged round a bend in the gorge and saw a sliver of starlight a short distance ahead, revealing the exit. Then he stopped. It was obvious that Brixus would have sentries at either end of the narrow passage, and those on the outside were likely to be far more vigilant. However, they would be looking for threats approaching the entrance, so would be facing the other way. All the same, Marcus slowed his pace and hugged the side of the gorge as he felt his way towards the opening. Beyond lay a small clearing surrounded by pine trees and covered in a thick blanket of snow. A path crossed the clearing, the snow trodden down by the passage of many men and horses. Marcus was steeling himself to emerge from the gorge and make for the pines when he saw movement along the treeline.

A small party of men was trotting up the path towards the mouth of the gorge. They were halfway across the clearing when a score of men burst from the trees on either side, spears levelled as they closed round the new arrivals.

'Who goes there?' a voice called out menacingly.

The men on the track stopped dead and their leader raised an arm as he responded. 'Trebonius of the scouts. Let us pass.'

'Trebonius? You weren't expected for days. You're supposed to be keeping watch on Caesar.'

'We have been. He's marching this way. Now let me pass. I have to inform Brixus!'

'Caesar's coming . . .'

Marcus felt a mix of hope and anxiety as he heard the news. If his plan was to succeed he must find Caesar as soon as possible, while there was still a chance to prevent a bloodbath. The men in the clearing were talking in low urgent tones that Marcus could no longer make out. But for a brief moment their attention was on each other. Taking a deep breath, Marcus crouched down and moved slowly out of the mouth of the gorge, staying close to the cliff as he made for the trees. It was only a short distance, no more than twenty paces, and he reached the nearest of the pines as the scout party continued towards the camp. The sentries turned and headed back to their stations. Marcus ducked under a heavily laden bough and heaved a sigh of relief as the clearing disappeared from sight. Then the sleeve of his tunic caught on the stump of a broken branch and the whole bough jerked, dislodging a small avalanche of snow.

'Over there!' a voice cried out. 'There's someone over there! Under that tree. Hey, you, stop!'

Marcus cursed himself for a clumsy fool, but was already in motion, scurrying under the low branches as he scrambled deeper into the trees. As branches swished past him he heard shouting behind, and the crack of twigs as his pursuers plunged into the forest.

'Don't let the spy escape!' a voice ordered. 'Kill him if you have to!'

Marcus stayed low and ran on, swerving round the tree trunks, barely able to make out the way ahead. He had no idea which direction to head in but kept running, steering away from the sounds of his pursuers. But he knew he was close to exhaustion. Perhaps it would be better to stop, press himself against a tree trunk and keep still while the men passed by. Then he could double back to escape in a different direction. Even as the thought raced through his mind, he knew he dare not risk being caught and killed on the spot, or taken back to Brixus. The veteran gladiator would not forgive his escape attempt. Though Brixus had been a close companion of Spartacus, his first loyalty was clearly to his fanatical hatred of Rome. There would be no mercy shown to anyone who betrayed that cause, not even the son of Spartacus.

That thought gave him an extra burst of energy and Marcus forced himself on, stumbling through the dark forest as the ground beneath his boots began to slope gently down. Behind him, the rebels called to each other as they kept up the chase.

After about a mile the trees abruptly began to thin out and he was suddenly in the open, on the edge of an expanse of uneven ground. A large stone enclosure stood at the bottom of the slope where the trees began again, a few hundred paces away, and Marcus guessed that must be a summer pasture for goats or sheep. If he continued down the slope, his dark cloak would stand out against the snow and he would be spotted the instant the rebels emerged from the forest. With a rising sense of panic, he turned back to re-enter the trees when a voice called out close at hand.

'Over here! Some tracks . . . He's been this way!'

A cold wave of terror raced down his spine. There was only one direction now and Marcus spun round and ran for his life. He had covered no more than thirty paces across the smooth sweep of snowy field when the first of the pursuers burst out of the forest.

'There he is! Just a kid!'

'Get him!' another voice called. 'He mustn't get away!'

Marcus risked a quick glance over his shoulder and saw several dark figures converging on him from the treeline, kicking up sprays of snow as they raced down the slope. He sprinted on, heart pounding, fear causing his stomach and chest to tighten so that he panted raggedly. When he looked back again they were much closer, their longer stride gaining on him. They were halfway across the field before Marcus realized he could not reach the shelter of the trees before they caught up. He felt the energy draining from his legs and there was nothing he could do.

In front of him lay the stone wall of the pen and he saw the sudden movement of a dark shape rising above it. Then another, and another.

'Heads up, lads! We've got company.'

Marcus slowed momentarily, unsure if these were more of Brixus's men. Then the shouts behind caused him to grit his teeth and run on.

'Kill him!' a voice cried out. 'He mustn't give us away! Kill him!'

Something dark flew close by Marcus's head and exploded into the snow. He saw the shaft of a spear as he ran by and any moment expected to feel the piercing blow as the next missile punched through his back and tore through his body. A short distance ahead, one of the men inside the stone wall reared up and drew his arm back.

'Get down, lad!' he shouted hoarsely. 'Down!'

With no time to think, Marcus hurled himself forward into the biting cold of the snow, rolling over towards the wall.

He did not see what happened next, only heard the thud and deep grunt from close behind him. Scrambling on hands and knees, he glanced back and saw one of the rebels collapse to the ground, a spear shaft protruding from his stomach.

'Get stuck in!' a voice roared from behind the stone wall and dark shapes clambered over, short swords in hand. Some carried large oval shields as they charged towards the rebels, shouting their battle cry. Swords clattered all around Marcus. With nothing to protect himself, he crouched low as he ran to the wall and clambered over the rough stones before dropping inside.

He landed heavily, forcing the breath from his lungs, and it was a moment before he took in his surroundings. The interior of the pen was filled with legionary marching yokes, and bundles of javelins leaned against the wall. A handful of men were still there, too late to take part in the skirmish outside. Marcus rose to his feet, gasping, and peered over the wall. The fight was already over. Most of the rebels had turned to flee, racing back up the slope towards the cover of the distant trees. Several bodies lay in the snow, some of them writhing and groaning with pain. The soldiers stood jeering, waving their fists and swords after the rebels.

'Right!' a voice called out over the shouts. 'You've had

your fun, lads. Get the wounded into the pen. Now then, where's that boy? I want a word with him.'

A tall, powerfully built man climbed over the wall and looked to either side before he caught sight of Marcus's slight form and strode over. He stood, hands on hips, and stared down at him.

'Mind telling me who you are and what that was all about?'

'Take me to Caesar,' Marcus replied, still breathless. 'I have to speak to him. At once.'

'You want to speak to the general?' the centurion asked in an amused tone. 'I doubt he'd thank me for waking him in the middle of the night.'

'He might just do that . . .' Marcus took a deep breath to calm his nerves and speak clearly. 'Once you tell him that Marcus Cornelius has escaped, and can show him where the rebel camp is hidden.'

22

'Marcus!' Caesar grinned as he looked up from his campaign desk. 'I'd given you up for dead. Where did you find him, Festus? The lad looks all but done in.'

'He was picked up by one of the forward patrols, sir. They were all for throwing him in with the slaves we've captured, but he said he had important information for you. So they brought him to headquarters. I was there when they arrived at dawn and recognized Marcus at once. I brought him straight here.'

Caesar gestured to Marcus. 'You're shivering. Come, sit by the fire and warm yourself. Festus, give him my cloak, then send for some food, something hot.'

While Marcus eased himself down on a stool in front of the brazier that warmed and lit the tent, Festus crossed to a chest and picked up the heavy woollen cloak. The thought of food made Marcus's stomach rumble and the need to satisfy his hunger was just enough to put off the need to sleep. A moment later Festus gently placed the cloak over his shoulders and Marcus began to feel comfortable for the first time in many days.

Once Festus had left the tent Caesar turned to Marcus. There was a brief silence before he spoke again. 'You might be interested to know that this isn't the first reunion of former comrades. It seems that Lupus survived the avalanche. He was dug out by the rebels.'

'Lupus is alive?' Marcus couldn't help grinning with pleasure at the news. 'Where is he?'

'With the rest of the prisoners. He was captured following our clash with the rebels.' Caesar shook his head sadly. 'I misjudged him. He was not the loyal slave he seemed. Of course, he will be punished in due course, before I send him to work on a chain-gang. Some hard labour on a farm or in a mine might teach him the price of treachery.'

At first Marcus did not know what to say. He could hardly believe that Lupus would willingly join the rebellion, but then again, why not? For all the comforts he enjoyed as Caesar's scribe, he was still no more than a piece of property when all was said and done. Perhaps Lupus had grasped that and decided he wanted a taste of the freedom his master took for granted. Marcus was determined to save his friend. 'Sir, Lupus had no choice. He had to join the rebels or be killed.'

'It was his duty to refuse. Do not feel sorry for him, Marcus,' Caesar continued as he read Marcus's expression accurately. 'Lupus deserves his fate. You refused to join Brixus and managed to escape. That's what Lupus should have done.'

'He was not trained as I was, sir.'

'That is no excuse as far as I am concerned,' Caesar replied dismissively. 'Anyway, enough of Lupus. I intend to forget all about him. It is your story I am interested in. So, you survived the attack on the baggage column. When they could not find your body I hoped you had been taken alive. That was some small comfort given that the tents and food supplies were lost. The only shelter left was this tent. Too big to make off with, I guess. My men have been forced to sleep in the open, and if we do not destroy the enemy within the next few days I will be forced to fall back on Mutina to resupply and begin the campaign again . . . Unless, of course, this information of yours changes the situation. Well, Marcus, what do you have to tell me?'

Staring into the flames, Marcus struggled to fight off the weariness that fogged his mind. If he revealed the secret of Brixus's camp, then Caesar would crush the rebels ruthlessly. Brixus and his followers would fight to the end and many thousands would die. The thought of all that bloodshed appalled Marcus and he decided that he must do all he could to prevent it, even if it set him squarely at odds with his former master. He cleared his throat and sat up straight as he turned to face Caesar.

'I know where the main rebel camp is. That's where they took the prisoners after the ambush.'

'You know where they are?' Caesar's eyebrows rose in surprise. He smiled coldly. 'Excellent . . . Then we have them. The rebellion is as good as over.' He paused and his eyes narrowed slightly. 'But I dare say you were not the only prisoner.'

'There were some others, including Tribune Quintus, sir.'

'Quintus is alive? I had hoped he would do the honourable thing and die rather than be taken prisoner. He has disgraced himself, and Portia, and therefore my family. If he still lives when this is over, he may as well give up any ambition to pursue a political career. Anyway . . . If there were others taken prisoner with you, how is it that only you have managed to escape? You had better explain yourself.'

Marcus thought quickly. 'I was with the others when Brixus and his men returned to their camp. He recognized me and ordered his men to release me.'

'You know Brixus? You know him and yet you did not seek to inform me of the fact?'

'I thought you knew, sir,' Marcus replied innocently. 'Brixus was at the same ludus as me, until he escaped.'

'Great Gods!' Caesar clenched his eyes shut for a moment as if furious with himself for not making the connection. He breathed in deeply before his tense expression eased. 'All right, so you knew each other. What happened after he released you?'

'He took me into his tent and we talked.'

'What about?'

'He tried to convince me to join his rebellion. He said that this time he will succeed where Spartacus failed. He also asked me about you.'

'Me?'

Marcus nodded. 'He knew that you had bought me from Porcino and taken me to Rome to continue my training. He wanted me to tell him what I knew of your character, and your plans for the campaign.'

'I see. And what did you say?'

'I told him I did not know the details of your plans. I also said that you were determined to crush the revolt as swiftly as possible, whatever it takes. I said you were not the kind of man to let any obstacle stand in his way.'

Caesar leaned forward across the table. 'How did he react to that? Did he find it unsettling?'

Marcus paused briefly before he replied. 'I think so.'

'Good, then we have him off balance. Anxious men are more inclined to make rash decisions. And it unsettles those who follow them. So what happened next? How did you escape?'

'Once Brixus had finished talking he left me to sleep. I waited until the rebels had settled down for the night, then crept out of the camp. I had almost got clear when I was spotted by some men on guard. They chased after me, until I ran into your patrol. You know the rest.'

Caesar had been listening attentively and now he smiled. 'Quite a tale, Marcus. You have been lucky, though you were quick-witted and showed great courage. But I'd expect nothing less from you. By now I think Brixus will be aware of your escape. He will be making plans to abandon the camp and flee. This is the moment to strike. We'll march on them at first light and bring this matter to a swift conclusion. Tell me, Marcus, where are they?'

This was the moment Marcus had been dreading. He felt his limbs tremble as he forced himself to speak. 'What do you intend to do, sir?'

'Why, catch those scum before they can get away. Those we don't slaughter will be made an example of. Never again will the slaves doubt what awaits them should they turn on their masters.'

Marcus nodded. 'That's what I was afraid you would say.'

The triumphant gleam in Caesar's expression faded and he stared fixedly at Marcus. 'What are you thinking, my boy? These are slaves we are talking about. Worse, they are rebels. They have destroyed hundreds of farms and fine villas, and murdered thousands of Romans. Do you question my right to destroy them?'

Marcus had his answer ready. 'Until a few months ago, I was a slave. One of the scum you mentioned.'

'And now you are free.'

'It takes more than that to shake off the experience of being a slave, sir.'

'Marcus, you do not pick sides. Fate does that for you. A year ago, you might have joined Brixus. But now you are on my side. On the side of Rome.'

'I may be free. But I have lived as a slave and I experienced the cruel, brutal way that they are treated. I can understand why Brixus and the others have rebelled. They had no other choice.'

'Choice?' Caesar looked surprised. 'What has choice got to do with it? Slaves have no right to choose. They must simply obey, or face the consequences. And I will show them, and every other slave in Italia, the price of forgetting what being a slave means.'

Marcus shrugged off Caesar's cloak and let it fall on the ground behind him. 'Then I cannot tell you where the camp is.'

'Cannot or will not?' Caesar repeated in an icy tone. 'You dare to defy me?'

Marcus nodded. 'If it will save lives: Romans as well as slaves. Sir, I have served you loyally. I am grateful that you set me free. I would not defy your will if I could avoid it.' Marcus clenched his fist and pressed it against his breast. 'I will not have so many deaths on my conscience.'

Before the confrontation could go further the tent flap rustled as Festus returned with a canteen and large bowl. The rich aroma of stew filled Marcus's nostrils. Festus hesitated briefly, sensing the chilly atmosphere between the two, and then continued to the desk and set the canteen, bowl and spoon down. Then all was still and no one spoke until Caesar gestured towards the bowl and muttered curtly. 'Eat.'

Despite his hunger, Marcus found that his appetite had faded and his nerves had left his stomach tightly clenched. He forced himself to pick up the spoon; anything to create a sense of normality.

As he took his first mouthful, Caesar chuckled. 'You missed an interesting moment, Festus. It appears that our young friend has decided to become something of a moral philosopher.'

Festus frowned. 'Sir?'

'Marcus is refusing to reveal the location of the rebel camp.'

Festus turned to Marcus with a look of incomprehension. 'What is this?'

Marcus swallowed his mouthful of stew and put the spoon down. 'I did not say that I would not tell you the location. It's just that I want a deal with you, Caesar. If I give you what you want, there is a price.'

'A price? What nonsense is this?' Caesar slapped his hand down on the desk. 'I will not make any deals. Especially not with a boy. An ex-slave at that.'

'Then I will say nothing,' Marcus replied firmly.

Suddenly Festus clenched his hand round the back of Marcus's neck and shook him hard. 'How dare you speak to Caesar like that? You will show him the respect he commands, boy!'

Marcus clamped his jaw tightly shut and endured the pain as he kept his eyes fixed on Caesar. At length the proconsul let out a sharp breath.

'Enough, Festus. Release him!'

Festus pushed Marcus's head forward, then let go. He kept his position just behind the boy, ready to act again at the slightest sign from Caesar. The latter folded his hands together as he returned Marcus's stare.

'What exactly is this price that you would have me pay for the location of the rebels?'

Marcus rubbed his neck tenderly as he carefully ordered his thoughts. 'I'll take you to the camp and you can demand their surrender. In return you will spare the lives of the slaves. They are to be returned to their masters unharmed.'

'What if they don't surrender?'

'If you move quickly they will be trapped, sir. They will have to surrender.'

'What if they choose to resist?'

Marcus thought for a moment. 'I pray that they will see reason, sir. If you guarantee their lives, then I think they would prefer to live than face death by the sword, or on the cross.'

'The ringleaders will have to be executed, of course.'

'No. They will be spared too.'

Caesar shook his head. 'That would not play well in Rome. The Senate and people will demand the deaths of Brixus and his companions.'

'You are the commander here, sir. It is your decision, not theirs.'

Caesar leaned back in his chair and drummed the fingers of his right hand on the desk. 'What is to stop me ordering Festus to take you aside and beat the truth out of you? He has a certain skill for loosening tongues.'

Marcus fought to keep the fear from his expression. 'You could torture me, sir. But I might endure it for some hours, by which time Brixus and his rebels would have escaped. I know that time is precious to you. The campaign must be finished before you can march against Gaul. This is your chance to put an end to it today. Otherwise it could drag on for months.'

Festus coughed. 'The boy has a point, sir.'

'Quiet!' Caesar snapped. 'If I ever want your opinion, I'll ask for it.'

'Yes, sir. Sorry, sir.'

Caesar ignored his bodyguard and kept his attention on

the boy sitting before him. Marcus stared back unwaveringly, but inside he was terrified. He felt small and alone in the presence of great danger, yet he knew that he had one powerful weapon on his side: time. Every passing moment increased the risk that Brixus and his followers would slip through Caesar's fingers. That was what he was counting on. If he had misjudged his former master, then Marcus was certain that he would be dead by the end of the day, and would be swiftly followed by thousands of others before the rebellion was over.

'Very well,' Caesar growled through clenched teeth. 'You have a deal.'

'I want your word on it.' Marcus swallowed. 'I want you to swear to it, here in front of Festus.'

'And what oath would you bind me to?' Caesar asked mockingly.

'One that I know you will keep. I want you to swear on the life of your niece, Portia.'

The blood drained from Caesar's face and Marcus feared that he had pushed the proconsul too far. Then Caesar nodded slowly.

'I swear, on the life of my niece, that I will not harm those rebels who choose to surrender.'

Marcus felt a wave of relief sweep through his heart and

was about to offer his gratitude when Caesar held up his hand to still the boy's tongue.

'I further swear, on Portia's life, that if you are misleading me, or if the rebels escape, then I will have Festus nail you to a cross planted on top of the nearest mountain so that all might see what happens to those who defy Caesar. Is that clear?'

Marcus nodded.

'Then there's no time to waste. You can tell me where to find the rebels while Festus gives the order for my soldiers to assemble.'

Marcus cleared his throat. 'That's not quite all, sir. There are two other things I would like your word on.'

Caesar glared at him. 'Speak.'

'You are to release Lupus. Set him free. When the rebellion is over, you will give me some men, and a letter of authority to help me find and release my mother.' Marcus nodded his head. 'That's what you agreed with me, months ago.'

'I agree,' Caesar said harshly. 'There. Festus, give the order.'

'Yes, sir.' Festus bowed his head and hurried out of the tent to pass on the proconsul's command. Inside the tent Caesar breathed deeply through his nose as he regarded the boy who had been his slave and one of his most promising gladiators.

'I'll thank you for my cloak before you leave. Wait in front of the tent.'

Marcus did as he was told and tried not to show his fear as he walked away. Outside the first dull gleam of light struggled to break through the mist that wreathed the mountains to the east. A handful of snowflakes swirled on the light breeze sweeping over the makeshift shelters that Caesar's men had erected. Marcus shivered. Not because of the cold, but for fear of what the coming day held.

23

Dull grey clouds hung low in the sky as Festus turned to Marcus. 'You ready?'

Marcus stood still for a moment. The dense ranks of legionaries stood formed in their cohorts, plumes of steamy breath rising up amid the dark shafts of their javelins. Behind them Caesar and his officers sat on their horses, waiting. In front of the Romans stretched the open space that led up to the entrance to the rebel camp. Even though he knew where the gap in the rocks was, Marcus could not make it out as he stared at the cliff rising above the forest that stretched away either side of the entrance.

Nothing moved. There was no sign of life, yet Marcus could sense the eyes of the rebels watching them, waiting for the Romans to make their first move. Then, for a chilling moment, Marcus was seized by a terrible fear that Brixus and the others might already have escaped. But there was only one way to find out. He nodded. 'Ready.'

'Then let's go.'

They set off across the snow accompanied by two legionaries carrying brass horns. They had gone a short distance when the air was split by three shrill blasts of the horns, repeated at intervals of twenty paces to give clear warning of their approach. Festus had explained this was the procedure followed when the general of an army wished to open negotiations with his opposite number. It was important that those sent forward to speak on behalf of the general were not taken for scouts, attempting to infiltrate the enemy's lines. Marcus flinched at the first sound of the horns, but kept his attention fixed on the cliffs ahead. There was still no movement and the only sound beside the flat blasts of the horns was the soft crunch of snow beneath their boots.

'Where are they?' Festus muttered. 'Should have shown themselves by now . . . If you're trying to pull the wool over Caesar's eyes, boy, you know what'll happen to you.'

Marcus tried not to think about the appalling fate that

Caesar had promised him should the camp prove to be abandoned. He swallowed nervously and continued trudging forward across the open ground towards the cliff.

'Are you sure there's a gap in the rocks?' asked Festus. 'I can't see a thing.'

'Trust me, it's there.'

In a blur of motion an arrow shot out from the rocks and struck the snow with a soft thud, a few feet in front of the small party approaching. They stopped and looked at the shaft quivering before them, dark against the snow. Then Festus cupped a hand to his mouth and called out.

'Show yourselves! We have come to speak with Brixus!'

There was a brief pause before Marcus saw a figure emerge from the rocks at the foot of the cliff. He recognized him at once. 'Mandracus.'

'You know him?' Festus spoke softly.

'Yes, he's Brixus's second in command.'

'Stay where you are, Romans!' Mandracus shouted. 'Take one step closer and I'll have you filled with arrows! What do you want?'

'To negotiate,' Festus replied. 'I speak for Caesar.'

Mandracus was still for a moment, then half turned towards the rocks as if conferring with someone hidden from view.

Then he nodded and cautiously made his way across the open ground, stopping twenty paces away. He glanced over the men and fixed his gaze on Marcus.

'Caesar's little spy got away after all. So you betrayed us.'

Marcus felt his heart skip a beat. It was madness to be here. Mandracus might reveal the truth about his father's identity at any moment.

'I led the Romans here, yes,' Marcus replied.

Mandracus smiled thinly. 'Then I was right to warn Brixus about you. If only he had returned to the camp later, you would be dead and the secret of the camp still safe. But nothing can be done about it now. What do you and your Roman friends want to negotiate about?'

'We're here to discuss the terms of your surrender,' Festus intervened.

'That's what I thought.' Mandracus nodded. 'All right, we'll talk. But not to you. To him.' He pointed at Marcus. 'And him alone. You and the others stay here.'

'No. I speak for Caesar. Not the boy.'

Mandracus shrugged. 'It's him or nobody. And if you attempt to attack, you will discover just how impregnable our camp is. If Caesar wants to talk, we'll speak with the boy. Those are our terms.'

Neither Caesar nor Festus had anticipated this and now the bodyguard frowned as he rubbed his chin anxiously. He looked down at Marcus and spoke in an undertone. 'Well? Are you prepared to do as he says?'

At that moment there was nothing Marcus dreaded more than being left in the clutches of Brixus and his followers. Yet unless he was prepared to risk his life, it would cost the lives of many more. He nodded quickly before he could change his mind.

'All right. But if there's any sign of danger then run for it. I'll wait here and come for you the instant you raise the alarm.'

Marcus smiled faintly at him. 'Thank you.'

'Very well,' Festus called out to Mandracus. 'The boy will go with you. But I warn you, harm one hair on his head and I will kill you with my bare hands.'

Mandracus laughed at the threat. 'You're welcome to try any time, Roman. Come, boy.'

Marcus felt his heart beating wildly as he forced himself to step away from Festus and cross the snow towards Mandracus. Then the two of them continued towards the cliff. As they drew near, Marcus could see that the opening of the narrow gorge was filled with armed men waiting in silence. At their head stood Brixus, ready for battle in his polished greaves and breastplate, some ten paces in front of his fighters. His face was set like that of a statue.

'I do not know what to say to you, Marcus,' he began. 'There are no words to describe the depths of your treachery. Why did you do it?'

'I told you, back in your hut. This rebellion is doomed to fail. You don't have enough trained men. This is not the right time. If they were better prepared and there were more of them, there might be a chance of success. As it is, you can only lead them to defeat and death.'

'That was why I needed you, Marcus. With the son of Spartacus at the head of our army we would have drawn slaves to our ranks in droves. Even without training, the sheer numbers would have overwhelmed Rome in the end.'

'I don't think so,' Marcus replied simply. 'And your battle with Caesar's men the other day proved me right. If I truly thought that you stood a good chance of defeating Rome, then I would willingly have joined the rebellion.'

'Instead you betrayed us.'

Marcus shook his head. 'I wanted to prevent pointless bloodshed.'

Brixus sighed bitterly. 'Your father would be ashamed if he could see what you have done.'

'My father died before I was born. I never knew him. I am not Spartacus. I am Marcus and I will lead my own life as I wish.' Marcus spoke with as much pride as he could summon. 'I am not yours to command, any more than I am Caesar's.'

Mandracus took a step closer, his fist clenched round the handle of his dagger. 'I've heard enough. Shall I silence his tongue, Brixus?'

'No . . . Let him live. Death would be too gentle a mercy. Let him carry the burden of shame and guilt that he has earned this day. Let that be his reward for betraying us.'

Mandracus pursed his lips and reluctantly released his grip. 'As you wish.'

Brixus turned his attention back to Marcus. 'Your secret is safe with me, since you have disowned your father, a man I loved as a brother. You are no son of his, it seems. Perhaps in time you will change your mind. I pray that you live long enough to understand and accept your destiny. Until then . . .' His voice caught and he paused to clear his throat. 'What does Caesar want from us?'

Marcus forced his exhausted mind to recall what had passed between Caesar and Festus some hours earlier. 'Caesar demands that you surrender at once. In return he gives his word that those who throw down their arms will be spared. All slaves will be returned to their owners as soon as possible.'

'And why should I trust a Roman aristocrat any further than I can spit him?'

'He gave a solemn oath, in front of witnesses.'

'And you think he will stand by his oath?'

'This oath, yes,' Marcus replied confidently. 'Besides, he needs a quick conclusion to the rebellion, and will do whatever it takes to end it.'

'We don't need to listen to this!' Mandracus interrupted. 'Let Caesar do his worst. While we control the gorge the Romans cannot force their way into the camp. We can hold them off as long as we want.'

'True.' Brixus nodded. 'But they could simply lay siege to us and starve us into surrender. There is no other way out of the valley for us all. Caesar does not need to force the issue.'

Marcus said nothing. He knew the proconsul needed the rebels to surrender at once. If forced to starve the rebels out, he would lose valuable time. Marcus had known Caesar long enough to believe that he would order an immediate attack on the camp. It would cost many lives and would fail, and Caesar would still be forced to starve the rebels out of their stronghold. In that case he would show no mercy to any who survived.

Brixus was gazing towards the Roman lines, and the cluster of officers waiting beyond. 'This guarantee of yours, does it include us all?'

Marcus nodded. 'Everyone. Even you and Mandracus.'

The latter snorted with derision. 'It's a lie. The Romans will want to make an example of those who led the rebellion. We'll go the same way as Spartacus and his comrades: hanging from a cross outside the gates of Rome. Don't be a fool, Brixus. You knew from the start that only two paths are open to us – liberty or death. Either we hold our ground as long as possible, or we cut our way through the Roman lines to escape. We could find a new camp, raise another army and continue the struggle.'

The rebel leader glanced at the silent body of men filling the gorge. 'If we defend the camp, we are doomed in the long run. To escape, we must abandon all the others in the camp: the old, the women, the children.'

'Then that is the price we pay to keep the dream of Spartacus alive.'

Marcus cleared his throat. 'Spartacus, my father, dreamed of putting an end to the suffering of slaves, not making it worse for them.'

Mandracus rounded on him angrily. 'Still your tongue, traitor, before I cut it out!'

'Enough!' Brixus snapped. His eyes blazed at Mandracus until the man backed off a step. 'The boy is right. We are trapped. We are dead whether we stay or flee. You and I and many of the others would prefer death to slavery, but we cannot make that choice for everyone in the camp. It is better that they live. Having tasted freedom they will never forget it, and in time there may be a better opportunity to rebel. But if they are butchered now, such a hope will die with them, and in the hearts of all others who are still slaves. We must accept Caesar's terms.'

Marcus felt a surge of relief wash through his body.

'You would give in without a fight?' asked Mandracus.

'We have fought for as long as we can, my friend. Now we must accept defeat.'

Marcus saw the anguish in Mandracus's face as he struggled to accept his leader's decision. 'This is your will? Your command?'

Brixus nodded slowly. 'It is.'

Mandracus's shoulders slumped and he bowed his head in utter dejection. Brixus turned to Marcus. 'Go back to your . . . master. Tell him we will surrender on condition that no one is to be harmed. I'll send out the men first, then the rest.'

'Thank you,' Marcus said quietly. He wanted to say more, to offer his gratitude for all the lives that had been spared. To explain that he shared the man's dream, and that of Spartacus, and had things been different then he would have counted it an honour to fight against Rome at the side of Brixus. But he saw the pain and despair etched into the veteran gladiator's face and knew that such words would only add to his grief. Instead he simply offered his hand. Brixus looked down and did not move for a while. Then he slowly extended his hand and they gently clasped each other by the forearm.

'Farewell, Marcus. I doubt that I will see you again.'

There was a painful lump in Marcus's throat as he replied. 'Farewell.'

Brixus looked deep into his eyes and spoke softly. 'Never forget who you are. There may come a day . . .'

'If it comes, I shall be ready.'

Brixus nodded, then released his grip and looked at the Roman lines. 'You'd better go.'

Marcus slowly turned and paced across the snow towards Festus and the others, his heart torn by the pain of their parting. He felt a tear at the corner of his eye and blinked it away. Overhead the sky was a sullen, heavy grey and he felt the full weight of the world on his young shoulders.

'Well?' Festus asked as Marcus stopped in front of him.

'He accepts. It's all over.'

Marcus sat in his saddle beside Festus as they watched the long, silent procession pass between the lines of legionaries either side of the entrance to the gorge. A short distance in front Caesar watched them with a haughty expression. A great pile of swords, spears and other weapons and armour lay to one side of the route where the rebels had dropped them before being marched away under the watchful eyes of the legionaries. The small number of hostages held by the rebels had been released earlier and taken away in a wagon to recover in the nearest town.

There was little conversation among the Romans, and the rebels were silent. Caesar had given orders that Brixus and his closest comrades should be the last to surrender. As the end of the column emerged from the gorge, the Roman commander clicked his tongue and led his entourage forward.

Marcus could see Mandracus and several others waiting there, still carrying their weapons as they eyed the approaching Romans.

'It is time for you to join the others, gentlemen,' Caesar said in a tone laced with contempt. 'Throw down your weapons.'

Mandracus stepped forward and glared defiantly at the Roman general before drawing his sword. Festus took a sharp intake of breath and reached for his blade. But Caesar did not flinch and after a brief pause Mandracus dropped his weapon, unbuckling his breast and back plates to let them fall into the snow before he stood aside. One by one his comrades followed suit. Marcus looked for the rebel leader but there was no sign of him.

'Which one of you is Brixus?' Caesar demanded.

There was no reply.

'Which one of you is that scoundrel who calls himself your leader? Step forward, Brixus.'

Mandracus crossed his arms as he spoke up. 'Brixus has chosen not to surrender. He has remained in the camp where he awaits you, sword in hand.'

'Indeed?' Caesar nodded gravely. Edging his horse closer to the rebel, he raised his proconsular baton and struck Mandracus on the cheek. 'You will call me master from now on, slave. I gave my word that you would be spared and returned to slavery. And I will treat you like any slave who dares to treat men without due respect! Do you understand?'

Mandracus was bent over, stunned by the blow, as blood dripped from a cut on his cheek. Marcus looked on with a sick feeling in his stomach. Even though he knew that this outcome was the only way to prevent the deaths of many, the guilt over his decision weighed heavily on his heart.

Caesar raised his baton again. 'I said, do you understand me, slave?'

Mandracus looked up and nodded. 'Yes . . . master.'

'Good. Then join the column.'

As Mandracus was led away, Caesar turned towards the gorge and took up his reins. 'One last rebel to deal with, it seems. Follow me.'

The secret valley was still and silent. Abandoned huts and shelters stood on either side of the track. Caesar and his party looked about them warily, suspecting an ambush at any moment. As they reached the small rise overlooking the heart of the valley, the large huts of Brixus's compound came into view. At once Marcus saw a thin trail of smoke rising from the largest building. A red glare showed in the thatch as a tongue of flame burst through and quickly spread.

'I want him alive!' Caesar called as he spurred his horse forward, and his men galloped after him. By the time they reached the huts the fire was raging across the thatched roof and the air was filled with red and black cinders floating on the breeze. The heat from the flames was intense and Marcus's horse shied away with a panicked whinny. Some of the officers jumped down from their saddles to approach the hut, but it was impossible. Then Marcus recalled the entrance that adjoined the rear of the building to a smaller hut, and trotted his horse round the fire until he could see it. The flames had not yet spread to the smaller structure so Marcus slipped down from the saddle, approaching the low entrance with his arm raised to shield his face from the heat. The fresh snow that had fallen around the hut was already melting, but Marcus spotted a set of footprints leading towards the mountains at the end of the valley.

He backed away several paces and looked around, but so far none of the others had joined him on this side of the hut. Quickly Marcus kicked snow over the tracks, concealing any trace of them, before he turned away.

'Marcus! What are you doing?' Festus was edging round the blaze towards him.

'I thought I'd try the rear!' Marcus called back. 'But it's too late.'

Festus nodded. They stood side by side, staring at the awesome spectacle of the fire raging before them, the flames lighting up the valley and painting the clouds above with a pink hue. At length Festus nodded to himself. 'So Brixus preferred death to surrender . . . A good death, under the circumstances. But Caesar is going to be furious.'

'Yes.' Marcus nodded. 'He will be.'

'At least he has a victory, of sorts. The rebellion is over. That will annoy his enemies in the Senate and leave him free to deal with Gaul.'

Marcus nodded absent-mindedly as he glanced up at the cliffs round the valley. Then he caught a slight movement in the rocks. He strained his eyes until he saw it again, one last time. Though it might have been a man, it was difficult to tell at such a distance.

'Marcus?'

He turned back towards Festus.

'What is it?' Caesar's bodyguard looked up at the mountains. 'Did you see something?'

'No, nothing. Just a bird. But it's flown off now.'

24

THE COAST OF GREECE,
THREE MONTHS LATER

'That's Lechaeum off the starboard bow there.' The captain of
the merchant ship raised his arm and pointed along the rocky
coastline. Marcus followed his direction and saw a sprawl of
white buildings with red tiled roofs spilling down the side
of the hill towards the sea.

'We should reach the port before the end of the day with
this breeze,' the captain added. Then, briefly looking up to
ensure the broad sail was drawing well, he made his way back
towards the stern.

Marcus continued to watch the passing coastline of the

Peloponnese as the ship rose and fell on the easy swell of the Gulf of Corinth. A handful of seagulls followed the ship, swooping round the top of the mast against the clear blue sky. It was a good day to be alive, he reflected, as the wind blew in his dark hair and the fresh sea air filled his lungs with its salty tang.

Despite the tense aftermath of the rebels' surrender, Caesar had kept his word. The slaves were returned to their masters unharmed and there had been no repercussions for the ringleaders. The intense heat of the fire had reduced Brixus's hut to ashes. No bones were found in the smouldering remains, but the blaze had been so fierce that it had consumed everything, even the sturdy timbers holding up the roof. Caesar had proclaimed that Brixus set fire to the hut before taking his own life, and no one dared question his verdict that the matter was closed. As for Decimus and his men, they had disappeared at once, no doubt making for Rome and the safety of the house of Crassus.

Later, back in Ariminum, Caesar had met Marcus for the last time and reunited him with Lupus. Since he was about to march on Gaul, surrounded by an army with a personal bodyguard of five hundred veteran legionaries, he no longer required his household protectors. Accordingly, Festus and two of his men had been instructed to accompany Marcus to Greece. Lastly, Caesar had presented Marcus with a scroll bearing his proconsular seal.

'That's a letter of introduction. I've asked anyone to whom it is presented to offer you assistance in finding your mother.'

Marcus bowed his head. 'I am grateful, Caesar.'

'I should think so. I do not take kindly to being manipulated by anyone, let alone a boy of twelve. My obligations to you are fulfilled, young Marcus. We shall not meet again. If you ever appear at the door of any of my houses I shall have you thrown into the streets.'

'I understand.'

With that they had parted, and Marcus left the general in his study to complete his plans for the campaign in Gaul. As he approached the door of the house commandeered by Caesar for his headquarters, he had heard footsteps behind him.

'Marcus, wait!'

He had turned to see Portia, breathless and agitated.

'I'm told you are leaving.'

'Banished, more like.' Marcus smiled. 'Your uncle never wants to see me again.'

'Oh . . .' Portia looked crestfallen. 'Then I shall never see you again.'

Marcus nodded sadly.

'How is Tribune Quintus?' he asked.

Disappointed by the question, Portia had shrugged. 'He suffered dreadfully in the cold. Frostbite, the surgeon says. But he should recover in time to join my uncle.'

'That's good.' Marcus nodded again.

They had stared at each other a moment before she took his hands and squeezed them gently. Marcus felt something pressed into his palm, then she turned and ran, brushing the corner of her eye.

Marcus had stood by the heavy gate to the street as Caesar's doorman opened it. With a last glance at Portia's retreating back, he left the house. Outside he had opened his hand and seen a heavy golden ring in his palm. A ruby gleamed brilliantly in its setting, like a tear of blood.

Now, standing on the deck of the ship, Marcus recalled the scene. Through the cloth of his tunic he felt the chain round his neck and the bulk of the ring at the end of it. Though saddened at the prospect of never seeing Portia again, there had never been any question of their friendship being more than a closely guarded secret. It was for the best, he decided reluctantly.

'What's the matter, Marcus?'

He turned to see Lupus, standing with feet apart, one hand grasping a rope to steady himself on the heaving deck.

'It's nothing.' Marcus made himself smile back. 'Just thinking.'

'You should be rejoicing. You're back in Greece. We'll soon find your mother, you'll see.'

Marcus nodded. Then both of them turned to the other side of the ship as a deep groan sounded across the deck. Festus stood hunched over the rail and his body heaved as he tried to vomit again.

Lupus chuckled. 'There's one at least who'll rejoice at the prospect of reaching shore. Who'd have thought that tough old Festus would have the constitution of a lamb the moment he stepped on board ship?'

Marcus laughed, then looked fondly at his companion. 'You're in a fine mood today.'

'Why shouldn't I be?' Lupus grinned. 'I am free. For the first time in my life. It's the first thought that fills my mind every morning. There is no better thing in this world.' His expression grew more serious. 'And I have you to thank for it.'

Marcus felt a warm glow of pleasure. Even though he had prevented a bloody massacre, those he had saved were still slaves. Only Lupus had been freed from bondage. But it was a start, he told himself. One small step along the way to . . . what? A greater destiny? Perhaps. But for now only one thing mattered. The single purpose that had carried him through Porcino's gladiator school, the vicious streets of Rome and the icy perils of the Apennine mountains – his burning desire to rescue his mother. Now that time had come.

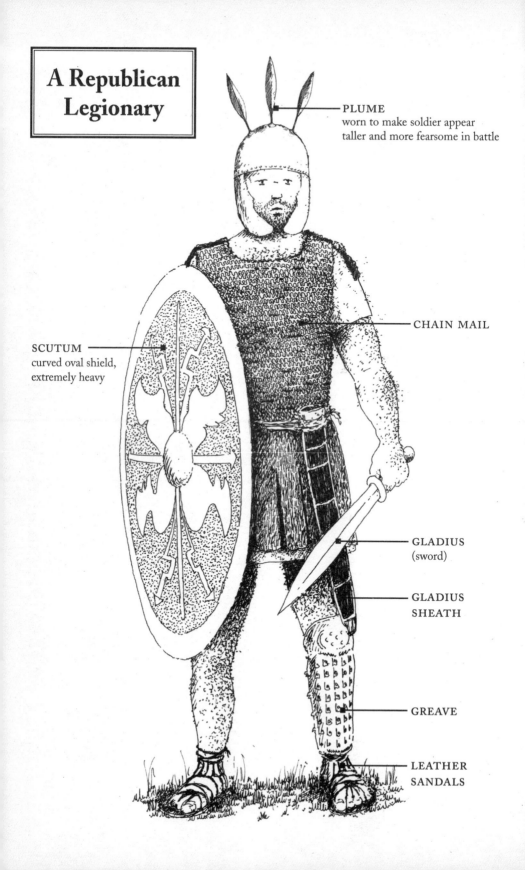

A Republican Legionary

PLUME
worn to make soldier appear
taller and more fearsome in battle

CHAIN MAIL

SCUTUM
curved oval shield,
extremely heavy

GLADIUS
(sword)

**GLADIUS
SHEATH**

GREAVE

**LEATHER
SANDALS**

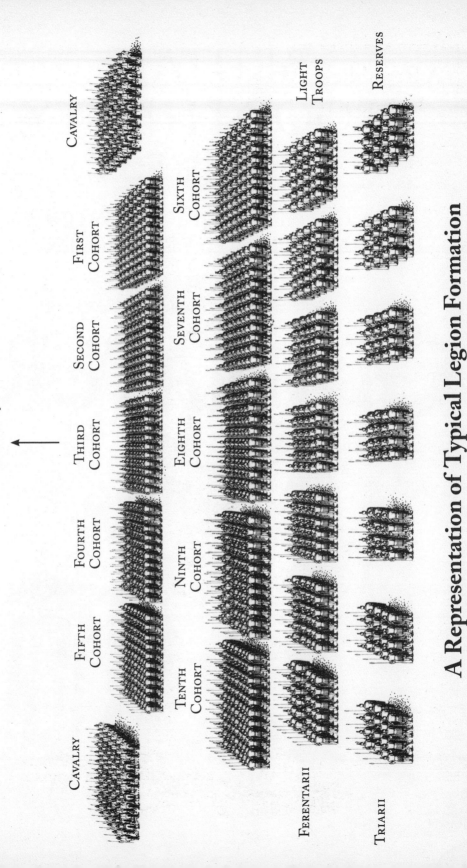

The Enemy

CAVALRY

FIRST COHORT

SECOND COHORT

THIRD COHORT

FOURTH COHORT

FIFTH COHORT

CAVALRY

SIXTH COHORT

SEVENTH COHORT

EIGHTH COHORT

NINTH COHORT

TENTH COHORT

LIGHT TROOPS

FERENTARII

RESERVES

TRIARII

A Representation of Typical Legion Formation

BRUTAL, BLOODTHIRSTY, BRAVE.

MARCUS'S HEROIC FIGHT CONTINUES – DON'T MISS THE NEXT EPIC ADVENTURE

COMING IN 2014

GLADIATOR

Enslaved by empire, he will rise a hero . . .